SYNCHRONICITIES
on the
Avenue
of the ## Saints

SYNCHRONICITIES
on the
Avenue
of the Saints

By
Deborah Gaal

ANCHOR HOUSE
PUBLISHING

Editorial and production management by Flying Pig Media with typesetting and cover design by Circecorp Design.

A CIP record for this book is available from the Library of Congress Cataloging-in-Publication Data.

ISBN: 978-1-7325896-5-0

For E, because you kept your promise.
I must keep mine.

To the "crazy woman" who saved my father.
You are remembered and loved.

THEN WINKS

Everything is clapping today,
Light,
Sound,
Motion,
All movement.

A rabbit I pass pulls a cymbal
From a hidden pocket
Then winks.

This causes a few planets and me
To go nuts
And start grabbing each
Other.

Someone sees this,
Calls a
Shrink,

Tries to get me
Committed
For
Being Too
Happy.

Listen: this world is the
lunatic's sphere,
Don't always agree it's real,

Even with my feet upon it
And the postman knowing
my door

My address is somewhere
else.

By Daniel Ladinsky

PROLOGUE

The Author Receives Divination and an Assignment

The shaman leaned over the runes spread atop the divination cloth, peering at the mess of tiny rocks and carved images from different angles, and hovering a finger over a piece or two while we sat in silence for a good five minutes.

At long last the man broke free from the fabric's pull and gazed up at me with a look of confusion. "Did you complete each task the ancestors assigned during your last divination? When were you here?"

"Two years ago."

"Ah." He nodded. "And in that two years?"

"I fed the birds as the Ancestors required. Both hummingbirds and seed birds." I burbled on, careful to avoid reportage of what I had neglected to accomplish. "By the way, that caused a spirited disagreement between me and my husband. We have bird poop everywhere in the yard." I laughed, but got no reaction from him.

"You and your husband don't like messiness," he stated flatly and stared at me with a hint of condescension etched on his otherwise smooth face.

"I guess not."

"Life is messy." He returned his gaze to the pile of detritus.

"Don't I know it." Another nervous laugh escaped my throat. "I also placed a whalebone on the fountain," I said hopefully. "And I'm telling you, finding one was no stroll in the park. But I discovered an artist in Nova Scotia who carves figures out of whalebone he scavenges off the beach. Doesn't look bad if you hide it toward the back of the fountain."

"Because you and your husband are concerned with aesthetics." The shaman leaned back in his chair and crossed his arms. "I see. So, you fed the birds. You placed the whalebone on the fountain as instructed."

"Yes."

"What else?"

I avoided his gaze. "That's it."

"Have you noticed changes?

I closed my eyes and took a deep breath, taking stock of events and trying to form a response that would get me off the hook. "I smell smoke in one of the guest rooms."

"The room where your son stays when he visits?"

"The very one."

"Is he a smoker?"

"Maybe. Probably. He hides it from me, I guess. But when I enter the room it smells like the rest of the house. Then suddenly, there's a strong smoke odor."

The shaman shrugged. "A smoke spirit is trying to

get your attention."

I nodded, even though I had no idea what a smoke spirit was or what it wanted from me.

The shaman leaned toward me and narrowed his eyes. "Your story is on fire. Yet, you're avoiding your assignment. The Ancestors want you to write a myth."

I had hoped the shaman had no memory of my last divination. Was I paying him to remember, or paying him to forget? Or perhaps this reading would show a different result. But the wiseman's mind was sharp, and the assignment unchanged. "You said this last time. And I told you, I don't write. And I still don't write."

"You want your son to stay in this world? To stay in your life? To be 'well.' You want him to 'find himself'?"

My heart ached to hear my deepest need and to know, apparently, of my unwillingness to go to all lengths to save my son. What kind of mother am I? "That's the reason I came to you. But there must be some mistake. The Ancestors got it wrong. I don't write."

"Nonsense. You were born in a mineral year. You carry stories in your bones."

"I've tried. Nothing happens. I'm a blank."

The shaman shook his head. "Just show up and be available. Sit at your computer. Stay with your pad of paper and pen. The Ancestors will commence from there. Take dictation. You said you want to get out of purgatory. That you've been miserable for...how long is it now?"

"His problems showed up at twenty-two. He just turned thirty-five."

"You don't have to be in purgatory for three-hun-

3

dred-million years. There is a way back into the light."

"You're telling me that if I just show up—"

"You have a huge team behind you. The Ancestors are filling this room as we speak. They hang from the ceiling, they sit on the floor. You have as much collaboration as you need. Show up. Let everyone else do the work. They are waiting."

"Tell them I'm sorry—"

"They are not angry. There's no such thing as that. They just need this story to make its way into the present world."

"I'm not the right person. All that sitting and thinking. My hips ache. My elbow is sore, maybe bursitis. I came to let the Ancestors know—"

"Stop boring the Ancestors. They do not make mistakes. Only stubborn people walking the earth. The world is in a dark place. It wants to come into the light. You want to emerge from the deep forest as well. You are feeling a frustration that you've cocooned yourself. The cocoon is at times pleasant and perpetually addictive, but your soul wants to be part of the daily conversation."

"I'm so tired—"

"Of being in business. You have told me this. You took a break."

"No, I'm tired of life. And I can't wait in silence and think about the things I should have done differently, the mistakes I've made. It hurts—"

"Stop. Your soul is saying, 'Enough.' It is time to birth a new world. Stories and myths will help the world make change in a heartbeat."

"A heartbeat? It will take me years of stillness."

"What is time? The story will surface on its own schedule."

"What kind of story? I have nothing to say."

"A story of the indigenous world and modernity coming together to heal the earth. A story of how all people must accept our mutual importance. A story of bad medicine and good medicine."

"This is the story the Ancestors want?"

"This is the story they always want."

"They've asked before? Has the story already been written?"

"Many times written. Many times ignored. The Ancestors know they must teach this lesson one person at a time.

"And this is how I save my son?"

"I do not know if your son needs saving. Perhaps you are the one who needs saving."

I was exhausted from worrying about my hapless son and yet I continued to resist this possible option of help. All that sitting. All those intrusive thoughts and self-analyzation and self-recrimination that show up unbidden. Why is it so painful for me to admit I am the cause of my own sadness? Perhaps, my journey has little to do with my son's. The pressure felt like a car sitting on my chest. Yes, enough. Tears of fear, inadequacy and frustration broke free, and I sobbed.

The shaman placed his hand on mine. "Start the story with your ancestors. It is always a good place to start."

THE ANCESTORS

Chapter One

Winter never ended in this godforsaken village. Without her husband, Chaim, Hadassah knew she would starve and rot. First, though, she would go mad.

A blizzard in April. The road lay buried beneath deep drifts that mimicked the mounds of white flour on her baking board. Her crooked fingers ached from the damp cold, and she pulled at them as she watched the relentless snow outside her window.

Driving a horse and wagon in this storm would be impossible; perhaps Chaim would not return. Please, merciful God, make the impossible possible. Dread brought the sting of tears to her eyes and heightened the throbbing in her hands.

Hadassah needed to stop this pointless vigil at the window and make the pastries Chaim loved so much. She'd baked a new batch of *rugalach* for him every day since the date of his scheduled return. Two weeks ago.

Already the townsfolk whispered of murder. They gossiped that he'd been slaughtered like an old cow.

"Such foolishness to make this trip."

"Like the czar ever favored a Jew."

"Hung or shot."

"A groyser tzuleyger, such a big shot...tutor to the czar."

Hadassah clung to the hope he'd just been delayed, but rumors of the execution of Czar Nicholas and imminent revolution raged among the villagers. They clucked like hens and left packages on her front stoop as though she already was sitting *shiva*.

During the night, she'd abandoned her bed and pried open a can of red paint. Chaim had brought it back from an earlier trip to Saint Petersburg to use in staining an old china cabinet. "Just like the czar's palace."

She'd stirred the paint with two fingers, marking her front door with the word *machashaifeh*. Witch. Perhaps now the villagers would leave her in peace.

What difference did it make what they thought? She couldn't bear to hear their talk or to look anyone in the eye. What did they know? She'd stopped going outside, shutting herself away from everyone.

She spent her days keeping watch and circling the one room hut. She'd examined Chaim's history books, something she'd never dared to do when he was home. Embarrassed by her inability to read, she had shunned Chaim's lessons rather than let him witness her struggle to interpret the jumble of letters. But now she found herself caressing the yellowed pages of print, seeking a connection to Chaim. A cornered page. A water spot. A sooty fingerprint.

Each day she pounded dough, cut out strips, sprinkled cinnamon, and pressed in little morsels of raisins and nuts she scraped together from her dwindling pantry.

The scent of cinnamon filled the small house. It permeated her skin, her clothing, and her hair. Now, the smell sickened her, because it reminded her of her longing and the futility of her efforts.

Again and again, Hadassah recalled their final exchange.

"What do you expect me to do if you don't come back?" she'd screamed at Chaim before his departure for Saint Petersburg.

"My Hadassah, my blessing, you already know. Tell me again."

She'd put her hands on her hips and glared. "I'm old. I don't remember."

He'd kissed her forehead, trying to soothe her anger, yet failing to grasp her anxiety. "Tell me, my sweet Hadassah."

"Hunh. Sweet like an onion. And you—also an onion with your head in the ground."

She'd relented in the end and given him what he'd wanted. "I'm to take the eggs to Pincus."

But she would never go to America without Chaim. At nearly sixty, she couldn't make the trip on her own. Another death sentence he'd imposed upon her. What if he returned to the *shtetl* to find her gone? There'd be no *rugalach* or lighted candles. Or his precious jeweled eggs.

She cursed those symbols of the church and power. The gems meant nothing in a village like Yompola. If they'd been chicken eggs, instead of gold and diamond eggs, there'd be something decent to eat. A hen's egg now cost four times what it had just two months ago. Women haggled in the market over the price, then left with nothing.

Hadassah cursed the czar and her foolish husband for traveling to see his beloved student one more time. Why? Why? For one more conversation? For one more priceless egg?

"Why do you cling to your czar?" she'd berated him.

"Hadassah, there is a special relationship between a tutor and his pupil. He is like the son we never had. Look at what he's given us."

"Hunh, an execution is what he wanted to give you."

"Nicholas released me."

"You had to convert or flee for your life. Now you go back?"

"His advisers threatened me, not Nicholas. He would never harm me."

"You're a fool, Chaim." She'd followed him out the door, shouting at him until she lost sight of his wagon as his horse plodded down the thin, muddy lane. "You're a fool." The whole village bore witness to her rant.

Now, she refused to open her door to her neighbors, hating their pitying offerings. A piece of dried-out chicken. A bowl of thin soup. She'd stopped eating. She would rather die than live without Chaim.

Hadassah paced in circles. She finally returned to the kitchen table, tossed flour on the board, and rolled the pin over the dough again and again until her arm muscles burned.

The white sky darkened to gray. The sun began its descent, announcing the Sabbath. Another week of despair at an end. The snow piled up outside the decaying hut as the wind howled around and through it. She pushed loose strands of brittle hair back under her *babushka* and tightened the frayed shawl around her bent shoulders.

The fire needed more logs, but she lacked the strength to bring them in and arrange them in the stove. She thought about removing a book from Chaim's shelf and throwing it atop the smoldering embers. Such sacrilege would serve him right. He'd mourn its loss when he returned to her, and she'd give him the tongue-lashing he deserved for bringing this terror upon her. Anger boiled her blood, but it failed to warm her.

"What did you expect?" she railed. No one answered. The cockroaches and the mice scurried for the corners.

She struck a match, lit two candles, and chanted the prayer over the Sabbath lights. Then, she sank to her knees and placed her folded hands on the flour-dusted table. "Blessed God, *Hashem Yisborakh*, bring Chaim back to me." She rocked back and forth. Back and forth. "Please, *Hashem*. I will never rest until he's home. I will never rest."

Snow blew in through cracks around the window. A bitter gust of wind raised a cloud of flour above Hadassah's head.

The smell of cinnamon wafted through the air.

Chapter Two

Noah Friedman felt even closer to connecting the dots. He sat on the edge of his seat at his favorite blond wood desk in the physics section of the library and braced for a download of knowledge to gush into the top of his head. He could feel how close he was to channeling complete illumination. An infinitesimal degree separated this knowing, and yet key fragments eluded him. The universe toyed and taunted, its answers suspended somewhere in the macrocosm, an attosecond away, waiting for him to pluck them from the ether. At twenty-four, he approached the age when Einstein had written his papers on relativity. Every clock tick marked the advance of Noah's creative peak.

Surrounded by the hardbound volumes of Galileo, Newton and the rest of the gang, he sucked in a deep breath and exhaled, comingling his zing with the molecules of musty, well-worn inspiration. Spikes of energy vibrated through his nerve endings, kicking his senses up to high alert. Eyes closed, he let his fingers hover above the computer keyboard. The fine hairs on his arms stood at attention, buoyed by electrical current, as his neurons coalesced. Abruptly, the tingling stopped.

He'd lost the thread. Power outage again, damn it. Lately, his meds seemed to be fucking with him. Perhaps his Selexikote dosage needed ramping.

Suddenly, the vision of a man floated into his brain and took shape. Distinct. Tangible. His skin shone like black ocean pearls, and his smile revealed a transparency as startling as an albino bird flushed from the bush—ascending, creating wonder.

This charismatic man laughed with such elegant joy, Noah briefly forgot about the drug, his research, the pending deadline, the importance of it all, and....what had he been doing?

Sinewy hands thumped a drum covered in animal skin. The drumbeat matched the rhythm of Noah's heart, and he listened, mesmerized by the feral call.

The man ceased his cadence, gazed at Noah, flattened a palm turned skyward and blew across the top of it. A ball of purple flame exploded from the heat of his skin, sending sparks of amethyst upward, spinning, splattering against the star-speckled black of the sky.

"The fire is within us, my brother. Come." He motioned Noah to follow.

Oh, how he wished he could.

In this instant of longing, Great-Grandma Sara's voice popped into his head. "Come, Bubala. Trouble's brewing."

His heart couldn't ignore Grandma's message. He must see her.

His brain jangled these two conflicting images, and it occurred to him he might be wrong about the Selexikote. Perhaps his dosage should be lowered rather than increased.

Opening his eyes, Noah reentered the present as defined by accepted space-time parameters. He shut down his laptop, zipped up the carry-case, and closed the leather-bound physics book, caressing it with his fingertips. He sighed.

His cell buzzed his thigh. Fishing it from his pocket, he read Mom's text. "Y no call back? R U Ok? Dinner 2 nite?"

Fifth message in two days. She'd keep bugging him until he called. Maybe later. After he visited Grandma and finished further research. Maybe.

Noah shoved the phone deep into his jeans pocket.

Leaving the cool cocoon of the library, he sprinted through the blistering St. Louis heat.

☀

The television blasted *Oprah* all the way out into the stairwell. Opening the door to Great-Grandma Sara's apartment, Noah was assaulted by a perfume derived from the essence of chicken soup, cat litter, and bleach. Window shades drawn tight masked the sun and heat of the afternoon, and it took a moment for his eyes to adjust to the dim light.

His shirt, soaked from his run in the stifling humidity, met an environmentally reckless air conditioning setting, raising goose bumps on his skin. Sara must have had a substitute caregiver for the day.

He marched over to the thermostat and turned the dial to the right, warmer for Great-Grandma's poor circulation.

Kitsala, Sara's black cat, pranced over to greet him, brushing back and forth against his leg. He reached down to rub her throat and enjoy the purrs rumbling through his fingertips.

Great-Grandma Sara slouched on the threadbare velvet love seat. Her head slumped on her chest and both rose and fell rhythmically. The cat trailed Noah into the living room, and they plopped down on either side of her.

He lifted one of her weightless hands and studied it. Prominent blue veins visible beneath translucent skin formed a large N. "N for Noah," she used to say when he was little. "You're my boy. See, even my body knows this is true." Noah traced the N with his index finger.

Her genetic code had skipped two generations and stamped him as her boy. They both shared the same blue eyes—cobalt, Co, atomic number twenty-seven—and trademark red hair—copper, Cu, twenty-nine, although her mane had long ago gone white and sparse. They both got that prickly feeling, sometimes at the same moment, when otherworldly energy was present.

Sara stirred. "Joe, is that you?"

"No, Grandma. It's Noah." he shouted over the din of the television. He found the remote control on the end table and hit the mute button. Sara looked up at him through slits beneath drooping eyelids, her chin revealing two long, gray chin hairs.

"Who the hell are you?"

"I'm your great-grandson. Sally's son."

Sara gazed blankly at Noah, her wrinkled mouth pursed like a cinched bag. Then, her thin lips stretched into a smile. "Oh, my *boychick*. Tonight, are you taking me dancing?"

"Yes, Grandma. You'll put on your purple dress with the gold buttons, and we'll go out on the town."

Sara displayed her coffee-stained grin.

"How are you, Grandma?"

"It's time for the ambulance to come get me. Real excitement that would be."

"Don't say that."

"What does it matter? I've got a message for you."

Noah placed Sara's hand on her lap and removed a small green notebook from his back pocket. On the cover he'd written *Synchronicities* with a thick black marker. He flipped through pages that chronicled dates and conversations in black ink. Yellow highlighter tagged Sara's quotes. Red stars and underlines emphasized patterns. *This came true.* or *What a coincidence.* had been scrawled in selected margins.

He wrote *July 10, 4:22 P.M.* on a fresh sheet of paper.

"Okay, Grandma, I'm ready. What did you want to tell me?"

She turned her head to look at him. "What?"

Her face registered how much effort small movements took at the age of ninety-eight.

"You said you had something to tell me?"

"I did?" Her eyes looked vacant. "I'm so *tsedreyt*. I don't remember." The wires connected. "Oh, I know what it is. You need a suit. You have to go to your mother's office."

"Thanks, but no thanks."

Sara wagged a demanding finger. "Your mother has

trouble. You have to help."

"Don't guilt me. Why don't you tell her she's in trouble?"

"Are you *meshuga*? She's not going to listen to me."

Sara squeezed Noah's arm, and he dropped the notebook and pen. "Ow, Grandma." His arm smarted where she'd pinched, and he rubbed the spot.

"Listen to me. A storm brews. It's the hay wagon story. Have I told you this?"

Noah picked up the notebook and flipped through the pages until he found the correct entry. "Fifty-two times, to be exact."

"Put that thing down and look at me." She motioned with two fingers pinched together that she would give him another *zetz*.

"Sorry, Grandma." Noah set aside the notebook.

She squinted. "Where was I?"

Noah waved his index finger. "I see it like it was yesterday. The Cossacks stampeded across the desolate plains of the Ukraine..."

Sara made a fist and shook it at him. "You think you're funny. A regular Milton Berle, you n*udnik*. A what for I'll give you."

He laughed. "Sorry. I couldn't help it."

"Oh, mine Noah. For you, always, I wish you could laugh." Sara's eyes clouded. Her papery hand reached for his.

"Why are you crying?" Noah scooted closer to her and put his arms around her frail body.

"There's a part of the story I've never told. I'm ashamed to tell you, but I must. Our family's done a terrible thing."

I see it like it was yesterday. The Cossacks stamped-ed across the desolate plains of the Ukraine towards the pitiful town of Yompola.

Into the shtetl they rode on one hundred black stallions. The giant steeds foaming at the mouth were hot and angry from carrying the weight of their masters' evil. The Cossacks brandished their death sabers, slashing at Jewish throats and trampling the fallen until the town was still.

The only survivors in Yompola were me, my sister Faigie, my brother Jossel, my mother Leja. And one other.

Your great-great-grandmother Leja had hidden us in a crazy woman's house. Hadassah, a machashaifeh who possessed the evil eye. The soldiers were afraid to go near her for fear they'd be turned into mice.

Hadassah offered to put a spell on us to keep us safe from harm while we journeyed from Yompola to America. She gave my mother a beautiful box made of polished ebony, sealed with a solid gold lock. In return, she asked that my mother deliver the box to her nephew, Pincus Goldberg in Brooklyn.

She warned us not to open the box. 'If you look inside, I'll know.' She shook a crooked finger in my mother's face. 'I see things. I'll know if you keep your promise to Hadassah, and I can curse as easily as I can bless. A broch tsu dayn lebn. May your life be worthless if you don't keep your word.'

I clung to my mother's skirt. 'Don't shake so, mine Sara,' she whispered as she stroked my hair with trembling fingers.

Your great-great-grandmother knew Hadassah possessed powerful magic. She'd once seen Hadassah give Shmuel-the-Butcher the evil eye, because he sold her a rotten chicken. A week later, Shmuel was dead. My mother yearned for Hadassah's protection. She agreed to deliver the box.

Hadassah huddled us together under the glow of a single candle. She placed her gnarled hands on our shoulders, and she asked God to grant us safe journey.

Standing close to her, I smelled a powerful fragrance like cinnamon, as though Hadassah wore it as perfume. Snow flurries fell through the rafters and swirled at her feet. Snow in August.

The four of us waited until midnight, crept out of Hadassah's hovel with the ebony box, and made our way to the border.

There, as if by magic, we found a horse-drawn wagon. We got underneath the hay spread thick on its floor. Little did we know the wagon transported soldiers across the border into Poland.

At dawn, the soldiers scrambled on top of the hay. One stomped on my neck, his riding boot strangling me. The fumes of cow dung filled my nose. Weight crushed my windpipe. I couldn't sneeze or wheeze. Noise would have meant certain death.

Then, as if under a spell, the soldier raised his boot. He might have had to scratch at lice or pick a scab. But No. Hadassah's blessing had reached God. I gulped air without the soldier hearing. Then, I prayed to be as still as a dead person, until we crossed the border, and the soldiers jumped off the wagon to run to the closest brothel.

Now, here is where the trouble begins. When we went through Ellis Island and my father met us in New York, my mother explained the promise we'd made to Hadassah. We went to Pincus Goldberg's address, but he had moved.

We asked a few people if they knew how to find him, but we didn't try hard enough. My father was in a hurry to get back to St. Louis and his chicken-plucking business.

'I promised,' said my mother. 'Hadassah is powerful.'

'A bobe myse, a fairy tale,' my father said. 'This is America. Your promise no longer matters.'

My mother felt torn between her vow to Hadassah and her covenant to obey her husband. She wrung her hands, but said nothing more. She decided to search for Pincus on her own from St. Louis. Until he could be found, she would safeguard the box.

My mother secreted the ebony box inside a cedar chest, placing it at the bottom of her wardrobe trunk at the foot of her bed. Each night she checked on the ebony box and prayed over it. 'Please God, help me find a way to keep my word to Hadassah.'

One fateful night my mother dug through the trunk and screamed, 'It's gone. We are cursed.' She ran to my father for help.

But it was my father who had taken the ebony box. With a pick and hammer, he'd broken the gold lock. There he'd found three jeweled eggs, brilliantly glazed in pink, blue, and yellow and covered in diamonds, emeralds, sapphires, and rubies.

'Leja, we have mouths to feed," he said. "The children need shoes and milk.'

'What have you done?' My mother sobbed. "Our lives will be worthless. We are cursed forever.'

'Stop crying, you silly woman.'

My father wasted no time in selling the eggs. He used the money to start his grocery business, the beginning of our family's fortune: money stolen from Hadassah's nephew in New York.

Sara grabbed Noah's face, pulling him toward her. "Hadassah isn't finished with us. In my dreams last night, she visited. She told me our family would pay for stealing from hers. 'A broch tsu dayn lebn,' she threatened."

May your life be worthless.

Noah had never heard about the ebony box. He'd grown up listening to stories about his industrious ancestor and the grocery store chain he'd founded. Decades later, it had morphed into a thriving pharmaceutical business. Noah had absorbed the lesson that hard work, ethics, and honesty equaled contributing to the world. Now, he registered another one of life's many disappointments: Sara had fabricated their family history.

"The Cossacks are rising," she said. "They're brandishing their death sabers." Great-Grandma Sara's expression revealed the terror of eighty-seven years ago. "Go see Sally. You're both in trouble. You must figure out how to make things right before Hadassah harms you. Promise me." Tears collected in the creases of her face.

Noah wanted to ask her to explain why she had lied all these years rather than trust him with the truth. Instead he rocked her like she was a small child, his arms around her thin, bent shoulders. "I promise."

Sara fell silent. She rested on Noah's chest, the weight of her story and its legacy now transferred to her great-grandson.

A blast of cold air hit Noah's face. It smelled of snow and cinnamon. His skin prickled.

Sara raised her head, rasping a guttural noise. She lifted an arm and pointed toward something in front of her. "Huh. Huh..."

"What, Grandma?"

She tried again to gesture, but her arm fell limp by her side. "Hadassah." She stared at Noah with a look of horror and her body slumped.

Kitsala hissed. Teeth bared, she leapt off the love seat. She clawed the air with one paw, back arched, black hair puffed and raised on end. She let out a keening yowl.

Noah shuddered.

Sara was gone.

Chapter Three

Noah hauled himself off his crumpled bed, crunched across crud in the carpet, kicked loose papers blocking the front door, and stepped outside into the electro-magnetic field.

Driving rain pummeled streets, bounced, and ricocheted sideways. He felt like a neutron in heavy water, but he muscled through the deluge, dodging potholes toward his target: Jimmy's Café.

He craved *Celeritas*: the adrenaline of exercise, the kick of caffeine. He ran from the sadness of losing Great-Grandma Sara and toward his life-long friend, Fleck McNulty.

For the past year, Fleck had been reporting for a television station in Des Moines. Communication had been sketchy at best. Hell, Noah hadn't even known Fleck had returned to town until he'd shown up at Great-Grandma Sara's funeral, wending his way through the condolence line.

Fleck had offered his sympathy before whispering, "I need your help. ASAP." They'd agreed to meet for coffee.

Noah's running shoes spanked the concrete. The smell of ions stirred his senses. He sloshed through a street puddle, darted under Jimmy's storefront awning, and pushed through the door.

The café buzzed with conversation and the click of laptop keys. Noah spotted Fleck's Cardinals baseball cap bobbing above a spread-open front page of the *RiverFront Times*.

He wove through tables of patrons who chatted, read or stared blankly past their cups. Floor space was at a premium, and he pivoted sideways, trying to avoid seated customers. Still, he dripped rainwater all over a businessman who then startled, bewildered by the sudden dampness.

"Sorry." Noah grimaced and rushed toward Fleck. He snatched his friend's newspaper, a surprise attack. "Caught you in the act."

Fleck saved his tipping cup and looked up with calm green eyes, the color between cucumbers and Gumby. "Act of what?"

"Gathering news from a reliable source."

"There's more news printed on this paper cup than in this rag." He studied Noah, then shook his head. "You still on a no-driving kick? Sheez. Sit down before you soak me."

"Never drive when you can walk."

"Never drive when you can swim is more like it." Fleck offered a napkin. "Mop up."

Noah swiped his wet face and settled into a chair.

Fleck pushed a lidded coffee toward him. "I bought your boring favorite."

Noah dug into his damp khakis for his wallet and

slid two twenties across the table.

Fleck's mouth scrunched below his pin-straight nose. "I think you know that, despite inflation, coffee's only three bucks."

"When you find a job, buy me an electric car. In the meantime...."

"How'd you know I lost my job?"

"Why else would you move back?"

Fleck's knees bounced beneath the table. "I gotta work on something more important than a small-town broadcast."

Noah understood—no explanation needed. They both shared a desire to make a difference in the world. Their constant search for a way to do it remained one of their strongest bonds.

Fleck shoved the twenties into his jeans pocket. "Thanks. I'll pay you back. Got something huge in the works." He scanned the room, but apparently didn't see what he was looking for. "You doing okay? You and Great-Grandma were close."

Noah felt awkward admitting he struggled with this. "She had a long life. I'm adjusting." In truth, Noah believed he would still have a connection with her somehow, if he could just expand his awareness.

"Still saving the world one discovery at a time?"

"Getting closer."

Fleck leaned in. "What're you working on?"

"You really want to hear this?"

"Tell me."

Noah sighed. "Just remember, you asked. I'm working on the theorem that awareness is the fifth dimension."

"There are five dimensions?"

"In 1919, Theodor Kaluza proposed there were more than four and even Einstein was intrigued by the concept. But only four dimensions fit our common experience: left-right, back-forth, up-down, and past-future."

"Three spatial dimensions plus time."

Noah smiled. "You got it."

"Physics osmosis. I've soaked up a few things from you over the years."

"String theorists suggest the universe actually has eleven dimensions. I'm working on describing the fifth dimension as low data-high data or awareness."

"And M.I.T. pays you a fellowship for this?"

"Enough to get by."

"I'm lost."

"Here." Noah took a pen from his damp jacket and grabbed another napkin. "I can pinpoint exactly where you are with four pieces of data. You are at a specific left-right dimension...." He drew a horizontal line on the napkin and the number one. "...A specific back-forth dimension...." He drew a vertical line through it and the number two. "...That represents the address of Jimmy's Café. You are at an exact height, or up-down dimension, about five hundred feet above sea level, since we're in St. Louis, and we're on the first floor." He inked a dot above the horizontal line, labeling it with a three.

"Additionally, it's 10:07 a.m." Noah wrote 10:07 on the napkin and the number four. "See? Four dimensions. So, if you said, 'Meet me at Broadway and Market in St. Louis on the third floor at 11:15 a.m.,

Tuesday, August 10, 2002, I got you, right?"

Fleck shrugged. "Right."

"Not right." Noah smiled. Fleck was such an easy mark. "Let's say I process dissimilar or more information than you."

Fleck rolled his eyes. "No duh."

"This is hypothetical."

"We both know you're smarter than me."

"That's not true. We just have different smarts. Anyway, this has nothing to do with intelligence. Information can be sensory, like sights, smells, or sounds. Creative connection. ESP. If I process more data, I have heightened awareness. Maybe I meet you at those coordinates on August 10, 2002, but if I'm focused on atoms, or photons, or a microbe, or an alternate universe, I'm not where you are. I can't find you."

Noah's senses spiked, his nerve endings tingling. "My brain has a different holographic experience than yours, depending on the amount or kind of data we each compute at any given place and time. Understand?"

He felt high on camaraderie and exchange. So high, it jolted him up and out. In a flash, a nanosecond, Fleck disappeared. The café and patrons became a pitch-black void. Brilliant color streaked across Noah's visual field. Miniature blue, red, gold, and purple comets.

Holy Einstein. It's so beautiful.

Noah was conscious of loving eyes. A shower of rose petals swirled through the nothingness, landing at his feet, making deep piles of velvety scarlet. He inhaled an overpowering fragrance of flowers, redolent of a memory: at the age of three he had held Sara's hand, walked through her garden, and sniffed a rose for the first time. Now, mixed with this scent, Noah detected a faint trace of chicken soup, cat litter and bleach.

Straight ahead, a path led to a garden gate covered with violet clematis vines. Behind it stood the seventy-something Sara of his youth.

Her hair hung thick, her face was vibrant. "Hello, *bubala*."

"Grandma, I found you."

"Is that so difficult? Listen. Stop moping about me and get to work. Easy it won't be, but you'll be fine. Shave and wear a suit. You look like a bum."

"I don't know what I'm supposed to do."

She touched his shoulder.

He felt rainbows, ocean waves, and dancing fire. "Grandma, is this where the energy goes?"

His high dissipated. He slipped down, down, surged away and slid back into his body. Sara disappeared, replaced by the noise of café patrons and the scents of java and sugared pastry.

"Kind of like *The Matrix*?" Fleck asked.

"What?"

"Is your theory like *The Matrix*?" Fleck asked a second time.

Noah found the thread. "I'm creating a mathematical formula to calculate awareness and synchronicity patterns of universal consciousness."

"I have no idea what you just said."

"This is why I don't bother to explain my work."

"It's worth it for me to see the look on your face. Your eyes light up and you get all red and intense. You love this shit." Fleck sipped his coffee, his eyes scanning the room before settling back on Noah. "I need to tell you what I'm working on."

"This is why you wanted to meet."

He nodded. "When I was in Des Moines, I researched companies that distribute AIDS drugs to African nations."

"You were assigned to local news. Is this why you got fired?"

"Whatever. Anyway, there's a large African community in Des Moines. I made connections. You remember the movie, *The Constant Gardener?*"

Noah shook his head. "Not again."

Ever since Noah could remember, Fleck had dug up media stories that reflected Hollywood blockbusters like *Casablanca* or *Blood Diamond*.

"Fleck, stop watching old films."

"I'm a journalist. How else do you think we find stories? And it paid off too, 'cause I'm onto something." Fleck chewed on his swizzle stick. "Here's the thing. It involves Sally."

Noah blinked in surprise. "My mother?"

"I found a shaman who tracks AIDS villagers on the drug Telaxiphentol. He's documented that patients on the drug do no better than those without the drug."

"What does this have to do with my mother?"

"She's offering to sell Friedman Pharmaceutical to Duschene International."

"What?" The news caught Noah off-guard. Apparently, he'd been more out of touch with Mom than he'd thought.

Fleck squinted. "You didn't know?"

"How'd you learn this?"

"Researching Duschene. Friedman Pharmaceutical was listed as an acquisition target."

Now his mom's incessant nagging about him coming to work for her took on more urgency. She wanted out. If he wouldn't be her successor, she'd sell. Noah felt lighter. Perhaps at last she understood his love of physics. "How is her sale connected to your story?"

"It's not. Here's the thing. Telaxiphentol is distributed by Duschene."

"You and this shaman think the company's doing something shady?"

Fleck spit into his right hand, slapped it on the table, then placed it over his heart, their childhood sacred oath. "Will you talk to Sally for me?"

"Right before Great-Grandma Sara died, she told me to wear a suit and visit my mother's office."

"See? A synchronicity. Anyway, you can't stay mad at Sally forever."

"I'm not mad. She just drives me crazy."

Fleck shook his head.

"Don't worry about it. We talked at Sara's *shiva*. I made a promise to Great-Grandma, and I intend to keep it. I'm just not sure how."

"Promise about what?"

"Long story short: my family pissed off a ghost, and I've gotta make it all better."

"Sounds like Hamlet."

Noah sipped his coffee, thinking how he might finish his research and absolve his family's curse at the same time. Einstein had worked for the Swiss patent office while he'd written his paper on special relativity. Anything was possible. "Every time I see my mother, she offers me a job. Thinks I should be in management, or something equally ridiculous. You've given me good news. Maybe if she's selling, I can work there for a short stint."

"I knew you'd end up pushing drugs. Will you talk to Sally?"

"Maybe. No promises." Noah removed his green notebook from his jacket pocket. "Tell me more about this shaman."

"I want you to meet him."

"Is he here? I thought he lived in Africa."

"He flies back and forth. People do that, you know. They drive cars, too." Fleck eyeballed the room again. "There's one more thing. Jean-Paul says he knows you."

Noah scribbled July 20 on a fresh sheet of journal paper. "I'd remember meeting a shaman."

"From his dreams."

Noah looked up. His skin got that prickly feeling all over.

"He said it's his destiny to meet you." Fleck lowered his voice. "Okay, I'm just going to say this. He said you're going to change the world."

Noah stared at his melodramatic friend. "Every living organism does that every second of the day. You know, a butterfly flaps its wings in South America...I've explained this."

"No. Transformative change."

"My theory." Noah slapped the table. Paper cups jumped, splashing trickles of coffee down their sides. "I must be closer than I thought."

"Here's the hard part. He says you're in danger."

"Huh?"

"I don't know what he means, but I trust this man."

"If you're fucking with me, you're doing a good job. I'm only a pill away from being a delusional paranoid as it is."

Fleck locked eyes with him. "You're on your meds, right?"

"Why would you ask me that?"

"You don't look like you're taking care of yourself."

Noah pushed his chair back from the table. "What the hell?"

"Just making sure you're okay. Anyway, you brought it up."

"I was joking. Apparently, you lost your sense of humor when you lost your job. Look, my mom bugs me about taking my meds every time I see her. I don't need my best friend joining in. I thought we had a deal."

Fleck's face flamed the red of his cap. "We do. I was wrong."

Noah rested his elbow on the table and offered his hand to Fleck arm-wrestling style. Fleck clasped it, and Noah nailed him in one move. "I've still got it."

"I let you win."

"Did not."

Noah could never stay mad at his goofball friend, and while they both got annoyed with each other from time to time, there was an unbreakable bond between them. "Don't worry about me. I'm on shots."

Fleck used the coffee dribbles on the table as paint, moving his swizzle stick through the puddles. "Just covering the bases."

"This is lame. I'm not even going to write this stuff

down." Suddenly, he felt the dampness from his clothes and shoes down to his bones. He shivered. "Man, Jimmy's cranked the AC way up. Is he around?"

Rain hammered the storefront window. A crack of lightning illuminated the sidewalk. Noah counted. One, two...thunder roared overhead. A whoop from the crowd washed over him. A few patrons clapped.

"Wow, that's close." Noah opened his Synchronicities Journal to the page where he'd jotted July 20. "Worse than when I came in here." Next to the date he wrote "Thunderstorm, omen, African shaman." He looked up at Fleck. "Slow down and tell me about this shaman again."

Fleck's focus shifted above Noah's head. He smiled. "He can tell you himself. Noah, meet Jean-Paul Amon."

A broad-shouldered man moved from behind Noah's chair and stretched a muscled arm in greeting.

Noah shook his hand. In his firm grip he felt rainbows, ocean waves, and dancing fire. Just as he had with Sara.

Jean-Paul insisted that Noah share his theory. Fleck excused himself, grumbling that he'd already heard the spiel and wouldn't understand if his brainiac friend explained it twice or a hundred times.

The shaman listened with his whole body, nodding like a drumstick keeping beat to a psychedelic trance band. Most people's eyes glazed over after about thirty seconds of Noah's rap. Insights on synchronicities

(Huh?) or multiple dimensions (Gimme a break.) made them shift in their seats. The conversations usually dead-ended with, "Gotta get going."

The shaman's eyes stayed glued on Noah until he finished. Jean-Paul Amon presented an odd mix of contrasts: modern and traditional, dark and light, tough and gentle, still and animated. He wore a blue and white woven cotton pillbox cap and matching dashiki pared with jeans and Nikes, a fashion statement that suggested he both honored his heritage and embraced change.

Jean-Paul closed his eyes and breathed in, an island of calm oblivious to the sounds of café clatter and patrons drifting past. He turned his hands face up on the table as if to evoke a higher power.

Noah sat transfixed, watching while the man breathed in and out, in and out, his body relaxed in the solitude he'd created amid the surrounding hubbub.

His midnight eyes opened again, and Noah envisioned people traveling long distances at great sacrifice to gather around this man. "You work on things no one else can see?" Jean-Paul smiled.

Cynicism, Noah thought. "Yes."

A chuckle became a laugh. "You work on making sense out of this nothingness?"

Noah felt a pang of sharp disappointment. He hoped he'd found someone who would understand the importance of his work. Guess not.

"You see that everything is connected?" Jean-Paul laughed harder.

Noah's face heated. "Yes."

His shoulders shook. "Then, my friend, we work on

the same thing. That is funny. The same thing."

Noah stared, confused.

"Never mind." Jean-Paul's laughter waned. "I have worked on this connectedness my whole life. As my father before me. As his father before him. Spirit work. We have so much in common."

"I'm studying physics."

"Same thing. Spirit work. Noah Freeman, you are my brother."

Noah weighed the pros and cons before adding anyone to his select circle. Usually the cons won. Yet, somehow, and he couldn't quite articulate it, he felt drawn to Jean-Paul. Could he join forces with him and Fleck? "What country are you from?"

"Burkina Faso, in Central West Africa."

"French speaking, right?"

"French is my native tongue. Here, of course, I speak English. Except when I am nervous. Then, everything comes out in French."

"So, when you speak French we're in trouble?"

"It takes a lot to make me nervous. You will hear me speak Dagara, the language of my tribe."

Jean-Paul told Noah about his villagers who suffered from AIDS and had sought relief through the drug, Telaxiphentol. He believed Duschene International had shipped either placebos or tainted drugs to his people. "The Ancestors tell me it is purposeful."

"Aren't ancestors dead?"

"Define death. They are not flesh and blood, but even so, they are with us all the time. In my village, the Ancestors guide all the decisions."

Perhaps Jean-Paul would understand Noah's encounter with his departed great-grandma. This cheered him.

"Never mind. I will teach you." Jean-Paul's brow furrowed and his arms edged the table. "I need proof before I accuse Duschene of shipping contaminated or diluted drugs. Fleck tells me you have contacts. Will you help?"

Begging a favor from his mom required reciprocal endurance of a cycle of dinners plus gratuitous super-vision. "Fleck exaggerated. I've no connections at Dus-chene, and I don't know if my mom does either. Why don't you ask your government or the United Nations for help?"

"All governments are on the take," the shaman de-clared. "Also, I cannot go to United Nations' officials without concrete proof. Otherwise, people will think I am crazy. I am sure you know what I am talking about."

Noah wondered exactly what Fleck had told the shaman. "What do you mean?"

"I have offended you. Do not be afraid of who you are. In my village, you would be considered a shaman in the making." He rested a strong hand on Noah's shoulder. "You carry important messages the world needs to hear, Noah Freeman."

"Friedman. Noah Friedman."

Jean-Paul lifted Noah's pen, scribbled on a napkin, and turned it on the table to face him. "No-a-free-man. You are free to do what you want. I need your help."

Noah spent his days in a fog: thinking, studying data, and imagining possibilities. "I don't know any-thing about corporations, governments, or international drug distribution. Crap, I can't even organize myself to clean my apartment or buy groceries. Why me?"

"Because you will be sympathetic to my people's cause. You understand how it feels to take drugs that kill."

Noah shook his head. Perhaps he'd misunderstood the man. Language barrier, after all. Still, his intuition bristled. "Excuse me?"

"My friend, this is what I came to tell you. The drugs you are on...you must stop taking them now."

BAD MEDICINE

Chapter Four

When Noah's kindergarten class gathered in a circle in the center of the room for playtime, Noah would walk around the group in a perfect square. *Walk toward the windows. Stop. Turn left. Walk toward the door. Stop. Turn left. Walk toward the blackboard. Stop. Turn left. Walk toward the art corner. Stop. Turn left. Walk toward the windows....*

"Noah Friedman, sit down," his teacher would call out. Noah couldn't sit. He would run to the sink in the art corner and wash his hands thirty, forty times, feeling the cold water wash away his imperfections. *Bad, Noah. You made a mess. Bad, Noah. Clean it up.*

"Noah Friedman, what are you doing? Stop that."

His hands chafed from cold water and the friction of constant scrubbing. His knuckles bled. They looked like those of the school cafeteria ladies who spooned out green beans and Sloppy Joes.

The principal told Sally to do something about her son, or she'd have to send him to another school more suited for special needs children. She handed Sally a slip of paper with the name and phone number of Dr. Roger DeMarko.

Noah held his mother's hand as she guided him down the hallway to the doctor's office. Her lotion smelled like Great-Grandma Sara's roses. His ear brushed against her polished-cotton sheath; it made a swishing noise in rhythm with her stilettos, clacking hollow on the terrazzo floor.

Sally met with the doctor alone while Noah played Lego's in the reception room. The blocks, sticky from candy or soda, prompted him to wash his hands at the water cooler. By the time Mom came back for him, he had built a space station and lunar rover, his hands cracked with fresh scrub spots.

Dr. DeMarko led Noah into his office so they could "play with dolls and talk."

Noah bolted underneath a table in the corner of the room. While drawing pictures of rocket ships, he bit his lips, shook his head, and stared at the doctor's crossed legs.

The doctor scribbled on yellow paper with a silver pen, one leg kicking back and forth, swinging higher and higher.

"Do you like chocolate chip cookies? I've got some here with milk." Fleshy fingers balanced a paper plate, and the man wore a smile that Noah didn't believe. He was bald except for spiky blond hair on the sides of his head that stuck straight out. His thick, black spectacles, bulbous nose and mustache reminded Noah of the gag eyeglasses at the five and dime.

Noah crawled out from under the table and walked around the perimeter of the office. He wanted to talk to the potted philodendron in the corner. It had much to tell him and kept trying to gain his attention with cries of help. *I'm thirsty. I'm dusty. Need sun.*

Walk towards the door. Stop. Turn left. Walk towards the plant. Stop. Turn left....

✸

A week later, Noah visited the man with the gag glasses again. His mom talked with Dr. DeMarko while Noah built a Lego launch pad. When she came back, her face was blotched red and shiny.

Mommy only cried when she and Daddy fought. "What's wrong, Mommy?"

Sally knelt, her knees making dimples in the carpet, and she put her arms around him. Her tears felt warm and wet on Noah's face, and he tasted salt mixed with face cream. "I'm crying because I'm happy."

It scared Noah when she lied.

"Everything's going to be fine." Sally hugged him too tight.

She took Noah to a Chinese restaurant where his father, Steven, joined them for dinner. His parents ordered a *Happy Family* meal but ate in stony silence. Noah went to the bathroom to wash his hands.

His dad marched in after him. "Noah, stop doing that. Don't make me come in here again to get you, or you'll be spanked."

Noah rejoined the silence at the table. He took a sip of his soda and accidentally set the tumbler on a chopstick. The glass teetered and fell, spilling the contents on the Chinese red tablecloth. A blood red stain spread disaster toward his parents.

Bad Noah. You made a mess. He wailed. He'd tried so hard to be good, but he always seemed to make his parents unhappy.

"It's okay, baby." Sally mopped up the soda with her napkin. "We'll get more."

Noah wailed louder.

"Stop it." His father's forehead beaded with sweat. "We're in a restaurant."

Noah strained his vocal chords. In the reflection of a silver teapot, his face turned purple.

"Stop it. Damn it." Dad grabbed his shoulder.

Louder. Red. Purple.

"Steven, lower your voice. He's scared."

"He needs to shut up. You're too soft on him."

The woman who owned the restaurant came over to the table. "I help you? Something wrong?"

Steven tried to lift Noah out of his seat, but he slid down in his chair, wrapping his legs around the table pedestal and squeezing tight. All eyes in the restaurant turned and stared. He'd upset his dad. He'd made both his parents unhappy. Bad, very bad.

"Sally, help me get him out of here." Steven and Sally each held an arm and pulled, finally freeing Noah's legs from around the table.

"Nooooo." Noah's teapot face turned violet, his neck bulged. His hands clenched in tight fists.

His parents dragged him, arms flailing, legs kicking to the nearest exit.

The Chinese restaurant owner ran after them into the parking lot with a to-go container of *Happy Family*. Tears streamed down her round face. "Don't beat him. Please."

Soon, Noah was visiting the man with the gag glasses every afternoon. Sometimes, Noah stayed underneath the table in the corner while the man jotted notes and said nothing until it was time for Noah to leave.

The medicine and the brain scans didn't start until 1986, when Noah turned eight.

Noah remembers the year, can pinpoint the month, because shortly after that, the space shuttle exploded.

The whole elementary school was watching when the Challenger blew up, the space teacher evaporating into the ether. Noah's view of an ordered world turned into trailing streams of ash.

Noah's teacher couldn't stop him from screaming. The principal tried to reach Sally, but her secretary said she was on the road. Steven was traveling on business as well, so they called the next person on the emergency list and Noah went home with his next-door neighbor.

He snuck over to his house for his Lego set, the one with the space shuttle assembly. It might take him all afternoon, but he'd snap all the small square pieces together, make the shuttle brand new, and then everything would be okay.

Laughter floated down the hall from his parents' bedroom. Mom. Noah wanted to talk to her about Challenger and how sad he felt. He peeked in.

Mommy was naked. It looked like she and Dad were play wrestling. His mother rolled over and now the man, bald-headed with blond spikes on the side, was on top. On the nightstand Noah saw thick, black glasses.

Dr. DeMarko looked up and let Noah know he'd done a bad thing. He should never have peeked. He hated when he made mistakes. Now Mom would be upset, and Dad would be angry. Noah vowed to try harder. He would be perfect from now on.

He didn't bother to get his Legos. He crept down the stairs and out the back, careful to close the door without making a sound.

Dr. Roger DeMarko's exam room remained unchanged in the almost fifteen years Noah had been showing up for injections and brain scans. The same leggy philodendron in the corner struggled to survive under fluorescent lights. A poster slapped against a mint green wall advertised the PBS special, *The Brain*, sponsored by Ciba-Geigy, manufacturers of Ritalin and Lithobid. Balloon labels designated hemispheres, lobes and cortexes of the mushroom-shaped organ. "Peer into the workings and structure of the living human brain and learn about science's remarkable drug advances." On the counter, a hypodermic needle filled with thick orange serum waited to be jabbed into Noah's arm.

The room looked the same, but Noah felt different. Jean-Paul's words looped like a recording on replay. *You must stop taking these drugs.*

Just stop. Simple.

Only it wasn't. Noah had experimented once by going off his meds and suffered the consequences. What had prompted Jean-Paul's advice? What did he know and how? Why, when Noah knew all that could happen to him without the drug, did the shaman's words make so much sense?

DeMarko had his faults. Okay, he was pretty much an asshole, but he'd kept Noah functioning at a high level. Noah maintained relationships. He suffered fewer mood swings. His OCD symptoms were under control. Sure, he might obsess over his research, but that was healthy obsession toward a goal, right? Compulsions like locking doors, checking the stove burners, patting his pockets, scrubbing his hands, had all but disappeared. DeMarko deserved much of the credit, which warranted Noah's trust.

Noah intended to discuss his options with DeMarko, man to man. Together, they would settle on a course of action. As an adult, he could use Depakote, Lithium, or other drugs. He needed to step up and take control of his treatment.

Roger DeMarko entered the exam room, closing the door behind him. He gifted Noah with a supercilious nod. "How's the Master of the Universe?"

Noah didn't take the bait. "Fine."

DeMarko's pudgy finger trawled through a bulky,

yellow file that rested on his protruding belly. "Liver's clean, blood level's normal. Everything looks good."

The file's weight gain reflected DeMarko's. Every time Noah saw him for another test or consultation, a few pages of notes entered the file, and a few more pounds expanded the bulk of the psychiatrist.

Noah decided to get right to it. He focused on sounding confident. "I'd like to look for alternatives to Selexikote."

DeMarko looked up, surprised and annoyed. "Why would you want to do that?"

He hated DeMarko's snot-nose tone. "I don't think it's smart to be on anything long-term. Side effects. You know."

"Selexikote's side-effects are minimal, barely noticeable. It's in your best interest to stay with the program."

DeMarko refused to make this easy, but Noah didn't miss a beat. "I'm thinking of moving to Boston, so the injections won't be practical. I'd like to be on pills."

DeMarko sank onto his exam stool. He adjusted his black glasses to the end of his nose, peering through them at Noah as though inspecting a foreign microbe. He smoothed his moustache and folded his arms. "I'm afraid that isn't possible."

"Why not?"

"You already know what happens if you go off the drugs."

"I'm not going off the drugs. I just want another option. Instead of shots, put me on pills."

"Who's going to monitor you?"

"I'm older now. You can trust me."

DeMarko smirked. "Your last manic episode was merely three years ago."

"Exactly. Just one time. Three years ago. I'll get a doctor in Boston. He'll test my blood levels."

"Another doctor won't have access to Selexikote."

"Give it to him. Or my mom will give it to him."

DeMarko flushed. "We've talked about this before. You know very well we can't do that when it's still in testing."

Yes, Noah recalled. Multiple discussions. Three years earlier, Noah had questioned his feeling that the drug accelerated his ability to think, making him feel like an intellectual athlete on steroids. DeMarko had told him that was nonsense, a symptom of delusion. He'd refused to listen, so Noah had refused to take the pills. After the manic episode, the doc had added a diagnosis of passive-aggressive to Noah's list of psychological issues. He'd put him on shots.

Noah pressed. "I'm moving to Boston to finish my research."

Sweat dotted DeMarko's forehead. "Have you discussed this with your mother?"

Noah hated DeMarko's habit of dragging his mother into their conversations. "I'm your patient, not Sally."

"Everything you tell me is confidential."

Noah laughed. "Sure."

"I developed this drug for you on Sally's behalf. Naturally, we talk about it. Particularly now."

"What do you mean?"

"Because of Duschene." DeMarko's face brightened. "The acquisition. They're interested in distributing Selexikote. They want to make it available to a wide market."

Noah felt a stab of surprise. "Really?"

"I've been meeting with Sally and the head of Duschene." DeMarko smiled, his upper lip disappearing beneath his moustache. "This could be an important development for kids with bipolar disorder. We're on the forefront of something big. You and me. I just need a few more tests."

Noah gestured to the binder DeMarko cradled like a case of Hostess Ding-Dongs. "You've got a file full of tests."

"The FDA needs tests for a prescribed length of time. You'll have been on this drug for fifteen years as of next February. No one has such a unique history. Stay in town. Help me. Do something important for the world."

Noah saw the doctor's wet palm prints where he gripped the manila folder. "Why so nervous, Doc?"

DeMarko looked at him accusingly. "You're deflecting. We're discussing the importance of contribution."

"I'm contributing," Noah said. "My research..."

"...about coincidence?" DeMarko broke in. "It's a sign of being manic."

"M.I.T. feels differently."

"It's a harbinger we shouldn't ignore. Maybe I should increase your dosage." DeMarko scribbled in the file.

Noah wondered what comments DeMarko noted. Every time he expressed an opinion, he wound-up labeled with another emotional problem. To hell with DeMarko's designer meds. To hell with his mother's opinion about what was good for him. He would find a new psychiatrist. "Coincidence happens all the time," Noah said. "I study the frequency, the repeat patterns. For instance, it's no coincidence you're always an asshole. You'd be a great case study."

DeMarko glared at him. He slammed the file onto the counter, making the hypodermic needle jump.

The wall intercom buzzed. "Dr. DeMarko, I have Charles Dalton on the line for you."

"Dalton? Great. Ask him to hang on a minute. I'll take it in my office."

DeMarko turned toward the counter and fiddled with the file. He wheeled around and shoved the hypodermic needle into Noah's left arm, gripping tight until all the searing liquid plunged deep into the muscle.

Noah yelped. "What the hell...Jesus, what did you do that for?" Blood trickled from the puncture wound. Stunned, he mechanically rubbed his arm.

"I don't have time to argue. I've got to take this call. We'll talk about this when you're back for your next injection." DeMarko opened the door, then spun around to face him. "You're very bright, in case you didn't know. I hope your research goes well." DeMarko scurried from the room.

Noah's arm pulsed. Blood banged in his ears. He felt pressure in his head, like his brain was an imploding, dying star. He couldn't believe what had just happened. This was way over the top, even for crazy-assed De-Marko.

The file lay on the utility counter. Bold letters on the tab of the folder called out to him: **NOAH FRIED-MAN**. DeMarko's haste created Noah's opportunity.

He wanted to study the contents. He desired self-knowledge, and he needed to understand the meds he'd been on much of his life. He'd incorporate every detail of the sad history into his DNA.

Surveying the room for the last time, he petted the potted plant, caressing a waxy leaf and wiping gritty dust from its surface. "Sorry, buddy. Good luck."

He hefted the record of his brain: categorized, charted, and dissected, every cell scoped, mapped and inspected. Hugging the evidence to his chest, he escaped DeMarko's office.

For: **Noah Friedman** file
From: Dr. Roger DeMarko
Re: Manic episode, March 23, 1999
Noah went off medication March 18. Unusually quick onset of full-blown mania. Selexikote stays in blood stream an exceptionally short time period. More tests needed.

Patient must stay on Selexikote. Prescribe shot regimen instead of pills. Concern: next manic episode will be faster onset and increased escalation.

Noah picked up by police. No hospitalization necessary. Taped interview with subject transcribed March 23, 1999:

It started with birds. I noticed one was following me everywhere I went. One morning I left the school library and a mourning dove (hey that's a coincidence, morning and mourning) landed a few feet in front of me on the walk. It fluttered its wings and flew off when I got closer, but then it landed again on a lamppost a few feet down the path. I reached the lamppost and it took off again, then settled with another dove on a mailbox in front of me. I walked by the mailbox and a pair of cardinals joined the doves. Then orange finches. Then two crows, a pair of blue jays, orioles, parrots, flamingoes, ospreys, a bald eagle. An ostrich.

I walked down the street with a flock of every kind of bird before me. Song clanged in my ears. High pitched noise. Then I noticed the birds chirped in unison. If I thought, 'I should work on global warming,' or 'I can solve world peace,' the birds validated my dreams by twirping. I would think, 'My work is important,' and the birds, every single variety of species in front of me on the path (there must have been dozens) would chorus, "Chirp. Chirp. Chirp." It was deafening, and it was beautiful.

There were so many birds they blocked the sun and noise of traffic. Feathers floated through the air; little wisps of gray, brown, red, blue, yellow, riding the breeze on their way to earth—not by chance, but orchestrated, making a thick floor of feathers upon the path for me to walk.

The chirping became a message. 'We're hungry. The world is hungry.' I ran into a hardware store and asked for birdseed. The clerk pointed to the back aisle; I grabbed a cart and filled it with bags. I didn't know which kind to get. Should I get finch food? Wild bird food? Parakeet feed? So, I filled two carts. I couldn't find my credit card so I promised the clerk I'd be back to pay for the seed.

I ran into the street, flinging seed everywhere—on the sidewalk, the street, on trees, passing cars, on people walking by. Polly seeds, bits of corn, nuts, flax seeds—all raining down. Birds flocked to convertibles, jeeps, trucks and to the pavement, scooping up seed with their beaks. "Chirp. Chirp."

I saw motorists shake their fists and make faces, their mouths red and angry, their knuckles white on the steering wheels. I created a torrential downpour, a flood of seed at the intersection. The birds told me to feed the world, and to start with them. I had to make sure they had enough to eat so they could tell me what to do.

What is it I'm supposed to do? I must deliver my gifts, and I need to know what they are.

The police showed up. I explained I was helping. If they would just let me feed the birds, the birds would tell me how to serve the world. I promised to go back to the store and pay for the seed, but they pointed fingers and pushed.

"Noah, we've had reports on your behavior before," the policeman said.

What does that mean?

"Stop bothering my daughter," he said.

Who is his daughter? What is he talking

about?

I felt sun on my face, searing my skin. It was so hot.

I looked up. The birds were gone.

For: **Noah Friedman** File
From: Dr. Roger DeMarko
Re: Selexikote testing, June 3, 1999
Neurogenesis in rats after twice-daily Selexikote injections initiated.

Autopsies revealed: By end of 10-day regimen, new neurons generated and integrated into circuitry of hippocampus region of rats' brains.

Noah's cognitive tests and EEG's, over a period of ten years, consistently show increased ability in learning and memory.

Findings: brain cell growth, particularly in the hippocampus area, increasing at accelerated rate due to Selexikote.

Recommendation: increase Noah's dosage and shorten testing intervals. Continue control groups.

For: **Noah Friedman** file
From: Dr. Roger DeMarko
Re: Selexikote testing, July 22, 1999
Additional side effects noted.
Documentation transported: CBDJFG

Noah sat on a park bench in the summer heat. A forest of trees converted into paper smothered the lower half of his body and weighed him down, as he tried to understand the implications evident on every page of his medical file.

Drugs were responsible for his intelligence? He was an impostor, an ordinary guy with average smarts who'd been duped by DeMarko. His head reeled and he felt nauseous.

He'd relied on his smarts ever since he could remember. A strong link connected genius to mental disorder, DeMarko had told him, and his mother had reinforced it. He'd read biographies supporting that assertion: famously bipolar people like Mozart, Sylvia Plath, Virginia Woolf, or Van Gogh; and closeted manic-depressives like Isaac Newton, Nicola Tesla, Abraham Lincoln or Winston Churchill. An endless list.

Noah wasn't a genius. He was just disordered, damaged, and bolstered by drugs.

He became aware of eyes watching. Something sinister wafted through the trees, swaying the branches of a nearby oak. Just his imagination. Just his body and brain sensing coming disaster. The file entries stated additional side effects. *Documentation transported: CBDJFG.*

Why had DeMarko hidden these test results? CBDJFG. A code? An acronym? Since he'd grown so many extra brain cells, he should be able to come up with the answers.

Fleck, Jean-Paul and Great-Grandma Sara had been right. Only Noah hadn't seen he was in trouble, and he didn't know if he could rely on himself to get out of it. He didn't even know who he was.

He watched a mourning dove fly overhead. Oh, to be small-brained and oblivious. It gracefully swooped down low, spreading its fawn-colored wings wide against a cerulean sky, and dropped a bird shit bomb on an EEG test-result authorized and signed *Dr. Roger DeMarko.*

Thanks, buddy, I get the message. A speckle of droppings landed where Noah's name had been printed on the binder tab. What a critic.

He wiped his name clean with his index finger, blurring the ink and staining his finger pad with the last two letters of his first name, *ah*, as though meaning was being revealed.

Two things were clear, and together they couldn't be reconciled: He needed to stay on his meds; He needed to get off his meds.

When he didn't take his medication, his world spun out of control. He still dealt with the aftermath of his manic episode three years ago, which had lasted two months before he could gain some measure of stability.

He'd racked up bills that swallowed his cash. They'd choked his kitchen table, spilling off onto the floor. Thick window envelopes had poured in month after month as though they mated in the mailbox, producing offspring. He still hadn't paid off his debts.

Noah's spending spree had included four state-of-the-art computers so he could be in touch with everything on the web and in the universe simultaneously. He bought a new Prius, then crashed it into a tree the following day. He purchased five Armani suits, coordinated with shirts and ties, and gave them to homeless people he found on the street. He handed out seventy-five pairs of ergonomically correct running shoes at a 10K fundraiser. He donated funds that weren't in his bank account to the National Resource Defense Council, Peak Oil Foundation, Save Darfur, American Red Cross, and the Rainbow Push Coalition. He bought a flat screen TV for his girlfriend's apartment as a parting gift the day he ended their relationship—an homage to their movie romance.

When he'd depleted his trust fund, he spent money he didn't have and took out loans to cover the debt.

Only when he'd come down from the high did he assess the damage and replay his crimes over and over in his mind, repeating the list like a psalm, a prayer that if God would forgive him for the turmoil he'd caused, he would forever stay on his medication. The guilt over his misdeeds carved a new neural pathway into his cerebral cortex, ensuring he would permanently remember the list:

One lost girlfriend: "I love you no matter what," she had cried when he told her the birthmark pattern on her thigh indicated she was of royal heritage and therefore, too good for him.

One lost job: As a physics research assistant. A concrete deadline conflicted with his police arrest and twenty-four-hour jailing.

Two police arrests: One D.U.I. and one public nuisance citation.

Three lost friends: They could no longer bear his obsession of linking facts, dates, and numbers that prophesied impending doom, and worse, talking non-stop about it. Their parting salvo: "For the love of God, will you shut the fuck up?"

Five months of debilitating depression. Most days he never got out of bed, and his mom had hired someone to watch him and make sure he ate something.

EIGHTy thousand dollars in expenditures.

The final tally: 1, 1, 2, 3, 5, 8. A Fibonacci sequence of catastrophes. Even in his mania, he'd constructed a pattern of mathematical symmetry.

One thing wasn't on the list, because in some ways it may have wreaked the worst damage of all, and therefore, deserved to be considered in a category of its own: one over-the-top-distraught-never-to-be-the-same mother. He wanted to make things up to her.

Three years after his last manic episode, he still worked to pay down the $20,000 not covered by his bygone trust fund. He refused to allow her to pay a dime of his debt. After his research workday ended, he waited tables and wrote science articles for fees.

When Noah wouldn't accept Sally's financial support, she'd offered him a research job at Friedman Pharmaceutical. "You'd be a great asset in the lab, and this way I can keep an eye on you." As much as he might have wanted to relieve her worry, he couldn't bear the thought of being monitored like a child.

Now, he'd gotten his life back in order. God knows what would happen if his next episode was more intense, as DeMarko's notes predicted. Noah had read other researchers' conclusions that successive bouts of mania permanently damaged the brain.

He couldn't go off his meds. They were his first line of defense against total insanity. After all, he'd made a promise.

But Noah couldn't stay on the meds. If Selexikote altered his brain, he was a phony. He'd known too many people in his life that pretended—people who wore masks of respectability for the world to see, while their authentic selves smoldered underneath. People like his father, like DeMarko, and recently, his mother. Above all else, Noah hungered to be trustworthy.

He sat with the voluminous folder on his lap, thighs sweating through his khakis, his body and brain feeling the heat and the weight of indecision.

Jesus, go home where you can get some shade. No. DeMarko knows where you live. Keep reading. Learn. Stash the file.

Whoosh. A cold chill blew through his body, evaporating his sweat. His teeth chattered. The pungent sweetness of cinnamon tickled his nose, and he sneezed.

Hadassah.

Noah's breath caught. Just as swiftly, the phantasm floated away, leaving a lingering calm.

Great-Grandma Sara's hand patted his knee beneath the file. Her voice cooed in his ear, "Don't worry, mine Noah. You have all the time you need."

Noah grabbed for her hand, flesh meeting spirit, then she too drifted away on a breeze.

You have all the time you need. DeMarko's injection would pump Selexikote through his bloodstream for two weeks. Then, if he didn't get another shot or pills, he'd be off the drug. Two weeks to think about what he should do. He needed to get closer to the research so he could decide the best of the worst courses of action.

Friedman Pharmaceutical could provide access. Great- Grandma Sara had told him it was time to wear a suit and go to the office. Help his mother. Fleck and Jean-Paul had asked for help researching Telaxiphentol. The shaman had said he was in danger.

He stared at his stained finger and the coincidences formed a coherent pattern, as orderly and formulaic as a fractal.

Ah.

He placed the file on the bench and dug into his pocket for his cell phone. Taking a deep breath, he thumbed Sally's number.

MODERNITY

Chapter Five

After a passionate thunderstorm, raindrops clung on jewel-toned flowers and twinkled against the backdrop of the cash colored lawn Sally Friedman viewed from her office window.

She sipped her fifth cup of coffee while studying the financials. Caffeine had kicked in to mask the effects of last night's wine, and now adrenaline added to the mix to create an edgy buzz of excitement, as Sally eyed the best damn bottom line performance she'd generated in three years. The results broadcast her unparalleled savvy.

Her timing synchronized with the next round of acquisition discussions with Charles Dalton, III. "Sell when you have a cash cow," she'd philosophized, and Friedman Pharmaceutical was a prime heifer. She'd embraced another daily mantra, a self-fulfilling prophecy, "I'd rather be lucky than good." Damn if she wasn't both.

Sally drew a wavering black circle around the bottom-line number and penned an unsteady smiley face next to it like a schoolgirl. She anticipated dinner tonight with Dalton.

Charles Dalton, III was CEO of the fifteen-billion-dollar pharmaceutical conglomerate Duschene International. He was notorious for cheating on his wife and had earned a reputation as a lion in the boardroom as well as the bedroom. He seemed genuinely interested in all aspects of her company: the employees, future potential of undeveloped drugs, the cash flow prospective.

His enthusiasm included her: a talented leader. Yeah, maybe, but she saw the way he inspected her. They'd only seen each other twice across a conference table with superfluous people in the room. Their conversation had been strictly business, but still, there could be something. Sparks tingled her palm when she shook his hand, signaling the two of them had the potential to be as charged as the night sky in an electrical storm. She wouldn't mind drinking a bit too much at dinner and losing all abandon.

Post dinner, she might fly a kite with a key on it. An orgasm would be the ideal jolt of lightning to climax this exceptional day.

Pushing the morning over the top, Noah had called to say he wanted a job. She had repeatedly offered him one in the past, but he'd never seriously considered it. What a fantastic turn of events and fortuitous timing that he voiced interest when she might be on the brink of selling.

Thirty years of rising at the crack of dawn, schlepping all over the country and working insane hours had left her beat and lonely. A constant queue of people asked her questions, begged her for favors, pleaded for raises and days off. They loitered in long lines like carrion crows on a telephone wire, lusting for a window of opportunity to fly in and peck at her piece by piece. Plus, the federal regulations and twists and turns she'd endured to get a drug approved were worse than having pretzel sex with that sadomasochist, Bob. Or was that Mike? No, Rick had been the one who was so damn creative she'd had to visit a chiropractor the day after sex. Five times. Bob was the one who...oh, for God's sake, it was so long ago. She was exhausting herself thinking about it.

Was it any surprise she needed an occasional diversion? Was it asking so much for a few drinks or a romantic roll in the hay every now and then to get through the craziness of her life?

Noah embodied her only chance to leave a legacy and gain a smooth, uncomplicated exit plan from career to retirement. She could already picture herself on a Caribbean beach, sipping a Purple Passion, a gold sandal dangling from her bronzed toe, while she read anything besides *BioPharm International* or *Applied Clinical Trials*.

But acquisitions didn't happen quickly and more than likely, they didn't happen at all. If Noah wanted a career working side by side with her, maybe she shouldn't sell. At the very least, imagining his interest allowed her to negotiate without feeling she might crumble if she didn't seal a deal. The future emerged with glorious possibilities.

She glanced at her watch: 9:25. Less than three hours until lunch and a glass of wine. Maybe she'd celebrate fat numbers by drinking a green apple martini, the verdant shade of high finance. She'd consume one, two at the most. No more. She'd be fresh and ready to share a bottle or two with Dalton at dinner. She raised her hand in front of her, her thumb and forefinger slightly apart, her pinky in rarefied air, practicing the way she'd clasp her glass.

A chip in the corner of her polished thumbnail exposed yellowed, aged layers of the nail underneath. It was a small imperfection, but more could peel away so easily.

The intercom screeched, pulling Sally out of her thoughts and setting her teeth on edge. Who wanted her now?

"Noah's here," Maggie announced. "Should I send him in?"

"Of course. Thanks, Mags."

Her office door opened and Noah filled her view, dressed in the suit he'd worn to Grandma's funeral. He'd combed his copper fringe off his forehead, exposing soulful eyes. His shoulder-length auburn hair, a shade that matched hers, was a bit too long for her liking, but he kept it shampooed and conditioned. A positive sign, she noted. He was cute, if only he'd realize it.

Sally rushed over and threw her arms around him. "Here you are at last in your future office. The next CEO of Friedman Pharmaceutical." She released her hold and made a show of giving him the once over. "You look great all dressed up."

Noah flinched.

Had she sounded a bit too anxious and condescending? Noah's reaction said she'd forgotten herself, and he saw her as cloying and desperate.

"Thanks, Mom." He hugged her back.

It felt genuine. She hoped it was. She searched his face to see if she could detect his mood. Up, down, nervous, calm, happy, sad, she catalogued his emotional range. She scrutinized his face to assure herself he stood on solid ground, trying to rid herself of a recurring sense of doom that any day the other shoe might drop. "You good?"

Noah wore his why-can't-you-just-leave-me-be expression on his face. "Nothing's changed since you saw me last week."

She wanted to start things off on the right foot so he would see how great it could be if they worked together. "I didn't mean anything by it." In her imagination, their relationship was one in which she didn't weigh her words.

Sally walked behind her desk and sat. "You want coffee?"

Noah seated himself, stretched his long legs and crossed them at the ankles. He fidgeted with his tie, pulling it away from his collar. "No, thanks. I'm short on time."

"Can't you stay for a little bit?" She'd hoped for a heart to heart.

"I need to wrap up some research if I'm going to be here for a while." Noah pointed to her desk. "You've collected a few more awards since I was here last time."

The granite table top showcased a laminated cover photo of her from *Magnate* magazine, a hand-blown crystal rose awarded for the Business Woman of the Year, a plaque for the Top Ten Small Business, a gold-plated figurine for the Entrepreneur of the Year, among other accolades.

"Maggie thought grouping them together might be good marketing."

"You're quite the role model."

"In younger days." She smiled at him. "You probably have a head for business just like me. You can do anything you set your mind to."

Noah snuck a look at his watch and stifled a yawn. "Sure."

"We'll get right to it. I've got a crazy day, too. There are a few possibilities for you to think about, all of them great background for management. There's an opening in the Marketing Department. Or, you could apprentice in sales, which would be a fabulous experience. Or you could work in operations."

He laughed and scratched the back of his neck. "You don't really see me in sales or marketing, do you? I was thinking Research and Development. That fits what I already do."

This might be her only shot to persuade him to love the business. "I was hoping doing something different would give you a chance to see if this was a career path you'd enjoy. We could map out a progression for you to take over the company."

He leaned forward in his chair, peering at her like she had three heads. "Mom, I love physics. I just thought I could be here for a break. That's all." His gaze fell on his loafers.

Scuffed. Cheap. She wondered if he noticed. A small hole peeked out of one sole. A negative sign, she noted.

"Hey, I've got an idea. You want to go shoe shopping? We should spiff you up for the office."

"What? Who cares? It's okay, Mom."

If he were to work with her she'd get to keep an eye on him. Shape him a little. That'd be a plus. She felt deflated, but something was better than nothing. She forced a smile. "Right. Well, I'll be glad to have you start wherever you feel comfortable."

"If you end up selling the company, I might not be able to try it later."

She hadn't mentioned the acquisition possibility to Noah. She frowned. "Where did you hear that?"

"I didn't. Just guessing. I mean, it's a natural possibility, right?" He rapped his fingers on his legs rhythmically, pinkies first, then the next, and the next, progressing to his thumbs, as if he played the piano or typed.

She hated when Noah did that. It reminded her of all the twitches he'd adopted when he was sick. He'd play the piano on his dinner plate. He'd type words on his bed sheets, whole sonatas on his thighs, research papers on the wall next to his bed. He'd performed more concertos than Van Cliburn. Here it was again, this endless drumming. Did it mean anything?

"Noah, stop that."

He looked surprised and stilled his hands in his lap. "Sorry."

"Well, no reason to hide the talks. I'm in early stages of negotiating a deal. If you like it here, it might change my decision to sell."

"Right. Great..." He pulled on his pants leg.

Was he nervous? "Are you on your meds?"

He lowered his head to his hands and exhaled. "Why do you do this? Every movement I make is not a result of being off my meds. Why can't you relax?"

It was so hard to let it go. "Just making sure you're grounded."

He looked directly at her. "I'm not the only one who needs to be grounded."

He said it kindly, but it unnerved her just the same. What was it he saw in her? Was it obvious she craved drunken sex? She forced herself to meet his cobalt blues straight on. "What do you mean by that?"

"I won't ask you about your drinking if you don't ask me about my meds."

She looked away. "I've been great lately. You don't need to worry about me."

"Fine."

She was great; she functioned, got out of bed every day, led, made decisions, made money. But the look on Noah's face, it was as though he knew what lurked beneath her bravado. She grinned so wide her face hurt. "Here's the plan. A job in marketing would be the way to go. You can train there for at least six months, then go to product development."

Noah squared his shoulders. "Mom, research is the only thing I want to do."

Sally sighed and gave in to the inevitable. "Okay, Noah. R and D. I'll set it up."

"Thanks, Mom." He stood and walked over to her side of the desk. "I gotta get back to the library." He reached to take her hand and help her up from her chair.

She didn't want to reveal her hands were clammy. She stood under her own power and hugged him, confident he wouldn't detect her wet palms through his suit coat.

Sometimes when the two of them embraced, when they were still, without words or movement, she hoped she was an adequate mother. She yearned to stay in that safe space. The lyrics to an old Helen Reddy song she used to sing when he was little floated through her head, and she resisted the impulse to hum, "You and Me Against the World." Her eyes burned hot and sharp, and her temples throbbed.

He kissed her cheek. "Mom, everyone has problems. We're here for each other. We're lucky, don't you think?"

He opened the door and loped down the hall. She watched him, gait wide, arms swinging with determination to return to his rightful universe.

Sally knew Noah didn't belong in her world. He was a much better person than she knew how to be. But it wouldn't hurt to pretend for a little while that he'd always work by her side, would it? She could fantasize he'd let her watch over him, protect him, ensure he survived unscathed, and in the process, maybe she could feel whole. At least while she weighed her options, considered Dalton's offer, and decided on her next steps. Life rarely unfolded the way she wanted. Her imagination was far more satisfying.

She allowed herself a brief indulgence of tears no one could see. Drops landed on her computer printout in dark splotches. Enough, now, she resolved, pressing against her eyes to stop the flow. She walked around her desk, shaking off excess energy, and bumped the table, upsetting her cup of coffee. *Fuck.* She grabbed a bunch of paper towels from under her credenza and mopped up the mess on the polished granite surface and her award collection. Wiping brown drips from the crystal rose, she lost her grip and it slipped, hitting the desk, chipping a piece of glass petal. *Fuck, fuck, fuck.*

Sally hated when Noah brought this weakness out in her and she fell apart. She had a company to run. There was no time for this bullshit.

She threw the glass chip and paper towels into the waste can, sat down, and took a deep breath. She picked up her glorious financials, wet from tears and coffee but still offering comfort and stability in smudged numbers. She'd kick ass at the meeting with Dalton and wow him with her business smarts. If she played her cards right, tonight she just might get laid.

She checked her watch. She could make it till lunch. Piece of cake.

In a secluded corner of a five-star restaurant, Sally stared across the white tablecloth at Charles Dalton, III.

A youthful waiter, great eye candy, rushed in to light candles. He placed a hand-blown vase with a single red rose in front of her. "For you, Madam." He winked conspiratorially at Dalton.

"I've heard roses are your favorite," Dalton said.

"How did you know, Mr. Dalton?" Sally nosed the crimson petals. No scent. Sally disliked roses with no scent.

"I enjoy due diligence." He smiled without showing teeth. "Please, call me Trip."

"As long as you call me Sally."

"It's a deal. Our first."

She studied the way he put an index finger to his lips as he scouted the wine menu. In one efficient swipe, the same finger summoned the waiter and pinned his choice on the list.

The young server charged in again, bending over Dalton's shoulder to approve the selection. His eyes glowed brighter than the tapers on the table as he evidently calculated his gratuity. Cha ching. Sally thought he might give Trip a high five. "Excellent bottle, sir." He scurried away.

Trip shrugged. "It's not the best year, but it's still Chateau Latour. When we close the transaction, I'll order something memorable. A DRC, perhaps."

Sally studied Trip while the waiter returned, made the ceremonial show of decanting the bottle, and poured a short glass. Charles Dalton III performed his part of the classically choreographed duet, holding the stem between two fingers and swirling the wine in the bell of the glass. He breathed deeply, his nose dipping into the aromas being released, and finally took a large sip, churning the wine in his mouth. He nodded, and the waiter filled two glasses.

Trip tapped her wine glass with his. "To success."

She eyed his dignified mouth as it moved beneath archetypal features. His tongue flicked purple.

"... earnings, EBIT were strong the last four years... the bottom line is..." He gestured with his right hand, showing off star sapphire cuff links on French cuffs monogrammed "CDIII" in navy thread. "...shareholders ROI...debt to equity...after we combine our companies..."

What had he just said? She took unladylike swallows of Bordeaux. She felt heat ignite between her thighs.

"Our combined assets...enormous market share... proforma impressive..."

She lost track of time and conversation as she gazed at his strong but elegant hands, which resembled those of a sculptor or surgeon. She wondered if she would feel shaped or healed by his touch.

"You're the kind of woman who should be a role model... not hidden in obscurity...you in the spot-light..."

She fantasized his fingers inside her, manipulating her like he massaged a deal, examining her assets, prof-iting from her bottom line.

"We'll have the foie gras." She heard him command some time later. "Almost Lutece standards...your role... board of directors possibly..."

A small shot of adrenaline coursed through her and she pressed her palms to her cheeks to hide the red. A momentary fear she might leave a wet spot on the silk upholstered chair surged up her spine. She squirmed in her seat, repositioned her skirt. She accepted a second glass of Bordeaux—or her third? —and tried to hide the fact that she gulped it.

Sally marked the passage of time with the arrival of salads and filets. She vaguely registered their waiter's drifting in and out with plates and wine refills, giving her full attention to the big hitter seated opposite.

Trip ate like a carnivore. She picked at her greens.

"Would you like to progress further with the deal?"

Had he said something important? "I'm sorry?"

"Would you like to progress?" His business-golf

tanned skin glowed against the tablecloth. "Would you?"

Oh, yes.

"I'll need three years profit and loss statements."

His tongue between my legs...

"I'll need access to your people."

His body pinning mine, his muscle, his power...

"A listing of assets and liabilities, of course..."

She heard a pop, smelled the geyser of Cristal. A new glass found a home in front of her.

"So, shall we proceed?" He crossed his legs to the side, revealing flawless Italian leather shoes, size twelve, maybe even thirteen.

Sally almost moaned. She took a long draw on the champagne glass. "Where to?"

"I mean shall we proceed with the deal?"

Oh. Yes. "The deal. Yes."

He leaned forward, edging into her personal space. "I think we can skip dessert, don't you?" Trip lifted his champagne glass. "To our combined synergies."

"To us." She smiled, clinked his glass, and drained her flute.

Sally woke to vivid throbbing in her temples, and opened one eye to a hazy vision of chocolate mints and a tented fine stationary card calligraphed with, "Sweet Dreams from the Ritz Carlton." A masculine, clipped phone voice sounded somewhere in the room.

It took her a minute, but she assembled the fragments of memory. She was a regular Sherlock first thing in the morning. Ritz Carlton. Charles Dalton III. They'd had dinner, they'd come back here. She pulled the Egyptian cotton sheet over her nose and sniffed the vinegary stench of too much wine.

Dalton paced on the far side of the suite with his back turned and his cell phone glued to his ear. His right hand sliced the air, making short, commanding karate chops to accentuate his points to the recipient of his voice waves. He gestured like he fucked: small, quick, forward, I'm-doing-this-for-me-and-not-for-you thrusts without much follow through.

He glanced her way and nodded, his cell phone cradled between his left ear and his shoulder. He was putting a cufflink in his right French cuff and a fistful of fingers waved a tepid hello across the room.

Sally surveyed last night's carnage. Her best siren-red power suit lay in a wrinkled mess by the side of the four-poster bed. One high heeled $700 sandal lay upside down, but she apparently stepped out of the other shoe somewhere else, or it ran away to escape embarrassment.

Dalton ended the call and strode toward her, pausing at the end of the bed. "Welcome back to the world of the living." His voice sounded cheerily patronizing.

What had she gotten herself into? The momentary thrill of drinks and sex continually clouded her rational self. And the morning after usually resulted in regret. She was far too old for antics. Why, oh why, didn't she stop? She forced a smile. "What time is it?"

"After six." He faced the mirror and smoothed the sides and front of his dark hair. "I've got a seven-a.m.

meeting. Breakfast should be here any minute."

"Thank you." Coffee would help, but she winced at the thought of eating. If only she hadn't drunk that last dizzying nightcap. She wished he'd hurry up, finish dressing, and get going to his meeting so she could die in the room alone.

"You sure you have to go?" She had to play her part, and play him, but her heart wasn't in it.

He gave her a look that let her know he thought she was a little person with an even littler brain. "Busy day." He turned back to the mirror, examining his hair part and his perfectly square jaw. "I had a chance to look at the financials this morning. I have questions I'll need your CFO to answer. I'd like the head of my due diligence team to spend the next few weeks at your office."

"I didn't realize we'd move forward this quickly." Sally propped a couple of pillows behind her aching head.

"Last night you said you were ready."

She wasn't up to starting a negotiation so early in the morning. "It's just a surprise, that's all." She tried to sound confident.

"I'm not a man who wastes time. When I see something I want, I grab it." He walked over to her side of the bed a bit too aggressively. "My office faxed over a letter of intent and a confidentiality agreement for your signature." He took papers and a pen from his suit coat and handed them to her, then sat on the edge of the mattress by her side.

His proximity to her was unnerving, and Sally couldn't focus on the small type. She was in no shape to make decisions. "I need my lawyers to look at this."

Dalton frowned. "They're boilerplate documents. Sign them, so we can move on to next steps." His business moves resembled a military command, like his forced-march lovemaking.

"You're rushing me," Sally said.

"There are a dozen other companies I can purchase at the drop of a hat. You're lucky I'm interested in yours, but there's a limited window of opportunity." He combed back her hair from her face with his left hand, making her feel like an eight-year-old. "I'm doing you a favor because I like you. I'm going to make you a top dollar offer. You and your shareholders will be thrilled. But if you waffle on me, I'll move on to the next deal, and I won't look back."

She avoided his disapproving eyes and gazed down at the blurred lines. She wasn't sure she wanted to sell, but she didn't want to blow the opportunity and not have the choice. She understood Noah would never be her successor, and not many companies could afford to make a cash bid on Friedman Pharmaceutical. If she wasn't careful, she could wind up empty-handed, with no plan to get away from the pressure of her daily grind.

She envisioned her future self, wrinkled and frail like Grandma Sara, single and all but forgotten, still trolling for men and wedded to her business.

Sally smiled up at Dalton, trying to look coy. "I got where I am by making thoughtful, considered decisions."

"If you want a place on my management team, you'll need to make timely decisions. End of today," he said. "After that, I'm on to the next deal. Don't test me, Sally." He smiled, his capped teeth glinting.

Christ, how predictable that he'd always need to win. She'd have to stroke his ego so often she'd wind up with tennis elbow. Could she muster the energy to work for him? She reached up to caress him, combing his already slicked-back hair and making it clear she could condescend as well as he could. "Now why would I test you? I already know you're the smartest boy in the class."

Dalton lifted her hand off him, relieved her of his pen, and slipped it back into his jacket pocket.

Sally shifted into business mode. "I don't want the word out to my team that I'm considering a sale."

"My due diligence team is discreet. I'm sending you my key guy. We'll let your team think we're looking to joint venture a specific drug. That shouldn't be too intimidating. You've had joint ventures before."

"No, but we've thought about it." The negotiations were galloping along, and she needed to sharpen up. Where the hell was the coffee?

"We'll say we're considering a joint venture."

He looked so smug. He had everything figured out.

"On Selexikote."

"Selexikote?"

Had she heard him correctly? "How do you know about Selexikote?"

"Sally, do you have a memory problem when you drink?"

Ouch. She blinked at him, wordless.

"You told me about Selexikote a few months ago at our first meeting. You suggested I get in contact with

Roger DeMarko. I did."

She couldn't recall saying anything about the drug. Why would she? Her company had other signature products out-performing the competition. Selexikote hadn't run the gauntlet of requirements for FDA approval. She'd made it available to a small control-group of volunteers with no other options, Noah being one of them. She wouldn't have promoted Selexikote as a company selling point. Had DeMarko gotten in touch with Dalton? Was Dalton lying to her?

A bell buzzed. Dalton rose and walked across the suite to the door.

Coffee. Oh, there is a God. She watched him sign a ticket and the wait staff rolled a table into the living room.

"What did DeMarko say about Selexikote?" she shouted across the suite.

Dalton glanced at his watch and marched over to his suitcase. "Something about it having been developed for your son. Why don't you fill me in?" He sorted toiletries, pigeonholing them into the proper corners of his travel bag.

The wait staff arranged serving pieces on the cart. Jesus Christ, they were slow. She longed to vault across the room to the coffee pot, but she lay naked beneath the sheets.

"Would you bring me a robe, Trip?" She batted her mascara caked eyelashes.

Dalton sauntered to the closet, found a Ritz monogrammed bathrobe, and tossed it to Sally before strolling back to the other side of the suite.

She fumbled her way into the terry cloth while still

under the sheets, managing to conceal her middle-aged breasts.

The wait staff departed at long last. She grabbed Dalton's documents, lunged across the suite to the service cart, and poured coffee.

"Are you going to tell me about Selexikote?" Dalton twisted his wrist back and forth, his cufflinks catching the light. His brow furrowed as he noticed something that fell short of perfection.

"Oh, right. Selexikote," Sally said, as she gulped down caffeine.

She hadn't anticipated due diligence on the drug, and she felt uncomfortable talking about Noah. Well, better for her to fill in the blanks than Roger. "De-Marko diagnosed my son Noah as bipolar when he was five. Bipolar disorder had been considered an adult mental illness, appearing in the early-twenties or later. DeMarko was one of the first psychiatrists to recognize its presence in children. No drug tailored for kids existed in the market, so I funded the research for DeMarko to come up with the right compound."

Dalton fiddled with his jewelry, apparently trying to decide whether sapphires or rubies were the right choice with his tie. Oh, for God's sake, what difference did it make?

"Noah's been on Selexikote since he was ten," Sally said. "The results have been terrific. A Godsend. All the same, we never followed through with FDA approval on the drug."

"DeMarko's disappointed by that."

Sally felt blindsided. Had they met secretly? "It's unsettling to me that the two of you talked without my knowing."

She shared a past with DeMarko—a one-night stand, rather an afternoon, technically speaking. She regretted the encounter more than any other, stuffing it into a chamber with her other obscure memories. The affair had been a desperate act of loneliness and stress, on the heels of Steven announcing he was leaving her and Noah. "I didn't sign up for this. I never really wanted a kid to begin with," he'd said, suitcase in hand after one of Noah's tantrums. And that was that. Out of their lives forever. Sally needed someone to talk to about her son's issues, and in DeMarko, she found a collaborator who might help Noah.

Her pride stung at the prospect of Dalton and DeMarko discovering they'd both had her in common. She pictured the two of them high fiving, silly ass grins plastered on their faces. She felt flushed. And yet, why should she feel embarrassed? She had every right to make her own decisions, even if they were bad ones.

Dalton strode over to her, his features sharp and dark as he towered over her. "It's not unusual for owners to hold back on damaging liabilities. I do my own reconnaissance as a matter of course. I know everything there is to know before I consummate a purchase, and I'm under no obligation to tell you my whereabouts. Are we perfectly clear?"

Insufferable. She was tempted to say *crystal* or tell him to go fuck himself, but she did neither. "Do you think Selexikote has a future?"

"I'm not sure the market it serves is large enough to cost-justify the FDA requirements."

"Exactly why we never went forward."

"Well, you'd better hope something in your product line has huge potential, or no deal." He stomped back over to his bag and zipped it closed. "I'd like to inspect the test results and history DeMarko has on your son. I hear he's bright."

DeMarko. Doctor Loose Cannon. What else had Roger told Dalton? She considered the details of Noah's medical history private. "Yes, he's sharp. He's going to be working for us in the research department. I'd love for you to meet him."

Dalton checked his watch again. "If your son is as smart as DeMarko says, he might be a great asset to the firm. Maybe he can research his own drug." Dalton chuckled and shook his head at his own funny. "What's DeMarko's story? He seems...distraught."

Damn DeMarko. Sally fumed. Where to start? She'd witnessed him getting more and more out of control, with a noticeable weight gain from year to year and a penchant for gambling. She often wondered if he'd thought of getting a psychiatrist for himself. "He's a gambler. The addicted variety," she said. "He lost most of his assets at the roulette wheel a few years ago. He owns fifty per cent of Selexikote distribution rights. He steered the R and D, I funded it. He has a stake if there's money to be made."

Dalton clicked his tongue. "I knew I smelled desperation. Good. He'll work hard to help with FDA approvals."

Dalton's phone sang out *Hail to the Chief*. "Excuse me." Dalton flipped open his cell and raised it to his ear. "Morning, darling. Look, I've scheduled the plane to touch down around three thirty, should be at his soccer game around five...I know it starts at four thirty, but that's the best I can do. Tell Quatro I want a goal today. I'm depending on him." He paused. "Love you, too. Bye."

Quatro? Give me a break. Sally laughed to herself and poured more coffee. As the caffeine kicked in, it dulled the ache in her head. The omelet smelled and looked fantastic. Miracle of miracles, she actually felt hunger, despite her unease. She read the confidentiality agreement. Standard stuff. To her benefit to sign, since Dalton intended to pursue clandestine due diligence. If he stole secrets, she'd sue him. She could play this game, too.

He returned his attention to her. "You'll receive a call from my guy later today to discuss next steps. If you don't ink the documents now, this is our last get together. Sally...." He smiled again. "...In case I haven't said this, I'm excited about the possibilities of what we can achieve together. You're a savvy businesswoman. The sky's the limit."

His cell chorused again, and he pressed it to his ear. A long silence followed.

Sally chewed forkfuls of gruyère omelet and a dry bagel. Her energy steadily returned.

She found her briefcase, purse, and cell phone on the coffee table, carried them back to her chair, and signed the confidentiality agreement. Then, she scanned the letter of intent. Nothing unusual.

She looked up every now and then to glimpse Dalton while he listened, his jaw increasingly more set.

"Uh, huh...uh, huh."

She texted her lawyer to inform him she was reviewing a letter of intent. When did he want to see it?

Dalton's patriotic phone chime announced another call. "Stuart, set up the meeting with Inviron for tomorrow," Dalton said.

Inviron? Her toughest competitor. Crap.

"The Friedman Pharmaceutical deal isn't going forward. I'm moving on."

Sally's cheeks heated. Her hand shook, sloshing coffee out of the bone china cup. She looked up and their eyes met. He returned a placid, steady stare. He would never blink first. She suddenly felt outmatched. His cell sounded again and his gaze broke.

Stay cool. He's bluffing.

She sipped her coffee, concentrating on newly arrived emails: *Research Cost Overruns Review Meeting moved to tomorrow; cost higher than earlier projections.*

Idiots. Couldn't they just once stay on budget?

PriceWaterhouse reports internal profit and loss statements overstated by $500,000.

$500,000? What the hell? Her best results ever were a consequence of voodoo accounting? Her CFO was incompetent, bordering on criminal. She should've fired him years ago.

Class action suit filed by users of Daxolax.

Fuck. A class action suit? Now? Was there any end in sight to this bullshit? Sally's forehead beaded with sweat. Shit. Hot flash.

Her cell vibrated; a return text from her lawyer. *At fax. Send document.*

Sally no longer wanted to wait for his sanction or hear any objections. Maybe she could get this deal done before the class action suit showed up in discovery. Then, it would be Dalton's problem to manage. Fuck him. Duschene had a floor full of lawyers at his disposal. No skin off his back.

She took her lucky pen out of her purse, the red Mont Blanc she used on important contracts. She stroked the tip across the signature line on the letter of intent, making the familiar, ordered loops that formed a truncated version of her name. Tramping over to Dalton, she placed the documents on the table before him.

He caught her eye. "Let me call you back," he said into the phone, then flipped it shut. He smiled warmly at her this time. "That's my girl."

Hail to the Chief. Again. Sally ground her teeth as he returned the phone to his ear. Perhaps he should have it surgically implanted.

She plunked in her chair, nabbed another bagel, and slathered on extra cream cheese. She deserved it. She felt hungry, relieved and—dare she think it—almost happy.

"Tell that little shit to stop complaining," Dalton bellowed into his cell. "He made a deal and he got over paid for his crappy little company. He's lucky to have a job. Get me out of the remaining year on his contract, and we're history. That's what I want. Enough with his bitching and moaning like a whiney girl. 'I had a great company before you bought it.' Get rid of him." He threw his cell phone, and it landed on the couch. He created drama, not folly. "God, I hate stupidity. Obtuse, fucking people." He shot a dagger-filled look at Sally, making her feel like he'd been referring to her. "I'm late. My guy will call you. Don't worry. He'll be discreet."

A piece of bagel stuck in her throat. She swallowed hard. "His name?"

"Goldberg. Bernard Goldberg." Dalton scooped up his cell, briefcase, and bag and disappeared out the door.

What's this? She frowned. The letter of intent still lay atop the table. In his sprint toward the next deal, Dalton bungled this one.

For a split second, Sally felt the impulse to run after him. No. This was perfect. An act of grace, and just what she needed.

What had she been thinking? She could solve her own damn problems. Hell, she still possessed enough fight to stay in the game. Sally Friedman was no one's girl, and she could never be his.

"God, I hate stupidity," she said.

She grabbed the document, tore it into confetti, and tossed it high into the air. By the time the trashed deal fluttered to the carpet, she stood in the shower.

For: **Noah Friedman** file
From: Dr. Roger DeMarko
Re: Letter from Dr. David Steinhauer and transcript of recorded therapy session with Noah Friedman, August 17, 1999
Dear Roger,
You asked me to record a therapy session with Noah Friedman for the purpose of your assessing first hand whether or not the dosage/combination of meds prescribed by you is optimum. I informed Noah of your request and asked his permission to tape the session.

I'm sure you would agree that it would have been unethical on my part not to do so.

I'd not experienced a display of Noah's anger in past sessions, and I'm concerned that he staged a performance for your benefit.

Based on the reference to you in this transcribed rant, it is clear to me that you and Noah have a relationship issue. To be frank, I encouraged Noah to see a different doctor.

You are to be applauded for your groundbreaking work recognizing children with bipolar disorder and the treatment regimen that has resulted from your research. I've always admired your early efforts in this field.

I'm certain you will agree Noah would be better served to change psychiatrists. Perhaps you could see your way to make the drug you developed and the regimen prescribed to him available to another doctor.

Sincerely,

David Steinhauer

Taped interview

Subject: **Noah Friedman:**

I notice things. Have you observed how colors pop on a dull day? Like how red, green, yellow, any crayon color seems to be brighter at certain times? You know the tuner you have on your TV? You can turn the knob to make the picture sharper or to make the colors more distinct. You can play with that. Human beings are just machines. Sometimes I turn my knob and the world seems less drab.

I notice things. My mother calls it my 'exquisite sensitivity.' For instance, I know what people mean beneath their words. Someone will call out hello, and I know they're saying, 'Help me. I need connection.' Or someone will shake my hand, and I can feel clenched muscle and sinews that are wound so tight, they're about to snap. I'll say, "If you need to talk, it's cool." The person will find me weird. He'll think I'm too intense, or something. We're disconnected from one another. How sad is the world?

I notice things. Everything has patterns. Traffic's a good example of what I'm talking about, because it's easy to see. If you climb up on top of a building and watch cars on the highway snake along in lines, you'll see they move in rhythm, as if they're orchestrated from above.

I'll stand on a rooftop and pretend I'm shouting out commands to drivers to speed up or slowdown in unison. Sometimes flocks of birds fly overhead, and the cars and the birds move at the same rate of speed. It reminds me of a ballet. It's beautiful. In that moment, I feel anything is possible.

I notice things. There's so much in the world if you just slow down and observe. So sometimes I'm quiet. People think there's something wrong with me 'cause I refuse to talk. Then at times I can't wait to tell you what I've perceived and I can't get the words out fast enough.

Ican'tgetthewordsoutfastenough.

Ican'tgetthewordsoutfastenough.

People don't understand what I'm trying to say, and they get nervous. Most of the time what people say or feel has more to do with them than it does you.

I see things. For instance, have you watched birds communicate? They play games and squabble like humans. If you get close to a bird, they'll make eye contact with you. In that nanosecond, I commune with them. They're worried about bird flu, bird strikes, and being singled out for genocide if there's a threat of pandemic. People think I'm cracked when I share this information.

Or I'll tell them we're running out of oil. That's why we've gone to war, you know. When we have no oil, we won't be able to fuel our lifestyle, and the world as we know it will no longer exist. If your office is more than five miles away, you'll have a problem. We have to take steps to be ready for the day when vegetables can't be shipped, or when they are, green beans will cost thirty bucks a pound. So poor people won't be able to eat green beans, or lettuce, or broccoli, or anything that doesn't have hydrogenated oil and trans-fat unless they find a plot of earth where they can plant a seed.

Everybody must learn to garden. If you don't grow your own food you're screwed, because there won't be fuel to transport it. When I say this, people look at me like there's something wrong.

The fact that I don't drive makes people think I'm crazy. Do they have any idea what's happening? Do they read the newspaper? Holy Einstein, would it kill them to read a book?

If we don't talk about what's going on in the world, then maybe everyone will stay content and live at the mall and spend money on stuff we don't need. We spend a zillion dollars anesthetizing everyone into believing they'll be happy if they buy a new car that, by the way, only gets ten miles to the gallon, or a new pair of glow-in-the-dark bikini underwear.

This morning, for instance, I channel-surfed, tuned into the Today Show, and caught a segment on how to tie a sarong. The world is turning to shit. We are numbing the American public into worrying about how to hide women's unsightly hips if they will simply tie the sarong correctly by putting the knot in the middle, which by the way, elongates your torso, don't you know. I like women's hips. Why should they hide them?

Sure, I'm the one who's crazy. I'm the one who doesn't have a handle on reality. I'm the one who needs to be on drugs, because I tend to get a little upset about these things. Speaking of drugs, this country should have universal health care and we don't. Do you know why? The drug companies are making a fortune selling at high prices. My mother owns a drug company, so I know about this. Ironic, huh? There's no profit in selling to poor people. If someone can't afford to buy their own drugs, then why should the companies worry about them? This is just wrong. I've said this to my mother and it makes her cry. "Oh, Noah, why can't you just have fun?"

When I say things, I'm told to calm down, told my meds need adjusting. "Let's put you on a higher dosage." Doctors don't listen anymore. They just push pills. Are you listening, DeMarko, you fat fuck?

We live in a world of hurt. We live in a country that's spending its cash reserves and sacrificing its people to war. All because we're running out of oil and we haven't developed alternatives. Oh, I told you this already. Sorry. Let's not talk about the war in Iraq.

Yeah, I'm the one who's crazy. The one who needs to calm down and chill. Because I'm not on the same drug that everyone else seems to be on. I'm on Svengali's secret formula.

I notice things. Everyone in this country floats above the grim reality at our manicured feet. Have a burger, a beer and chill. Let's not worry about poverty, obesity, abuse, murder, war, the dying sun, black holes, nuclear bombs, nuclear waste, terrorism, pandemics, climate change, species extinction, and genocide. Chillax. Let's go see a movie. Let's watch beautiful people while we eat a tub of popcorn with faux butter and drink a trough-sized soda and sit on our fat asses for three hours and escape.

Yeah, I'm out of touch. Lock me up, put me on drugs, stupefy me like everyone else.

Pass the Selexikote.

HADASSAH
AUGUST 1919
YOMPOLA, RUSSIA

Hadassah crouched by her window, watching Leja's family steal across the deserted road toward the foothills leading to Poland. Leja held her youngest's hand, little Sara—such a *ziskayt*, a sweetie. The child, oblivious to the night's danger, skipped to keep up with her mother.

A full August moon guided them through the night. That same cruel moon might aid their capture. Bands of roving Cossacks, lusting for more rape and murder, could spot them and finish them off.

Hadassah feared for their safety, yet envied them. At least that family's future held mystery and, therefore, hope. Hadassah's future contained no riddle. She would know only loneliness, hunger, and certain death.

She wondered what she'd done to anger God. Why had Leja been blessed with children and a husband who already earned money in America, while Hadassah had been fated to a barren life? Yet, God had spared her the horror of the night's pogrom.

Only God controlled her fate. Life had turned out so

differently then she'd planned. She'd once been a woman of means in St. Petersburg, married to the Czar's tutor. Life had held promise and a late-in-life pregnancy, until the Czar's henchmen had insisted Chaim convert to the church or die.

Chaim and Hadassah had fled to poverty-stricken Yompola, where she'd never felt welcomed. Where Chaim had had little work. Where she'd lost their baby.

Irony of ironies, her naïve Chaim had returned to St. Petersburg for one more egg. A payment promised by the Czar out of contrition.

God decided who would live, who would die, when and how. God preferred Hadassah to die of hunger, rather than the sword. It had been inscribed in her book of life, and she accepted this as her destiny. She refused to leave Yompola.

Leja had begged Hadassah to join them. "How will you eat? If you stay here, you'll die."

"What do you care?"

Leja had shaken her head, her smooth face filling with compassion. She'd hesitated before telling Hadassah the truth.

"You've been waiting for Chaim more than a year. He isn't coming home."

"If I'm not here when he returns, he won't know where to find me."

"You have asked us to find your nephew, Pincus Goldberg. Chaim will find him, too. Come with us. Bring the box yourself." Leja's eyes had brimmed with tears.

Hadassah had turned her back. "I don't need your pity. I will pray for you. In return, deliver the box."

Now, she kept vigil at the window until well after they'd disappeared into the shadows. The *shtetl* slept, exhausted and bereft after the night's horror.

She fell to her knees, her throbbing fingers pressed to her forehead, and she rocked. "Blessed God, guide this family safely to America. *Got zol aykh shoymer un matzil zayn.* Watch over them, protect them from harm. Help them deliver the eggs to Pincus."

She rocked in deep meditation, rocking, rocking, her lips twitching the prayer she'd implored every morning, noon, and night for over a year. In her heart of hearts, she knew God had abandoned her, but while she still had breath, she must try. "Hashem, bring Chaim back to me. Send someone, who, in Your infinite wisdom, will bring Chaim to me. Send me someone. I will never rest until he's home. I will never rest."

Chapter Six

Sally stared out her office window. Thunderheads, steel grey and thick, blackened the sky and threatened a wild storm. Another soaker. Second one this week. A great morning to hunker down in her office. She studied her day-timer and felt lucky to have a day with only a few internal meetings noted. No reason to schlep outside.

She scrolled down the uncluttered page, imagining a string of white space days all in a row. What would it be like to have a pressure-free life? Someday. Today, she'd optimize her unstructured time by rededicating herself to running the business like someone who intended to keep it. She jotted down her goals for the month, her priorities for the week, her tasks for...

The intercom buzzed. Just when she was on a roll.

"Doctor DeMarko is here to see you."

Poof. The morning was blown all to hell. He'd called a couple times already, but she hadn't gotten back to him. What did he want from her? Sally felt like turning him away, but thought better of it. She'd keep it brief, get him out, and get on with her day. "Send him in, Mags."

He rushed in, navigating his way between her desk and the guest chair. His ass bumped against her award collection.

The "Chamber of Commerce Woman of the Year" glass vase tottered. Sally caught it before it hit the desk.

He wedged himself into the leather chair opposite her, his body spilling over the sides. He must have gained another twenty, maybe thirty pounds since their last encounter.

Sally couldn't believe she'd once slept with this man, despite the loneliness of losing Steven. What the hell had she been thinking? Then again, she couldn't believe she'd slept with Dalton either. At least Dalton was great looking, even if he was an over-the-top megalomaniac who turned out to be less than so-so in the sack. There was nothing redeeming about Roger.

Thank God she was turning her life around. No more drinking and indulging in one-night stands. She'd be a good role model for Noah by pouring herself into maintaining the company she'd built.

Roger DeMarko pulled his glasses down to the edge of his nose, an annoying habit that foreshadowed his delivery of either criticism or bad news. She wondered which was coming.

"What's so urgent, Roger?"

"We've got a little problem," DeMarko said.

She hoped he wasn't going to ask her for money. He was always looking for a handout. "Look, I've already loaned you—"

"I didn't come here for that." He pretended to be insulted. "I'm worried about Noah."

"What?" She'd just seen Noah a couple of hours

ago, during her management-by-walking-around tour. He'd been in the research department, seated at a computer. He'd even waved hello. "Noah's fine."

"So he might appear. Nevertheless...." He stroked his moustache. "Noah stole a file from my office."

She didn't believe DeMarko. "Stole a file?"

Roger shook his head. "I didn't think he would tell you. He was angry with me. A sign of mania, I'm afraid."

Mania. Just hearing the word sent a jolt of fear through Sally. Noah had seemed a little restless the day he'd visited her in the office, but we all have days like that. Noah was on shots, wasn't he? Had been for the last three years.

All of the test subjects received injections ever since that little girl, Rachel, had died from a Selexikote overdose. Horrifying incident. Her parents' fault for not following the correct dosage. Since then the controls had been tightened to avoid risk to another child.

"I don't understand. He's on his meds. You're giving him—"

"He needs further evaluation." Roger pushed the glasses back to their proper position as he cleared his throat. "Noah might say things...." His lip spasmed. "Doctors and patients have falling-outs. This happens sometimes. If he tells strange stories about me...."

"Strange stories?"

"I need to know about it. He might be cycling into another manic episode."

Sally's stomach clenched. "Oh, God."

Roger reached across the desk to pat her hand.

She pulled away. "I've asked you not to do that."

"I'm just being a friend." Fish-eyes blinked at her through opaque lenses. "Listen for indications of paranoia, and let me know if you hear anything. Don't give him too much responsibility around here. Stress isn't good for him."

"He's been fine." How could she have missed the signs? Or perhaps Noah had reasons for stealing the file.

She picked up her cell phone and punched Noah's number. While it rang, she searched DeMarko's features. Twitchy lip. Narrowed eyes. Furrowed brow. She made her own diagnosis: off target fabricator. DeMarko was wrong. Or DeMarko lied. What was his agenda?

Noah's recorded voice sounded in her ear. She pressed the END button, replacing the phone on her desk.

"Is there anything else?" she asked DeMarko.

"Trip tells me the sale isn't going through."

She sat motionless, letting it sink in for a moment that DeMarko owned a membership to the inner nickname circle, and he was up to date on her progress. "You've been in touch with him behind my back. It's a bad way to do business. I don't like it."

His face reddened. "You're not doing anything with Selexikote. It has potential to do so much good, and you're sitting on it." DeMarko's eyes accused her. His attempts to feign sincerity fell short.

"I had no idea you were such an altruist."

He looked surprised. "I want to buy your half-interest."

"With what?"

His eyebrows lifted above the rim of his glasses.

"Do you have any money?" Sally asked.

He jabbed a finger at her and leaned forward. "You owe me. I've bent over backwards to help your son."

Oh. My. God. The guy was desperate. She hadn't realized just how desperate.

"I've paid you well for everything you've done, and I've helped spotlight you in your field. The half interest in Selexikote I gifted you was a gesture of kindness."

He pounded the desktop with his fist. "When do I get my pay-off?"

"We don't have approvals." Sally kept her voice low and calm. Scraping him off the ceiling certainly held no appeal. "I don't even know how to value Selexikote. Now you tell me something is wrong with Noah? Maybe it's the drug."

"Noah's complicated. Most subjects are doing well. Selexikote has been a life-saver for these children." DeMarko pressed his fingers to his eyes, his glasses tilting at an odd angle. Tears dribbled around his fingers, behind the lenses and down his round cheeks. He made a snorting noise.

Oy vey. "What's wrong?"

He removed his thick frames and dried them with a frayed handkerchief. "I want to help other children. You're preventing me from helping the world."

Give me a break. "Roger, calm down," Sally urged.

"I could achieve so much good. That's all I've ever wanted."

What a performance. Either DeMarko was in real trouble, or...could he possibly be sincere? It was true. Sally hadn't released Selexikote. She also wanted to help other kids, as Noah had been helped, but the drug served a small market. Then, of course, that accidental death had thrown their liability insurance into a whole new bracket. She couldn't justify the bucks required for FDA approvals.

Dalton had agreed with her assessment. The money she'd poured into funding the drug development and monitoring the control groups hadn't been good business, but an act of motherly love. Even so, if Roger could change Dalton's mind, and if Dalton provided additional investment capital, she saw no harm in Roger's exploration of the financial potential of Selexikote.

"You have my blessing to talk to Trip. I haven't ruled out a company sale, but if that doesn't happen, I'll help you make a deal on Selexikote. Or I'll make a deal for you to buy my ownership with future earnings." She smiled, trying to appease him.

Sally didn't lack sympathy or compassion for others, but she wanted DeMarko out of her office before he completely fell apart. He struck her as a man on the verge of a breakdown.

More importantly, she wanted to keep him away from Noah. She scribbled a note in her day-timer so she'd remember to talk to her son about it.

Roger seemed pacified. At least he'd stopped sniveling.

She put out her right hand. "We'll make it a proper business transaction."

His hand in hers felt slippery and hot. He pumped her arm eagerly.

Sally's cell phone sang out, announcing Noah's return call. She was glad for the interruption. "Hi, Sweetheart. Just checking in with you. Everything okay?"

"Mom, you just saw me." Noah sounded hesitant. "I'm fine."

She felt a little foolish, but relieved. "Great. Talk to you later," she said, ending the call.

DeMarko laughed. "Noah's ring tone is 'Here Comes the Sun'? Sally, you're so droll."

The intercom buzzed. "You have a floral delivery. May I send it in?" Maggie asked.

"Sure. Thanks, Mags."

The door opened and a delivery boy, weighed down by a massive bouquet of over three-dozen red roses, purple orchids, stargazer lilies, and hydrangeas, stumbled into the room. "Where to?"

Sally motioned to a corner of her desk. "Here. Thanks." The display broadcast an intoxicating scent.

The delivery boy set the arrangement down and wiped his brow. "Man, somebody thinks you're special." He left the office rubbing his arms.

"They're beautiful," DeMarko said. "Who are they from?"

She searched through the green. "I don't see a card."

"I got it." Roger grabbed the white envelope off the floral stick at the back of the bouquet and opened it before she could protest. His face broke into a smile. "It was a wonderful night. Sorry things ended abruptly. Let's talk. Trip."

He stroked his moustache and studied her.

Under his contemptuous gaze, she felt exposed.

"Oh, I see," DeMarko said. "Just ensuring a proper business transaction?"

Sally had barely pried DeMarko out of her office when Dalton's due diligence guru, Bernard Goldberg, appeared on the scene. So much for an undisturbed catch-up day.

She'd debated whether to tell Dalton she'd decided not to sell Friedman Pharmaceutical, and then his flowers had arrived. Goldberg strolled in a few minutes later. She wondered if the timing was accidental or planned. Knowing Dalton, he'd probably staged the floral delivery as Goldberg waited in the wings. What the hell. She decided to take the meeting and see what developed.

Goldberg sat on the opposite side of her desk. About her age. Full head of hair. Height-challenged. Sally could barely see the top of his head above the huge bouquet. Either she died and didn't know it, or she'd reminded Dalton of the winning horse at the Kentucky Derby. Goldberg must be her jockey.

Goldberg blew his nose, using a handkerchief he'd pulled out of his jacket pocket. "Excuse me." He gestured to the floral hulk. "These are particularly fragrant."

"I'll have Maggie remove them." She reached for the intercom button.

"No, it's fine. I'm used to dealing with them. He likes to send flowers."

Sally felt the air deflate from her I'm-so-fucking-attractive-and-great-in-the-sack balloon. Oh, who was she kidding? At fifty-something her boobs sagged, her ass dragged, her face puckered, and her left foot had a bunion the size of a sixth toe. Dalton had assessed her flagging equipment, observed the parts had depreciated, and rushed funereal flowers to the nearly departed.

"These blooms are extremely generous."

Emphasis on extremely. Goldberg must have noticed a change in her demeanor, but his attempt at kindness fell short.

He eyed her with a face practiced in the art of masking emotion. "You know he's married," he said.

Sally felt her face flush. She shot him a look meant to pin him to the chair. "I never mix business with pleasure."

"Of course." He stared at her with no hint of unease or apology, and she suddenly felt angry with him for being so—damn his arrogance—for being so honest. Who did he think he was?

He squared his handkerchief and returned it to his pants pocket.

What a funny little man, she mused. Like a relic from the past with a Victorian air of holier-than-thou. The sort of man she could never have interest in sleeping with. Not bad to look at, however. She noticed his proportioned nose and generous mouth. Gentle eyes. Fit, trim body...oh for God's sake, Sally, stuff it. Old habits would be hard to break, but she would change. Starting right now. Jesus, he wasn't the least bit good-looking. No sense of humor. No sex appeal. He'd make it a breeze to concentrate on the business at hand.

Goldberg removed a pocket watch from his jacket, placing it on the desk beside the bouquet. Sally leaned forward to examine it. A diamond-studded design of a Star of David surrounded by six falling comets decorated its gold case. The antique looked like one of a kind. Affected, but oddly charming, the watch seemed to fit this anachronistic man.

"It's beautiful." Sally smiled at him through the Amazonian foliage. "I've never seen one like this. May I hold it?"

"Of course."

She picked it up and cradled it in her hand, running a finger over the diamonds. "What's its story?"

Goldberg shifted in his seat. "This watch represents the sum total of my inheritance. The heirloom reminds me to consider the gravity of buying a family business. Legacies are precious, Ms. Friedman. Like diamonds or falling stars. Generations spend decades, sometimes more than a century, to build a company. After Duschene International consumes it in one fell swoop, its singularity is gone forever."

"You make a company sound like a living thing."

"I believe it is." Goldberg took a pen from his pocket.

Sally wondered if this was all part of the game. Did Goldberg play good cop to Dalton's bad cop? "Whose side are you on?"

"The side of the deal, of course."

She wondered how Goldberg and Dalton's relationship worked. Goldberg might be playacting as a way to massage the deal, but he appeared sincere.

"You're surprised." Goldberg pulled a legal pad from his briefcase.

"I expected something different, that's all. What exactly is your role at Duschene?"

"I'm the one who takes the blame. If the acquisition

under-performs or the culture isn't a fit, Trip has some-one answerable to the board."

Sally detected a hint of bitterness in his tone. "Does that work for you?"

Goldberg looked down, jotting a note on his legal pad. "It pays well."

"You sound dissatisfied."

He looked up at her. "Large companies have pit-falls."

"Family businesses do, too."

"Of course. Is that why you want to sell? Because your business has pitfalls? Or, are you the one with issues?"

Goldberg seemed willing to say anything. "What do you mean?" she asked.

"If you think a change in ownership will result in a change in your life, you'll be disappointed. If you're looking for that, I can't give it to you. Are you, Ms. Friedman?"

He looked at her, his Kahlua eyes unblinking. She averted her gaze. Something about his unabashed frankness made it impossible to lie. She felt stripped bare. "I don't know."

"That's the most critical concern you must resolve. If you want to continue a career in the pharmaceutical business without ownership, I can give you that. Or, if you want your freedom from the chaos, I can give you that as well. But you will still be Sally Friedman. Do you know what you want?"

Her hands shook, and she hid them in her lap. It surprised her to feel the sting of his question. It surprised her that she wanted to answer it. "No."

"It seems your due diligence may be more difficult than mine."

Who the hell was this guy? How could someone she knew for less than ten minutes create this stir of unrest inside her? "What are your impressions of me?" she asked.

"I barely know you. It would be unfair."

"Please."

He put a finger to his lips. "Well, it's hard to see the woman through the jungle." He pretended to peek through and around the flowers, and Sally noted he possessed a sense of humor after all.

He shook his head. "I'm concerned you may be a lonely woman who's hoping a change in your business will mean a change in your life. I promise you it won't. As someone whose only inheritance is a pocket watch, I'd hang on to my family legacy until I'd exhausted all other options."

Goldberg took the watch from her hand, his fingers brushing against her open palm. He pressed the push-pin, and the gold cover flipped open. The tick of the timepiece filled the room, and they both listened in silence.

"Tempus fugit," Bernard Goldberg said finally. "Shall we look at the numbers, Ms. Friedman?"

Sally's back ached from sitting in her desk chair all day while Bernard Goldberg conducted an archeological dig of company records and peppered her with questions. She glanced at her watch. Six-thirty, and she desperately needed a cocktail.

"Would you mind if we call it quits?"

Bernard flipped open his pocket watch and looked surprised. "Sorry. I had no idea it was this late."

"You seem to get lost in the work. You must love it."

"It's a good escape to focus on minutiae. And when you travel, long days make for short nights." He picked up a legal pad from the table. "Let's go over the list of what I still need, and we're done for today."

She sighed. He must think she had short-term memory loss. Any idiot could have memorized the list by now.

Bernard looked down at his pad, ticking entries with his pen. "I need projections for the Data Storage and Recovery Division." Check. "A list of any pending lawsuits." Check. "Compliance data and history on Ambitag, Dreximen, and Biocytrate." Check, check, check. "A meeting with your C.F.O."

"I've asked Paul to free his schedule for you all day tomorrow. Cheryl Hopkins in marketing and Stan Anderson in legal will handle other details." She frowned and waved a hand dismissively. "On second thought, I don't want Stan involved. He'll panic if he thinks I'm selling. Cheryl and Paul can take charge. Here's a list of phone extensions so you can schedule or change appointments." She ripped off the top sheet of her memo pad and handed it across the desk to Bernard. "I've also reserved conference room one-hundred for you."

"Thank you." Bernard looked up from his list. "That's it for now." He opened his briefcase and crammed in his legal pad and the reams of computer printouts Sally had produced throughout the day. He forced his bag shut. He appeared to study her, and the beginnings of a smile appeared on his face. "Sally, I want to say something I usually don't. You've done a terrific job building your father's company. He would be proud. I hope you are."

She shrugged. "Sometimes." The truth was she'd lost her mojo in the past few years, and couldn't relate to her former self, the hard-charging dynamo who'd grown the company thirty-fold.

Perhaps in all his digging, Bernard would excavate some relic of the woman she'd once been. If she could see it dusted off and exposed through his eyes, just maybe she'd rediscover herself.

She jumped on an impulse. "How long will you be in town?"

"A couple of weeks, give or take."

"That's a long time to be away from your family. Will you go home to Minneapolis over the weekend?"

"No. No reason to go home."

"You're not married?"

"I'm a widower. Fifteen years." He tapped his foot.

"I'm sorry." She suddenly regretted having asked him about his private life. Yet she couldn't stop herself from performing due diligence on him. "Any children?"

"A son. He would have been twenty-four next week."

"The same age as my son, Noah. Would have been? My God, I'm so sorry."

"Me, too." His mouth twisted, and he exhaled raggedly.

He removed his antique pocket watch, opened the

case and handed it to her. A photo of a woman—mid-thirties, long dark hair, her arms wound around a young boy—had been pressed into the case cover. Bernard's wife had been a stunner, and the boy—dark Buster Brown haircut, cuddly and adorable—suggested how Bernard might have once looked.

"They're lovely," she said.

His eyes misted, and he cleared his throat.

"We don't have to talk about this."

"No, I want to. Caroline and Joshua are my history." He crossed, then uncrossed his legs. "They were coming home from a baseball game. The Twins had beaten the White Sox, six-to-three. I met Caroline at the stadium from work, so I had my own car. After the ninth, I left the parking lot no more than two minutes ahead of her, maybe less. I'd been home thirty minutes when I knew something terrible must have happened. I was on my way out the door to find them when I got the call. An eighteen-wheeler had fallen through the guardrail of an overpass and landed on my wife's car. Caroline and Joshua died instantly."

Sally and Bernard sat frozen, each of them staring past each other into space. His watch ticked. The wind gusted through the trees outside the window.

Sally possessed no words. Nothing clever or comforting chattered in her head. She tried to imagine what it would be like to recover from this tragedy. How would it be possible to find the strength if something ever happened to Noah?

She gathered her courage to break the silence. "How do you get over it?"

"You don't. You keep busy. You focus on minutiae.

A minute passes. An hour. Then a miracle transpires—you endure an entire day. The human spirit survives."

"I would not survive the loss of my son."

"Don't say that." His voice and his color rose. "We can't predict what life brings. We persevere, and in that way, we honor those we love."

"How?"

"I became a student of life. I try to understand my true purpose. Every day I ask: Who am I? Why did I live and not them? Why did my car, traveling two minutes ahead of them on the same highway, arrive at home?"

"Have you found answers?"

He shook his head. "Not yet."

"So, you keep searching for who you are."

"Humans are a complicated species." He opened his palm on the desk, and Sally placed the watch into his hand. He returned the heirloom to his pants pocket.

She wanted an opportunity to learn more about this solid man, who had revealed himself as strong, gentle and forthright. What a remarkable friend he might be, and how refreshing to converse with a man void of sexual overtones or business gamesmanship. "Bernard, would you like to come for dinner Friday night? I'm not a bad cook when I get the chance. It beats eating in restaurants."

"This isn't a pity meal?"

"You'd be doing me a favor."

He studied her and nodded. "Thank you."

"Seven o'clock? It'll force you to end your day at a reasonable hour."

He smiled. "Seven, then." He rose and walked to

the door. When he reached for the handle, he turned back to face her. "I'd like it if you'd invite your son."

She smiled. Maybe all three of them might find something they needed. "I think Noah might like that, too."

Late afternoon sunshine poured through the beveled glass windows of Sally's kitchen and splashed rainbows across the white subway-tiled walls. She'd forgotten her kitchen's serenity. For years, except on weekends, she'd only viewed the room before dawn and after dusk. She'd also forgotten the relaxed enjoyment of cooking with Noah, who'd arrived early to act as her sous-chef. Domesticity still lurked beneath her faux tough business machismo, begging for occasional attention.

Tomatoes and red and green peppers sat on her gleaming stainless counter ready to fulfill their ultimate purpose as gazpacho. Noah towered over them, cubing and dicing, his eyes watering from an assault on the onions.

He'd always enjoyed making a science of chopping, cutting each vegetable into symmetrical pieces. Then, he'd reassemble the chunks into a jigsaw puzzle of its original shape. Pieces of garlic formed a large clove. Chunks of onion configured a bulb. He'd been performing this act since he was ten, and to Sally's delight, he entertained her once more.

She noticed how his steady, sensitive hands gripped

the knife. No hint of tremor, eyes centered on his culinary targets.

She discounted DeMarko's recent spiel about Noah, and the nonsense of his having stolen a file. He seemed grounded and calm. She'd meant to talk to Noah about the file, as well as DeMarko. Later. Just mentioning DeMarko might come across as meddling and dredge up old arguments. She wouldn't risk breaking the magic spell present in her kitchen.

Mother and son had cooked together on Sundays until a few years back. Before his episode of mania. Before she'd started to obsess over him, probing him every few minutes as to how he felt, what he thought, what he'd done in the last few hours, when he'd last seen DeMarko and last taken his meds. Before Noah finally stopped answering her calls.

Now, he stood in her kitchen and worked at her company, just as she'd wanted. For the first time in a long time, she enjoyed an activity without craving the urge to anesthetize herself. Miracle of miracles, a man was coming for dinner, and she cooked up chicken instead of schemes for sex. The smell of spices and Noah's companionship filled her with joy, and the knowledge that all things would be good again.

"Mom, what does Bernard do for Duschene?" Noah picked up two peppers and plopped them on the wooden cutting board.

Her son seemed to have a newly found interest in business. When he'd learned Bernard worked for Duschene, Noah leapt at Sally's dinner invitation.

"Bernard examines the financial past and future potential of companies to see whether they're good risks for acquisition." She stuffed fresh basil and pine nuts into the Cuisinart.

"Would he know how Duschene operates?"

She raised her voice over the pulse of the appliance. "Of course. He'd have to have intimate knowledge of Duschene to understand how other companies might fit in."

"So, he could answer questions about the drugs they develop? Or how their drugs are distributed?"

"I guess."

"Do you think he'd know about their international contracts?"

She laughed to herself. Noah had barely inquired about Friedman Pharmaceutical, and now he threw questions about Duschene at her like a carnival knife-thrower. "Why the interest?"

He shrugged. "Just learning the biz." His cheeks turned pink, as though he felt embarrassed or exposed.

She had an urge to ask him which, but she remembered her vow and resisted.

Noah looked down at the cutting board and resumed chopping, alternating slices of red and green and placing the pieces on a plate.

The oven beeped. Sally carried over a roaster crowded with marinated chicken, opened the door, and slid the pan inside.

"How did you meet these Duschene guys?" The color had faded from Noah's cheeks, and he busily assembled his pepper mosaic.

"They're clients of my Data Storage and Recovery Division."

"You don't talk much about that business."

Sally turned to the sink to wash lettuce. "It's a small money-maker. I provide the infrastructure and the computer back-up for decades of pharmaceutical records."

"Why did you get into that?"

"I saw a market for it when I attended industry conventions. I heard everyone complain about devoting real estate and managing systems for F.D.A. requirements. Consolidation makes it efficient and cheaper."

Noah cocked his head, seeming to consider this. "Duschene's drug records are in your warehouse? Telaxiphentol records?"

"What? How do you know about Telax—"

Noah whistled through his teeth. "Amazing coinci...." He mumbled something else, but Sally couldn't make it out.

It shocked her that Noah seemed not only curious about business, but astute. She was barely versed on the drugs in Duschene's portfolio. "What's going on?"

"I just read stuff, you know that. Anyway, it's cool that you make money off your competitors."

Something was up. She felt it. But she'd made a vow and needed to let go of her impulse to grill him. "Since I was forced to schmooze at all those cocktail parties, I decided to make a buck at the same time."

"You're smart, Mom." He smiled at her. "So, what does Bernard think of your empire?"

"Not sure. I don't know how I feel about selling, either. Based on your budding enthusiasm, maybe I don't have to."

Noah cocked his head again, giving her an impish look. "So, is tonight's dinner business or a date?"

"Neither. Bernard's a nice guy stuck in town, and

I'm sharing our family. I can be just friends with a man, you know."

"Sure, Mom." He angled the plate of peppers toward her so she could admire his completed design of a red and green pinwheel, the vanes in the shape of jalapeños. "Not bad, huh?" He beamed, still craving her approval, and his face reminded her of a younger Noah.

Sally laughed out loud and felt her heart expand. If time could just stand still and she could hang on to this moment, it would be enough. It struck her anew that a rich life consisted of small joys. All the straining to achieve the illusion of success didn't measure up to this simple moment. Standing side by side with Noah, chopping, laughing, the sounds of the knife on the board, the smell of onions, garlic and peppers filling her kitchen, made her feel complete.

The doorbell rang. Was it time? She glanced at the wall clock. Bernard had arrived twenty minutes early. No matter. He could visit with them in the kitchen.

"Hey, Mom?" Noah looked up at her.

"What?"

"You look nice."

Without her permission, her eyes moistened, for after all, she still craved his approval, too. "Thanks, sweetheart."

She wiped her hands on a dishtowel and dabbed at her eyes. She floated through the hall, fluffing her hair, smoothing her blouse, arrived at the front door, and opened it.

A boyish looking man stood in the doorway sporting a red polo shirt, jeans, and a shy grin. For an instant,

Sally stared in confusion at the face, trying to recognize it in a new context. Then, she smiled at Bernard, shed of his suit and tie and holding a short bouquet of yellow daisies and purple pansies.

He handed her the stems. "If you put these on the table, I promise we'll still be able to see each other."

※

Surveying Bernard and Noah's sated expressions and the carnage of her dining room table, Sally felt the contentment of a job well done.

The platter of balsamic chicken had been thinned to a single wing. Only two pesto linguini noodles survived unclaimed in the pasta bowl. The gazpacho, the almond-crusted goat cheese salad, the herbed bread, all had been fawned over and polished off.

"Ready for apple pie and coffee?" she asked.

Bernard groaned and shook his head. "Noah, I think your mother's trying to kill us. Is there anything she does half-way?"

Noah scraped and stacked plates. "Haven't found it yet."

Sally smiled. The banter and the laughs had flowed all evening. The only thing she'd failed to provide was an opportunity for Bernard to know Noah one-on-one. For a reason Sally couldn't name, she wanted that, too.

She rose. "Noah, I'll finish up. Why don't you take Bernard for a walk and help him work up an appetite for dessert?"

"Sure." Noah leaned close to Bernard's ear. "You

don't want to skip Mom's pie."

"That good, huh?" Bernard asked.

"Nah, it's just okay. But you don't want to tick her off."

Sally feigned outrage. "Noah."

"You'd better come with me, Bernard. She turns crabby if you disrespect her pie."

Sally wadded her napkin into a ball and threw it at Noah. She missed.

"Nice try, Mom," Noah joked. "Hey, Bernard. It's basketball."

Bernard looked confused. "Basketball?"

"Something my mom does halfway."

Cassiopeia hung bright in the August night sky and helped create a black and white postcard scene of Sally's block. As Noah strolled with Bernard, a light breeze blew from the west—humid, foreshadowing possible rain tomorrow. The air felt balmy, almost tropical.

Bernard broke their silence with a moan. "Why did I have seconds?"

"It's hard to say no to Mom. We'd better pick up the pace if you want that pie." Noah lengthened his stride.

Bernard groaned again, and stretched his short legs to keep pace with Noah. "I don't want pie. But as you pointed out, Sally won't let me say no."

In the dim light, the neighborhood of Noah's youth looked peaceful. Mature, leafy dogwoods lined both sides of the street. Lush bush roses and verbena cascaded onto thirsty lawns, defying the one-hundred-degree heat and humidity that characterized St. Louis summers. Noah admired the grit of Mid-west florae—all the more beautiful for their perseverance through icy winters, tornado filled springs, and scorching summers.

He wished he could spot a red tail fox, the only thing missing from Noah's picture of an idyllic Missouri night.

No sooner had Noah created the thought when he saw a shape streak out of the trees, dart under a streetlamp, and reveal its furred shock of red.

"Bernard, look over there. A fox."

"Where?"

"There. Sorry. Too late." Noah removed his journal and pen from his pocket as he walked over to the streetlamp. He noted the coincidence of his thought and the subsequent fox's appearance.

"What do you jot down in that notebook?" Bernard asked as he caught up to Noah. "I noticed you writing during dinner."

He looked up. "I track synchronicities. Or coincidences, if you prefer. For my physics research."

"Synchronicities?"

"I'm working on a theorem that awareness is the fifth dimension."

"The fifth dimension?"

"You know the four dimensions—height, width, depth, time. Synchronicities are markers for the fifth dimension. At least, that's what I think. Expanded awareness determines where our consciousness resides."

"This is physics?" Bernard shook his head.

Noah laughed. "You'd be surprised what scientists work on. This isn't considered even slightly goofy. Physicists have mapped synchronicities since the turn of the twentieth century."

"I'm familiar with the concept, but I didn't know they'd been mapped."

"A guy named Paul Kammerer was the first. He kept a log of coincidences categorized by names, words, numbers, letters, dreams and disasters. He published "The Law of the Series" in 1919. Only, no one took him seriously, so he blew his brains out."

"Rejection can be tough," Bernard said.

"It sucks." Noah returned the notebook to his pants pocket. "We'd better keep moving."

Bernard kept pace. "You do research in your spare time?"

"I'll go back to it full time as soon as I...." As soon as I finish researching Selexikote and Telaxiphentol, he almost said, but caught himself. "I'm taking a break to learn Mom's business."

"You seem like a business natural to me. At dinner you asked lots of good questions."

"Just trying to make the most out of the job Mom gave me." Noah noticed Bernard's habit of looking at him instead of where he walked. "Watch out you don't trip." Noah pointed to a buckled slab of sidewalk in front of them.

"How do you feel about the possibility of Sally selling the company? Is that okay with you?"

Noah hadn't considered his feelings in the matter. He welcomed a sale, if it would relieve the weight of Sally's stress. In a way, it might relieve his too, since she tried to guilt him into management. Relentlessly. Another one of those things Mom didn't do halfway. Still, selling to Duschene? What if Jean-Paul's suspicions proved true? Surely Bernard wouldn't work for an unethical company. Noah needed answers, and quickly. "If she sells to the right company, it's fine."

"Because once it's sold, there's no going back." Bernard gestured with his hands. "If you have any desire to take over your mother's company, now would be the time to express it to her."

Noah struggled to imagine a future scenario when he would embrace business over physics. Would he regret that he'd tossed his family legacy aside like used furniture or last year's computer? Nah. "She should sell it if she wants to."

"Human beings are such a complicated species," Bernard said. "We don't desire the things we have, and we don't have the things we desire. My father wanted his own business, but couldn't afford it. He was always waiting for some mythical family fortune to show up. Only it never did. I grew up with his unsatisfied hunger lodged in my craw."

"So why don't you buy or start a business?"

"Life took me down a different path."

"It's not too late."

"I'm afraid it is." Bernard tripped and caught himself.

Noah reached for his arm. "You okay?"

"I see what you mean about the sidewalk."

"Winter tears up the cement."

"That happens in Minneapolis, too. So, any other synchronicities you noted tonight?"

Another street lamp caught Bernard's profile, and Noah studied it. Instinctively, he felt he could trust him. Out of the shadows emerged the perfect opportunity to broach the topic of Jean-Paul's problem. Noah took a deep breath, and gathered his courage. "It's no coincidence you came for dinner."

Bernard shrugged. "Of course, not. Sally invited me."

"I mean her asking and you accepting were part of a bigger picture—an implicit order. You and I were destined to have this conversation."

Bernard shook his head. "Based on what's happened in my life, I don't believe there's an implicit order, or a rhyme or reason for anything. But for the sake of discussion, why do you think we're supposed to have this conversation?"

"The reason is different for each of us. I know my reason. I'm supposed to ask for your advice."

"With what?"

Noah blew out his breath. "I have a friend who thinks his African village's supply of AIDS drugs may have been intentionally tainted. He's asked me to help find out if he's right."

Bernard halted on the sidewalk and the color drained from his face. "Why you?" His brow furrowed. "Because your mother's in the drug business?"

"Yes. He thinks I can help him uncover a crime. I think you can help me."

"Why?" The tenor of his voice deepened. He gaped up at Noah. "Are you making this up?" His face twisted in apparent pain. He stepped backwards. "My, God. You know about me, don't you?"

"Know what?"

"How did you find out? Who told you?"

Noah floundered. "I have no idea what..."

"Have you said anything to Sally?"

"No. Bernard, I really don't know what..."

"...because I'd like to tell her myself."

Noah moved closer to the street lamp and positioned himself to the full light. "Bernard, look at me. I don't know what you're talking about. If there's deeper meaning you've attached to something I've said, it's another example of synchronicity. Your internal thoughts matched an acausal external event. That's all."

Bernard stood still on the walk for a moment. Then, he made his way to Noah and stared up at him. "I see." Bernard cradled his face in his hands and laughed. "That's funny, isn't it? Is this the kind of thing you'd note in your book?"

Noah nodded. "Under the category of 'meaning synchronicities.'"

"It's a coincidence."

"Yes."

Bernard shook his head. "Forgive me. I'm haunted by my past. It rears up and surprises me sometimes." He walked into the shadows and stood alone in the dark.

Noah resisted the urge to follow, and he left Bernard to his own thoughts. Cricket chirps marked the passing seconds. Noah moved away from the streetlamp. He glanced up to the heavens to search for the faint glow of Sagittarius, visible only in the month of August. He thought he found it low on the horizon. When he looked down, Bernard stood before him.

"Before I handled due diligence for Duschene," Bernard said, "I used to head their operations. Something happened, and my position in the company changed. I'm afraid I don't have the credibility with Duschene to help your friend, nor can I put myself in that position. I'm truly sorry."

Noah felt disappointed, but he understood. "Okay."

"I'll give you this advice. Be careful. Don't say anything to anyone until you've gathered the evidence. Otherwise, the information will be hidden. Files will disappear, papers will be shredded, and you'll never discover the truth. Do you understand?"

"Yes." Noah nodded. Simply having this conversation had been a risk, but Noah's gut had urged him forward and had assured him he'd be safe with Bernard.

Noah puzzled as to what troubled the man. Bernard stood rigid, his fists clenching and unclenching. His face lost all trace of his former, relaxed demeanor.

"Bernard? Whatever might have happened...I can tell you're a good man."

"Can you?" Bernard looked into Noah's eyes. "It's hard to tell the good guys from the bad guys." He put a finger to his lips and appeared to be thinking. The crickets' songs filled the long silence. At last, a smile materialized on Bernard's face. "Now I know my reason for having this conversation with you." He slapped Noah on the back and turned to walk toward Sally's house. "When you and your friend find what you're looking for, tell him to see me."

Noah smiled, knowing he might be able to gain Bernard's support, after all. The two walked side by side in silence. The wind rustled the branches. Noah spotted the rounded shape of cumulus clouds off in the distance. Maybe rain would move in sooner than tomorrow.

Suddenly, the smell of cinnamon tickled Noah's nose. He felt the hairs rise on the back of his neck. Hadassah.

Just as quickly, the ominous feeling melted away. She'd either floated off, or meant no harm. Or, more simply, Noah's imagination had run wild in the night.

How ironic and synchronous, Noah thought. Like attracts like. Bernard felt haunted by events from his past. Noah felt haunted by a specter from the past.

"Remarkable," Bernard said, a look of surprise on his face.

"What?"

Bernard quickened his pace. "We're a block from your mother's house. But I swear I can smell her apple pie all the way out here. Coincidence or not, I'm ready for a piece."

Chapter Seven

A glossy layer of sweat covered Noah's body, and his hair was plastered to his head. With no rain that day to break the summer heat, the air felt like hot taffy.

No egregious-energy-guzzling-planet-sucking air conditioning for him. No way, no matter how muggy it got. Like all great catalysts for change—Gandhi, Nelson Mandela, or Abbie Hoffman—Noah suffered for his ideals.

He lay awake for the third sleepless night in a row, thinking about Jean-Paul's warning. "Nighttime is daytime for spirits," he'd said when Noah had discussed his desire to moonlight his research. Noah thought the advice ridiculous. He could be accomplishing some aspect of his theorem.

Anxiety added to the heat. In a few hours at the crack of dawn, he, Fleck and Jean-Paul would break into the Friedman Pharmaceutical Data Storage and Recovery Division warehouse to hunt for the Selexikote and Telaxiphentol files.

Noah had made no progress uncovering information on Selexikote in the two weeks he'd been at his new job.

The paper files were missing from the office, the computer files deleted. Today, he'd get closer to answers.

The cable box glowed against the pitch-black room, announcing time in glaring orange numbers: 3:55, 3:56, 3:57....

He closed his eyes and tried meditating himself to sleep by naming landmark physics discoveries in chronological order: 1604, Galileo, The Law of Falling Bodies; 1666, Newton, Universal Gravitation; 1687, Newton, Laws of Motion...Try as he might, his mind kept traveling back to his own research, and his squandered chance to add a contribution to the list.

He heard the low buzz of mosquitoes and pulled the sheet up to his chin for protection. Too late. His chest itched, like a whole swarm had invaded the room.

Noah turned on his bedside lamp to view the damage. His chest displayed a perfectly outlined 'n,' or an upside down 'u,' as though someone had written on his body with a red-Anopheles-marker. The shape below it formed a three-hundred-sixty-degree circle. He willed himself not to scratch as he puzzled over the uniformity and precision of the insects' work.

Nature amazed him, but he couldn't stay in the moment to relish the universe's beauty. He wanted to jump out of his skin. The itch drove him crazy. He needed Benadryl and calamine lotion. Noah threw aside the damp bed sheet and swung his feet to the floor.

Kitsala hissed, and Noah watched the ball of spiked fur scurry under the bed.

"What's wrong, girl?"

The dead air outside his bedroom window came to life, flapping the curtains against the wall. What started as a breeze increased in intensity until a blast of wind roared through the window. The room's temperature plummeted. Noah's teeth chattered. A frigid mist sifted into the room and encircled him; snow flurries swirled around his naked body.

"Impossible," he said. "I'm dreaming."

White snow dust glowed against the room's shades of gray, and he left footprints on his way to the shower. He turned on the bathroom fluorescents. Briefly blinded, he blinked. Then, he saw his nakedness in the full-length glass. Holy Einstein. Bite patterns dotted his thighs. Raised welts the size of marbles itched uncontrollably. In the mirrored reflection, he saw a message.

His ribs displayed a "U", his stomach an "O", his right leg an "M", and his left leg an "E".

You owe me.

His legs went weak, but he managed to stumble to the shower. He turned the knobs and stood under a hot stream, trying to warm up, lathering soap over the welts, scrubbing, scratching until he thought his skin must have surely been bleeding. All the while, Noah hoped he could wake from this nightmare.

He stayed in there an eternity or ten minutes, way too wasteful of a shower. Water evaporated from the planet at an alarming rate; how dare he contribute to the excess. Noah forced himself to turn off the tap and pat his skin dry. He stepped out of the shower.

Condensation covered the bathroom mirror and the walls; it dripped from the towel rack. H2O molecules detached and traveled separate ways at an accelerated speed. The words "You owe me," clung to the mirror and then bled down the surface.

The room resembled a steam bath. Yet Noah breathed in a frosty waft of cinnamon, so icy and dry it bit his nostrils. His senses felt spooked, but his brain remained coherent. He knew who was responsible.

"Hadassah, what do you want?" he screamed at his blurred reflection. "Tell me, and I'll do it."

The remaining fog cleared, revealing a shape across the room behind him. The mirrored image sharpened to a woman dressed in black, a babushka tied around her head.

His heart throbbed in his ears; his impulse was to run, but there was no escape. He turned to face her.

Hadassah raised her arm and extended a bony finger. From six feet across the room the arm stretched longer and longer, until the pale finger touched his forehead. "*Kumen*," said the ghost.

Come.

Noah reached for a towel and wrapped it around his waist. It embarrassed him to be nude in front of an old woman, whether or not she was of this world or from another plane.

He moved on autopilot, grabbing his clothes and hopping one legged to pull on his jeans. The cotton of his t-shirt scored the u and the o when he jerked the hem down to his waist.

Hadassah's hooded eyes were inescapable. Noah tried to look away, but he couldn't. Fully clothed, he still felt naked under her mesmerizing glare.

Hadassah raised both arms, and Noah's bedroom disappeared.

Noah found himself in a large room. Gold-embossed chairs with red upholstered cushions stood on oriental rugs, spread randomly atop high-glossed wood floors.

"*Vos iz?*" he heard himself say, but the voice was husky, not his. The words, Yiddish. Apparently, he processed ideas in both Yiddish and Russian.

He experienced random thoughts that didn't belong to him: his favorite soup was beet borsht, he loved to ice fish, and he couldn't wait to see his wife again, and enjoy a batch of her rugalach cookies. His right foot throbbed from wearing tight boots.

Noah realized with a start he was occupying someone else's body.

With a stranger's hands, he explored a foreign face. He discovered thick, soft hair in the shape of a short beard, moustache, and long curled sideburns. As he fingered deep horizontal crevices in his forehead and vertical lines on the sides of his mouth, he surmised his age as late fifties or sixty.

His fingertips grazed a tall, rounded hat. Beaver fur? He glanced down at a black button-down vest and a matching coat that flowed down to the top of polished knee boots.

From the vest's bottom button hung a gold chain that snaked into his pants pocket. A muffled song chime sounded. Four measures of a minor-key Russian lullaby. He withdrew the pocket watch, the eighteen-karat cover studded with diamonds in the design of a Star of David and surrounded by six falling comets.

Noah fingered the etched pattern before he pressed the push crown. The front flipped open, revealing gold hands on a Roman numeral face and the sound of rhythmic ticking. Three-thirty. What day? What year? He wondered.

Someone else stood in the room, but not Hadassah. The man wore a red military jacket adorned with medals. He sported a well-clipped beard and moustache, and shorn hair. With his right hand, he placed a gold and silver Fabergé egg into Noah's open hand.

The weight of it surprised him. He thought it the most intricately detailed and magnificent piece of art he'd ever seen.

The egg was embellished with sheaves of emerald bulrushes, ruby roses and sapphire laurel leaves. One side displayed a portrait of Peter the Great, which Noah knew because he could read the small inscription in Russian on the bottom. The other side of the egg showed a portrait of Czar Nicholas II. A cartouche of gold and diamonds encircled each picture.

Did this egg match Hadassah's collection? Was this one of the three eggs that Noah's family had failed to deliver to Pincus Goldberg? Was this egg the reason Hadassah had transported him through time? For what purpose?

Noah realized that he stood in the presence of Nicholas II, the last czar of Russia. He sucked in a sharp breath of shock.

"Chaim," the czar said. "You've been a wonderful friend and a patient tutor to both me and my children."

"Thank you for this gift, Your Excellency," Chaim, or Noah, said. He wasn't sure how this system worked.

The Czar extended his hand. "Safe journey."

Noah heard the pounding of footsteps on the stairs outside the room. Men shouted in Russian. Their voices gained volume a moment before something heavy slammed against the doors.

The wood shuddered and splintered. Soldiers in dusty gray coats barged inside, surrounding Chaim and the Czar in a tight circle and pointing rifles with bayonets.

The tutor stood there, motionless, cradling the egg.

"Come on, dude. Say something. Do something." Noah's thoughts screamed at Chaim. He could feel Chaim's heart thundering, an older heart. Noah feared it might explode. This experience held no fascination. Only terror.

A soldier jabbed Chaim hard in the ribs. Noah felt the rifle butt. "Move. We must take you tonight," the Russian said in a hoarse voice.

Czar Nicholas' eyes contained a look of somber resignation as he rested a hand on Chaim's shoulder. "I'm sorry, my friend. It appears you have stayed too long."

The steam had cleared from the bathroom mirror. The air felt damp and smelled faintly of cinnamon.

Hadassah had returned Noah to his apartment. She hovered before him, her eyes like a dark abyss. She raised her hand and pointed at him.

"Four losses you will suffer," she howled. "First, loss

of freedom." She lowered her bony index finger. "Second, loss of memory." The middle finger came down. "Third, loss of family." She bent the ring finger. "Last of all, loss of life. *A broch tsu dayn lebn.* May your life be worthless if you don't make things right with me."

Noah's muscles cramped with fear and confusion. What did she want? Was he supposed to find the eggs? Should he return the money? Who was Chaim? Why wouldn't she just tell him what to do?

There had to be a pattern, a synchronicity. "How do I make things right?" he shouted.

Hadassah's form melted before Noah's eyes. She became one with the mist, which scrawled her answer on the mirror, the steam script stretching across the glass.

Noah read the letters and heard her reedy whisper inside his head.

"Find Chaim."

Sally pressed her face to the glass door of conference room 100, cupped her hands around her eyes, and watched Bernard.

He sat hunched over a computer printout, a pencil dangling from his hand, ready to underscore some minute detail he'd failed to previously detect. With his free hand he blindly fished his legal pad from his briefcase, never taking his eyes off the page.

Today it might be tough to distract him. Since Bernard Goldberg's arrival, Sally had invented excuses to spend time with him—an offer of coffee, an invite for lunch, a request for his attendance at a marketing meeting. She'd played a secret game, betting how many attempts it might take to force him to abandon his reports. His tenacity made her laugh, but she'd win eventually, collecting her prize of a conversation with him in her office.

She liked Bernard. That's all it was. Yet it surprised her when she found herself fretting over her attire each morning, or feeling disappointment when he failed to notice. She combed her fingers through her bob, straightened her skirt, and pushed through the door.

He startled, looked up, his face and neck flushing. "Good morning."

She beamed her most charming smile. "Hope I'm not interrupting your train of thought."

"Not at all. I have great news. Today's the day," he said. "I'm finished with due diligence."

Her heart fell. Sally stared at him. "You said you'd be here for two weeks."

"Yes, well, it's been ten days."

"Are you sure you've been thorough enough?"

"Excuse me?" Bernard gave her that bemused little-boy grin she liked so much.

"You owe me four days." She shook her head. "Just kidding." For God's sake, she sounded idiotic. "Sooner is great."

"I leave tonight."

She forced herself to keep her smile in place as she met his gaze. "I can finally have my conference room back."

He laughed. "I'm sure you can put it to better use. You'll be getting a formal offer from Trip any day now.

He also intends to make an offer for Selexikote. Since you only own fifty percent rights, that's a deal I suggest you take."

"It's a surprise Trip wants it, but Roger DeMarko will be thrilled."

"You should plan on making a visit to Minneapolis soon. Trip insists on signing documents at the corporate office."

"Of course."

"I'm sure he'll want to take you to dinner." He frowned. "To celebrate."

She felt the impulse to clear the air about sleeping with Dalton. She wanted to apologize to Bernard, admit how stupid she'd been. She didn't need his forgiveness, but apparently, she wanted it. Jesus, Sally, let it go. "What about the other deal? Do you think I should sell Friedman Pharmaceutical?"

Bernard looked away, drumming his fingers on his legal pad.

"Is there something you want to tell me?"

He met her gaze straight on. "Don't sell your company to Trip. The two of you aren't a good fit. Hang on to your legacy. I think you should find someone to manage Friedman Pharmaceutical if you're tired of the day-to-day."

"That's easier said than done. I've tried."

"I know someone who would be the right fit. If you turn down Trip's offer, I'll help you pursue that option."

It warmed her to know he wanted to help her, and that she might have alternatives. She studied him for a moment, admiring his strength, his calm, and his candor. She sensed he wanted to say more. "Isn't this conversation highly unorthodox?"

"Highly? Off the charts. I should be fired for saying it. Instead..." he paused..."I offered my resignation this morning. Effective after I've completed this assignment."

"What?" Color me stunned, Sally thought.

"It's time. I've been hiding out in this job."

"I don't understand. I thought you enjoyed--"

He raised his hand. "There's a lot I need to explain, but this isn't the time. When you come to Minneapolis, after you've decided what you want to do, I'll tell you my story."

A faint, high-pitched chime interrupted their tête-à-tête. It seemed to be coming from under the table. The music, a fragment of a song from the past, sounded far too delicate to be a cell phone ring.

Bernard reached into his pants pocket and removed his antique watch. "Funny, it's been going off at the most inopportune times. I didn't even know my watch had a working chime. Now, I can't get it to shut up." He looked up, his brown eyes wide and fixed on her.

Sally experienced a sudden surge of loss, isolation and anxiety. Her stomach fluttered and her legs felt leaden. She sank into a chair beside Bernard. "The watch is telling you it's time to go." She lowered her head. "I don't want you to leave," she whispered.

"We'll see each other."

"People say that, but they never mean it."

"I do." He took her hand, positioning it palm up on the table. He gently smoothed her fingers flat. "Here." He dropped his watch into her hand. "Keep this for me."

"Bernard, I can't."

"You'll return it to me in Minneapolis."

Sally shook her head. "You told me to keep my legacy. How can you give me yours?"

"Because, in this case, I'm putting it in excellent hands." He closed her fingers around the watch and let his hand linger atop hers.

Her eyes watered. "Why do you trust me?"

"Sally, is it so hard to believe you deserve to be trusted?"

She blinked back the tears forming in her eyes. "I've made so many mistakes."

"You must have done something right. Noah's wonderful."

"That's a credit to him, not me. I've been a terrible role model."

"Human beings are a complicated species. Complicated and flawed, but we can all be redeemed. Even you, Sally Friedman." He smiled warmly. "I trust you. When you come to Minneapolis, you'll return my legacy. I'll tell you my story. And if you decide to trust me in return, you'll tell me yours."

THE INDIGENOUS WORLD

Chapter Eight

Noah crouched in the flowerbed, his back pressed against a monument signpost that read, "Pharmaceutical Data Recovery, a division of Friedman Pharmaceutical." He felt wired with anticipation and lack of sleep. Jean-Paul had pointed out that nervousness and excitement feel the same way. "Control your thoughts about your feelings. When you are nervous, imagine you are inspirited," the shaman had said.

Oh boy, he thought, am I inspirited. It was 5:25 a.m. He scanned the horizon for Fleck and Jean-Paul. The twilight sky glowed faint silver, the constellations twinkling brightly. To the north, he spotted Polaris. Not far away, he located the International Space Station.

He pulsed to the summoning chirp of male crickets, their wings rubbing frantically in the warm air as he counted the beats per minute. He tried to pick up additional sounds, leaves shifting or twigs snapping. Nothing.

He hoped he hadn't arrived too early. Jean-Paul had insisted they not meet until the Bird of Dawn announced to all nocturnal species and spirits that it was time to hide from the light. Only then would Noah be safe from Hadassah.

"What time is that?" Noah had asked.

The shaman pretended to consult his invisible watch. "Do I look like I have eyes that glow in the dark and feathers protruding from my backside? I am not the Bird of Dawn."

Noah had already experienced the result of ignoring Jean-Paul's warning that "nighttime is daytime for spirits." The thought of risking another spookadelic trip to Russia terrified him.

"Next time you travel to another world, you might not find your way back," the shaman had counseled.

Noah had checked the United States Naval Observatory's website for official twilight time, 5:17 a.m. Surely the Birdbrain of Dawn would crow, or tweet, or peep, or whatever it's supposed to do by sunrise, 5:48 a.m. If they were lucky, the chicken might decide to wake a bit early. They couldn't risk being at the warehouse past 6:30, when some aggressive, driven, I'll-prove-I'm-worthy-to-be-C.E.O.-type employee might show up. That gave them forty-two minutes to locate the file stacks, unlock the drawers, and remove and photograph the Selexikote and Telaxiphentol records. Two thousand-five hundred-twenty seconds and counting.

An owl hooted in the distance. "Why do you hide like a rabbit in the bush?" The shaman's voice echoed from nowhere and everywhere.

Noah's heart jumped. Suddenly, Jean-Paul's muscled frame towered over him.

Noah lost his balance and fell over in the flowerbed.

"Jesus, you scared the hell out of me. Where did you come from?"

The shaman laughed from his belly. "I will teach you to hunt without making noise."

"This makes at least sixty-five things you've promised to teach me."

Jean-Paul offered an outstretched hand. "It is pitiful what little you know."

Noah grabbed it, and Jean-Paul effortlessly pulled him to his feet.

"Hey, guys. I'm coming." Fleck's gravelly whisper sounded from across the parking lot. He lumbered toward them with a camera, a tripod, and a camcorder strapped around his neck.

"What's up with the extra equipment?" Noah asked. "Are you making a documentary?"

Fleck panted, red-faced. "You never know when this stuff comes in handy."

Noah turned toward the building. "Let's go. It's getting late."

"Wait." Jean-Paul said. "First we must invoke the ancestors."

"Awesome." Fleck fired up the camcorder and moved a few feet back from Jean-Paul. "Don't start until I set up."

Jean-Paul put a hand on Fleck's shoulder. "My curious friend, turn off the machine. Sacred ceremonies must remain secret, or they lose their power."

Fleck sighed and pressed the off button.

"Jean-Paul, we don't have time for this," Noah said. He was more nervous by the minute.

Jean-Paul ignored him, removing his medicine bag

from around his neck and loosening the drawstring. He walked stooped over, pouring ash onto the grass to form a large white circle, then sat cross-legged. "Sit."

Noah checked his watch, a tangible one with hands that glowed in the dark that Sally had given him for his birthday. It was 5:40. "We've only got—-

"Sit." Jean-Paul slapped the grass on both sides of him outside the perimeter of the ash. "First, we will honor the ancestors and ask for their guidance."

From the pouch he removed a short, knotty tree branch. A red feather was attached to one end, and some species of animal tail, perhaps a lion or giraffe, decorated the opposite end. He tapped the wand three times in all directions; in front of him, north toward Polaris; behind his head, south towards Cassiopeia; to the east, Orion; to the west, Betelguese.

"Por a saminay. Por a saminayo. Por a maminay. Por a maminayo." His chant echoed sonorous. "Come, Father. Come Mother. Guide us with your wisdom. Help us with our quest. Por a saminayo. Por a maminayo. Aah."

The breeze whistled a faint strain. The trees nearby swayed gently in concert, as though they danced a ballet. Their rhythm and coordination bedazzled Noah, and he was astounded to realize the trees seemed closer than they'd been a minute before. "They're moving toward us," he shouted. "How is that possi-"

"Holy shit." Fleck's crossed legs beat up and down like windshield wipers on high speed.

"Shh. Do not break the energy field." The shaman's eyes remained closed. He sat composed, a panther at rest.

The trees sambaed closer. The three of them sat encircled in a forest of pine and oak. The sharp scent of needles and desiccated late summer foliage teased Noah's nose. Smoke rose from the circle of ash in thin lines, swirled above their heads and took the shape of spectral beings. More than a dozen smoke creatures slalomed around the trees, the vegetation and vapors performing an otherworldly pas de deux.

"No one's gonna believe this ever happened." Fleck's eyes widened with wonder. A stream of smoke swirled through him, emerging on the other side. He laughed. "That tickles. Stop it, man."

A hazy presence floated before Noah, as silent and soft as a sigh. The smoke drew a face, a delicate pencil sketch with defined features: lips pursed like a cinched bag, drooped eyelids and two long chin hairs.

"Grandma?"

The mist seeped inside him, entering through his nose and mouth and infusing him with a feeling of love. Tears flowed down his cheeks. He felt as though his heart might burst, and he thought if it did, that would be fine. His tongue tasted mun cookies from Petrovsky's Bakery, Great-Grandma Sara's favorite. The flavor of poppy seeds tingled his tongue. The warmth of hot tea with honey slid down his throat. His teeth bit the glass.

A vision of Sara as a young woman stood before him, her skin opalescent, copper hair flowing behind her in waves as she waltzed. Someone, dark-haired and Roman-nosed, held her tight. Noah's head spun as Sara and the man twirled round and round and round. Noah sensed Sara's warm hand in his. He inhaled a combination of chicken schmaltz and rose petal perfume.

"*Bubala*, you are loved." Her words chimed inside his head. "There is nothing but love."

Then, she flew out of his torso. His chest collapsed for a flicker of an instant. Emptiness. He felt bereft. Then his atria expanded, his ventricles contracted— steady, rhythmic, and strong. Lub-dub. Lub-dub. Heart music vibrated through his body, reinforcing the splendor of being alive.

Sara's essence dissolved into thin wisps of silver-gray cloud, and floated toward the other specters. They commingled, the smoke vapor creatures fusing into a solid charcoal plume, which danced in loops high above their heads. The gray mist, distinct against the soft blue of dawn, skywrote across the heavens: V, U, U, R. Then, the solid column of smoke floated toward the warehouse.

"What does V-u-u-r mean?" Noah asked the shaman.

"Spirit. *Vuur* means inner spirit." Jean-Paul's eyes glowed against his dark face. He returned the wand to his pouch, pulled the drawstring tight, and slipped the strap over his head. "Come. It is time." He surged to his feet.

Noah checked his watch. 5:55. Thirty-five minutes to achieve the impossible. But then again, he had just experienced the impossible.

Noah, Fleck, and Jean-Paul raced across the office park, over pavement, grass and flowerbeds, following the smoke vapors to the side entrance of the warehouse facility.

The cloud of dark mist hovered before the steel door for a moment before disappearing through the alloy.

Noah fumbled with the keys he'd stolen from the security office, found the red-tagged one, and inserted the key into the lock. His hand poised over the alarm keypad, ready to press the code he'd pilfered from security's files, 102379. Sally must have assigned the company codes, because that was the date of his birth. He pulled back the key from the lock, feeling uncertain. "Wait."

He faced his partners in crime. Fleck's face gleamed beet red. Perhaps he'd heated from the run, but most likely he flushed from the excitement of breaking a story. This might be his moment to shed light on wrongdoing, proving he was a serious journalist. Jean-Paul appeared unflappable, not a bead of sweat creased his brow. Just another day in the bush. Just another chance to serve his embattled people.

They made an unlikely trio, but together, they would figure out this puzzle. Get on with it, Noah thought. Courage. Spirit. *Vuur.* "Let's go over the plan one more time."

Fleck sighed. "A little anal, are we?"

"Jean-Paul, Fleck, you find the Telaxiphentol file drawers."

"Gotcha," Fleck said. "I photograph the file pages."

Jean-Paul patted his medicine bag. "I speak to the Ancestors and guide them to where they are needed."

"I'll go to the Selexikote stacks," Noah said. "Fleck, text messages only. If you see anyone or anything, the code is…"

"T." Fleck said.

Jean-Paul looked quizzical. "T for trouble?

"T for T*sures*. Yiddish for trouble. My great-grandma used *tsures* for when trouble arrived."

"Your Ancestor." Jean-Paul smiled, his teeth reflecting a ray of breaking light. "It is good that she participates in our plan."

"Meet back in the parking lot by 6:30, no matter what," Fleck said.

"No matter what." Noah patted his pockets. "Everybody check your stuff. Cell, camera, flashlight."

Fleck and Jean-Paul tapped their jackets and jeans. Fleck jabbed the air with a thumbs-up. Jean-Paul nodded in agreement.

"Let's trick or treat." Noah raised a fist.

Jean-Paul and Fleck followed suit, joining three fists in a knuckle-grazing salute of solidarity.

Noah inserted the key in the lock and tapped 102379 on the keypad. The pinprick red alarm-light turned green. He turned the key to the left, felt the lock release, and pushed open the door.

The smoggy vapor had dispersed into separate apparitions, several spooks waiting for them in the hallway. One specter, seven feet tall with a hazy bone protruding through its fog-nose, tapped a filmy foot and shot them a look of utter disgust. It shook its head and a wake of gray smoke spikes waggled in the air.

Noah felt like he should apologize. "Sorry for the delay."

Fleck pointed his Nikon and clicked a succession of shots.

The smoke creature shook a disapproving fume-finger at Fleck, then floated toward the end of an entry corridor.

The three followed. Noah strained to detect light waves (or were they particles?) in the pitch black. He perked his ears and heard nothing other than the sound of Fleck's uneven breathing.

He fished out his flashlight and turned it on. The beam lit on file drawer after file drawer. Cold, forbidding steel boxes. Beyond the cabinets, the dark sucked the photons into the void.

"Extinguish your light," Jean-Paul whispered.

Noah complied. Black silence. "I can't see."

"Wait."

Noah heard Jean-Paul open his medicine bag. He muttered something soft under his breath.

Suddenly, the darkness turned to shades of gray, and Noah could make out shapes in the gloom. The expanse of the warehouse loomed before them. The file drawers formed four-foot aisles, approximately fifteen feet high. The rows stretched five hundred feet down the length of the building, and about two hundred feet across its width.

"Man, it's so big," Fleck said.

"100,000 square feet," Noah said. "I told you."

"Didn't sound big. But to see it…"

Jean-Paul whispered, "Silence is the word of the hunter. Come, Fleck." He grabbed Fleck's arm and guided him down the aisle in the direction of the Telax-iphentol records.

Noah watched the two disappear into the shadows. He groped his way along the numbered aisles, counting to locate aisle fourteen. He clicked on the flashlight and read the identification plate, number thirteen. Light off. He moved over one more aisle, then turned to the right and counted drawers, sliding his hand along the smooth metal handles until he thought he might be near 1463, the number for the Selexikote storage compartment. Light on. Number 1476. Light off. He backtracked along the stack, counting thirteen drawers. Flicking on his flashlight, he let the beam rest on the number. 1463. Bingo.

Conflicted emotions weighed him down like a g-force. He couldn't wait to release the information inside the drawer, but he also couldn't bear the thought of revealing it. Perhaps, there'd be no surprises. Then again, he might uncover a truth that could steer the course of his own fate.

He removed his Synchronicities Journal from his pocket and aimed the flashlight on it. The glow of the beam illuminated the green notebook, making it look phosphorescent. He flipped through the pages until he found the one titled, "Telaxiphentol documentation transported, CBDFGJ. Possible code combinations."

He scanned the list of number patterns he'd come up with to translate DeMarko's gibberish into the winning code that would open the file drawer: Number-for-letter, Caesar cipher, monoalphabetic substitution, keyword cipher, polyalphabetic crypto, word pattern, and transposition cipher. Something would work. He'd get what he came for.

The first number combination on his list, 3245670, was ridiculously easy. No way would DeMarko pick a simple number-for-letter substitution, but Noah had to list the obvious. After all, DeMarko wasn't the brightest specimen in the galaxy. Noah would stick to the plan, trying the codes in order, from easy to difficult.

The file keypad buttons were laid-out like the face of a calculator. Noah pressed 3-2-4-5-6-7-0. Enter. Nothing.

On to the next code. A Caesar Cipher...

He felt a jump in his hip pocket. A low-toned hum vibrated. Holy Einstein, he'd just gotten started. He reached for his cell phone and flipped it open. In the blue light he saw "T."

Tsures. Headed his way. Crap.

Where should he go? He couldn't crawl inside a file drawer, even if he could open one. He couldn't vault himself on top of the stack. Too high. The yellow glow of the exit sign beckoned to him. In the shades of gray, he might make it without being seen.

Leather soles slapped the concrete. The sound grew closer. More than one person. A pinpoint stream of light bobbed.

His heart thundered. He fought to control his breathing. He sent mental vibes to Jean-Paul, Great-Grandma Sara, Einstein, God. Help.

The smoke vapors seeped over the top of the file stalagmites and descended around him in curls. A chorus of voices spoke in different tongues. He recognized a few words of Dagara, the language of Jean-Paul's Ancestors, and Yiddish, the language of his. There were other patois, and Noah could only guess at the dialects. Swahili? Hausa? Yoruba? Dutch? Russian? German?

The smoke cloud discoursed like the Tower of Babel and he feared that anyone coming his way might hear.

Yet the sound also comforted him. Even though Noah couldn't translate the words, he understood their message. "We'll hide you. You are safe."

The fog enveloped him. He prayed he'd appear as nothing more than a shadow.

Footsteps pounded like hammers. Definitely two people. Their distinct cadences reverberated. One set, heavy footed, a man of some weight. The other set, athletic, almost graceful.

The click-clack boomed. The stream of light swelled. The two advanced to the same destination. File drawer 1463.

Noah slid along the steel structures past 1465...75...80...the smoke following his every step, blocking his view, but hiding him, he hoped.

Men's voices. He froze, straining his ears to pick up on their conversation.

"You won't be sorry." The vocalization sounded pompous and nasal, a tone that declared the speaker's intellectual superiority. He recognized the voice. De-Marko.

"I'm not accustomed to being summoned in the middle of the night, Roger. It's so retro CIA."

Noah couldn't put a name to the second man. His pronunciation was exact, almost English in its precision, with clipped consonants. The smoke and darkness prevented him from seeing anything but shadows.

"The documentation's here. I'll show you," De-Marko said.

"That you developed a drug that grows brain cells?

A drug that makes average people smart, and smart people brilliant? The next Viag..."

"Trip, this drug will make Viagra's success a dim footnote in the annals of pharmaceutical history. It dwarfs Lipitor and Nexium. Every person on the planet will wait in line for it. If they can afford it, they'll pay a king's ransom. If not, they'll steal for it."

"If your claims are true, I'll make you a very rich man."

"No, Trip. I'll make you a rich man."

Laughter echoed in the steel and concrete cavern. Arrogant. Patronizing. Someone who condescended to DeMarko.

"I'm already rich," the man called Trip said, "but I do love the game. My God, I love this game."

"I need to discuss a problem." DeMarko faltered.

"Side-effects?"

"How did you know?"

"There are always side effects. It's a question of managing risk versus reward."

"We can discuss it when you view the records..."

"I'm not weeding through your rat studies. Tell me."

Fingers tapped rhythmically on a steel file drawer. Noah smelled the sweat of fear.

"There's a slight problem with memory loss," DeMarko said.

"Don't spill the details. Let me guess. This is the part of the game I love most." Trip paused, clicking his tongue. "Selexikote exponentially grows brain cells. Users become geniuses. Users gain the ability to master anything they choose. Users invent, shape companies, forge new horizons. They transform that crappy, long-forgotten novel into lilting prose. They morph a lackluster jingle into a timeless symphony. Then one day, the party's over. Brain cells dry up, plaque up, shrink, and tangle. Neurons coat with protein. Poof. Alzheimer's."

Noah's heart froze. Hadassah's curse galloped through his brain. "May your life be worthless." This would be worse than worthless. This would be worse than death.

"Do I have that right?" Trip asked.

"You're a quick study," DeMarko conceded.

"How long before the side-effects evidence?"

"Fifteen years. Maybe a little longer. I have one patient who's been on the drug for fourteen years. He's doing great."

Yeah. Just great, Noah thought. But for how long?

"Fifteen years of glory is more than most people living lives of quiet desperation will ever have. Seems like a fair trade. Maybe a user will create a break-through that propels humanity forward. Yes, I can justify the risk. Think of the income we can rack up in fifteen years. You can stash your cash and go where they'll never find you. I'll be retired. Out of it by then, but not before I've created a paper trail leading to someone else. I have just the right person in mind. Get the file."

DeMarko shuffled his feet. His shoe connected with something. It skittered, thudding against the file stack.

"What's this?" DeMarko asked.

A flashlight beam swiveled and found its target.

Through the smoke, Noah saw a green glow. Phosphorescent. Like kryptonite. His brain filled with blood. Throbbing, throbbing. His chest ached. He wanted to fly away. His hands fluttered, searching, patting his jacket and pants pockets. Surely, he had it somewhere. He found his flashlight, his keys, his cell phone. A receipt from the cleaners. A balled-up Kleenex. Three pennies and a nickel. Where was it? Stupid. Stupid. Stupid. How could he have been so careless?

"Synchronicities Journal?" Trip read the cover.

"Why, that little shit," DeMarko said.

"This means something to you?"

"Sally's son. He's snooping around."

Noah heard the sound of buttons being punched. Confident. No hesitation. The right keys to the right combination. The storage compartment grated open.

"The file's here." DeMarko blew out his breath. "He didn't get it."

"Take care of him, Roger, or there won't be a deal."

"What's today's date?"

"August 20th."

DeMarko chuckled. "Just three days. Don't worry. He won't be a problem in three days."

"Three days?" Trip said. "There's a board meeting in Minneapolis to approve the purchase of Selexikote. Maybe, the purchase of Friedman Pharmaceutical as well. Is that it?"

"No," DeMarko said. "But what a synchronicity. What a coincidence. Perhaps I should make a note in Noah's notebook."

"What?"

"Never mind. He'll have no credibility in three days. He's gone off his meds. No one will listen to a spiraling-out-of-control nut-job in the midst of a manic episode."

Noah thought his head might explode. He wanted to reach through the smoke and the dark and deck the son of a bitch.

He felt one of the smoke spirit's gentle restraint. "Not worth the risk," it whispered. "You have more important work."

Three days. August 23rd. More than two full weeks since his last Selexikote injection and then he'd be in full-blown mania. Not a news flash. He'd known since reading DeMarko's file notes.

Look at the bright side, Noah thought. He'd broken into the warehouse seeking information on Selexikote side effects to determine whether or not to continue the drug. He'd gotten what he'd come for. In spades.

The decision turned out to be a no-brainer, pardon the pun. Stay on the drug, lose all brain function. Get off the drug, lose all reason. What a genius. He'd pick door number two and take his chances.

For the moment, he remained rational. Maybe, just maybe, he could thwart DeMarko and Dalton, preventing the drug from reaching the public. Multitudes were at risk.

His legs felt weak. He locked his knees to prevent a tumble to the concrete. He needed to get out of there in one piece. He wanted solitude to sort things out. Every second mattered. Time accelerated, dissipated, and contracted.

Just three days.

Noah hunched over the desk in his apartment, tension running through his muscles. His pen sped across the journal page so fast he could barely read his own handwriting. Images bombarded him as he raced to compile an oddly mixed list of things he wanted to remember: Sunrise, pizza cheese strings, ice crystals, the smell of women's perfume...

He'd document his mental photographs before the pictures faded away and fuzzed, like dried-out Polaroids he'd seen in his mother's childhood scrapbooks.

His first kiss—Rebecca had tasted like Cracker Jacks, salty and sweet. The feel of her glossed lips had imprinted his brain. Forever, he'd thought. No, only for now. For the moment. He could still transport himself to that kiss, to a time when he thought of limitless possibilities. Was he destined to be alone?

He hoped he'd remember how his favorite music engulfed him in vibration. He inserted his earplugs, scrolled the list on his iPod, clicked, and let Radiohead's "Fake Plastic Trees" wash over him while he wrote and wrote and wrote.

Conch shells. Mozart. Crème Brûlée. Silly Putty.

Holy Einstein, how he yearned to always remember. He prayed the images in his brain wouldn't fade too fast. If he were lucky, they might slip away slowly, silently, one at a time, so he wouldn't recognize the pain of loss.

The minute he returned to his apartment, he'd begun Synchronicities II, a new journal to replace the one he'd dropped in the warehouse. He planned to chronicle everything. Names and phone numbers of the people he cared about, even though now those digits were imbedded in his fingertips and all he had to do was conjure up a face and his fingers mindlessly punched the right buttons. The title of his favorite book (*Einstein* by Walter Isaacson), films ("Ferris Bueller's Day Off" and "Donny Darko"). Royal Blue, his color of choice. Jokes...he'd need to laugh, wouldn't he? The dates of physics discoveries. Species of birds. The Big Bang.

So much seemed important. He wondered what made a person unique. Was it the activities pursued or the emotions expressed? Was it doing or being?

The side of his left hand had smudged black with ink. It cramped. He took a break to massage it. His gaze rested on the collection of memorabilia from his youth that hung on the wall: science fair blue ribbons, a Certificate of Scholastic Achievement from the Talent Identification Program, an early acceptance letter from M.I.T. Useless, pathetic totems framed by Sally and earned courtesy of the modern miracles of drug therapy.

His thoughts were the essence of his life, he decided. Without a record of who he was, what he'd held a passion for, or what he'd spent his time on, he might as well have never existed. He refused to believe he resulted from the product of random luck and biology. He served a purpose, didn't he?

His hand blocked the sun streaming in through the window before his desk and cast a shadow on the journal page, spreading darkness over the word "exist." Synchronicity? Or was there no pattern or reason for the things that happen to us after all? Had there been any point to his work?

Noah remembered being six years old and staring out the window of an airplane gliding along at thirty thousand feet. Cookie-shaped scattered clouds had stretched for miles, as though spread across a blue baking sheet. The sun had cast cloud shadows against the earth, repeating identical shapes across the landscape for as far as he could see. Each individual cloud was part of a larger picture. A fractal.

Noah had felt awe in knowing that he played a part in something bigger than himself. There remained so much mystery in the world to uncover. If he could unlock one puzzle before he forgot to care, it would be worth everything.

Kitsala rubbed against his leg, meowing for his attention.

"Hey, Furball."

She jumped on the desk and nuzzled his hand. He rested the pen, rubbed her chin and stroked her jaguar coat. He'd promised Great-Grandma Sara that he'd always take good care of her, but he'd have to arrange for the cat's care before he started the downhill slide and forgot to feed her.

"I'm sorry, girl."

Would Fleck, Jean-Paul, or Sally take her in? He'd wait until he had no choice but to reveal his fate to anyone. He hoped he'd know when that would be. If he told his mother what was in store for him, she'd fall apart. Everyone thought she was so tough, but he knew better. He didn't want her or anyone else to know he'd soon spiral into mania, let alone the long-term prognosis of Alzheimer's. Fleck and Jean-Paul would want to watch his every move. No. He'd been monitored throughout his life. Enough already.

Maybe if he told Jean-Paul, the shaman would find an antidote to Selexikote in his medicine bag. No. He and Fleck needed to expose the truth about Telaxiphentol. They had their own full plate and ticking clock. Jean-Paul's people were dying. Noah would keep his problems to himself.

Kitsala cocked her head, her golden eyes narrowed to examine a bug on the floor. She jumped off the desk to chase it. Noah picked up his pen, adding to the list of things he loved and wanted to remember. Cat fur. Purrs. Kitsala.

He needed to see Sally. He had to warn her not to sell her company or her half interest in Selexikote. They would have a face-to-face, mother and son, C.E.O. and physicist. He removed his earplugs and punched her number on his cell, the third time he'd tried in the last hour. After one ring the call went to voice mail. She usually called back within minutes.

He punched in another number.

"Sally Friedman's office."

"Maggie, it's Noah. Is my mom there?"

"She went to Dallas for a short meeting, then on to Minneapolis. Didn't she tell you?"

Minneapolis. She was going early for the board meeting. She wouldn't be back until after the twenty-third. Noah's heart lurched.

"Noah, you still there?"

"Yeah. Sorry. She's not answering her cell."

"...Probably flying." Did he detect a hesitation in her speech? A wariness in her voice? "Do you want to leave a message for her at Duschene headquarters, as well?" Was she loyal to Sally? Or was it possible Maggie had been paid by Dalton to snitch?

A surge of fear stabbed Noah with the realization that he shouldn't leave his mom a message—not at Duschene or anywhere else. What if DeMarko and Dalton monitored all communications? What if they hacked into her voice mail? Crap. Noah would have to go to Minneapolis.

"Noah? You want the number?"

Could he trust Maggie? He'd check out Duschene's website for the address and phone number himself. "Hey, Maggie, don't tell anyone I called. Okay?"

He didn't listen to her reply and hung-up, already thinking about a quick up-in-the-morning, back-at-night flight to find Sally. Just in case—mechanical difficulties, whatever, you never know—he inked a note for his next-door neighbor:

```
Dear Mrs. Von Berg,
I might be gone for a couple of days.
Please look in on Kitsala and feed her
for me. I left food on the counter. I'll
call you when I'm back.
Thanks much.
Your friend and fellow cat lover, Noah.
```

Someone pounded the door.
"Noah? You in there?"
Fleck sounded pissed.

Fleck burst into Noah's apartment, his face flushed. "Where the hell did you go?" He bent over to catch his breath.

Jean-Paul glided into the room behind him. "The Ancestors told me we would find you here." He dropped into the only available armchair, a small celery-shaded silk wingback Noah had taken from Great-Grandma Sara's apartment. The juxtaposition of Jean-Paul's powerful frame and the diminutive chair made Noah laugh. The shaman responded with a wide grin that eased Noah's spirit, reminding him to include Jean-Paul's smile in his list of things he wanted to remember. "Glad you are safe and sound, my friend." He tossed his medicine sack on the floor.

Fleck paced, oblivious to the scattered research papers and old copies of "Scientific American" that crunched beneath his wide gum-soled shoes. "We said we'd meet in the parking lot. No matter what. Don't scare me like that."

Noah bent to rescue his fieldwork from Fleck's path. "Sorry."

"What happened?" Fleck plopped down on the floor next to Jean-Paul and crossed his arms and legs. "Well?"

They both stared up at Noah—one face aflame with impatience, the other composed and cool—demanding his logical explanation.

What a relief it would be to share the conversation he'd heard in the warehouse. Tell them everything. There must be some game plan they could brainstorm. Instead, Noah said, "I want to hear what you found."

Fleck's features transformed from annoyed to excited. "Everything was in the file: the original drug compound, memos from meetings, a contract with the United Nations and the governments of Ghana, Ivory Coast and Burkina Faso. There's a letter from the head of operations to Duschene's C.E.O., saying drug production costs were way over budget," Fleck said. "Another memo from the same guy suggested they look at ways to recoup their losses. We digitized it all."

"The head of operations?" Noah said, thinking of Bernard and hoping the subterfuge happened before his tenure. "Do you remember his name?"

Fleck put a finger to his lips. "Umm...Goldman, Goldstein, Goldbloom..."

Noah felt a pang of disappointment. "Bernard Goldberg."

"That's him. Do you know him?"

He shrugged. "Had dinner with him once."

"His name's all over the file like a bad smell," Fleck said.

"Do not look so concerned, my friend," Jean-Paul said. "We will learn more before we jump to conclusions. For now, we must test samples of what was shipped and compare the results to the original formulas in the file. If they differ, we will have enough proof to approach the United Nations and the press."

"Noah, we could bust this story wide open in less than a week." Fleck punched the air with his fist.

"I'm encouraged that soon we will secure the right assistance for my people." Jean-Paul's muscular arms gripped the sides of the chair, and he leaned toward Noah. "Now, my friend. Tell us. How was your hunt?"

A light breeze blew through the window. Kitsala meowed, jumped onto Noah's lap, and nuzzled his chest. He hugged her tight to calm her.

Suddenly, Noah smelled the aroma of chicken soup, cat litter, and bleach. He felt Great-Grandma Sara's hand on his shoulder.

"Tell them, *bubala*. Tell them the truth," she breathed into his ear.

She's right, he thought. Tell them you might be out of control within three days. Ask them to watch out for you. Tell them you might not be able to remember their names, or their faces, or that they were part of your life. Tell them it could happen anytime—you don't know when or how soon.

"*Boychick*, listen to me," Great-Grandma Sara whispered. "You must tell them."

Noah studied Jean-Paul's face. Open, kind, capable, the face of a man willing to tackle any problem.

You don't need to do this alone, Noah told himself. You're part of a team. The Three Musketeers. Remember?

"Courage, mine Noah," she murmured.

He looked at Fleck, his face brightened with possibilities, poised on the verge of an important breakthrough. Finally, he'd uncovered a story that would make a difference to the world. He knew Fleck would drop his quest in a nanosecond if he thought Noah needed him. If so, Fleck and Jean-Paul would fail to take advantage of the UNAIDS conference on the twenty-third – a chance to present solid proof about Telaxiphentol directly to the Executive Director of the Joint United Nations Program on HIV-AIDS.

Noah refused to let them miss their window of opportunity. "I got nothing," he said.

Sara pinched his shoulder. "Stubborn dumkopf."

He ignored her. "The file wasn't there. But I found out my mom went to Minneapolis for a board meeting. Looks like she's selling the company after all. She has to be warned about these jerks. I'm going up there to stop her."

Jean-Paul nodded. "Yes. Before she finds herself in harm's way. We will accompany you."

Noah cut him off. "No, you both go to the conference. I'll go to Minneapolis."

Jean-Paul stood, walked over to Noah, and looked down at his young grasshopper, the intensity in his dark eyes softening. "I shall not dissuade you from pursuing your destiny. Be careful, my brother. Your mother plays with powerful people."

Fleck rose to his feet. "Sure you don't need us?"

Noah nodded. "I'll fly up and back in a day. No problemo."

Jean-Paul embraced Noah. "May the Ancestors be with you. Heed their counsel. They will guide you."

"Hunh," Sara harrumphed in Noah's ear. "If you won't listen to me, listen to him."

Kitsala nipped Noah's hand.

He flinched. She'd given him more than a love bite.

The cat hissed and jumped off his lap.

Fleck's eyes followed Kitsala. "What's with her?"

Noah thought about asking Fleck and Jean-Paul to search for him if he didn't return by the twenty-third. What if he got into trouble and couldn't make it back? He cleared his throat. "Hey, guys..."

"What?" Fleck asked.

"Nothing." Noah shook his head. "Nail those S.O.B.'s."

Chapter Nine

C harles Dalton, III, smiled at Sally from across the wide expanse of his glass and steel desk, a commissioned work of art by preeminent master metalworker, Albert Paley. Without a doubt, the desk had cost more than her house, so what was another twenty million?

DeMarko lounged in the butter leather chair beside Sally, smiling and wiping his glasses.

She gripped the letter of intent, all those zeros in a row, managing to keep her game face on while she struggled not to blurt out something ill-advised like, "Are you whacked-out on your own pharmaceuticals?"

If Dalton wanted to gift her and DeMarko ten million dollars each for a drug that had a limited market and hadn't been through FDA testing, who was she to second-guess? She'd just won the lottery.

Dalton's pencil-thin lips curled up on one side. "I take it the terms are satisfactory?"

She slowly sipped Japanese Finé Water from a red Czechoslovakian cut glass tumbler, while she waited for an appropriate response to form. Should she yell yippee or bargain for more?

"Did you know Roger was such an effective business negotiator?" Dalton asked. "Of course, you knew, or you would have handled this yourself. Checkmate, Sally."

DeMarko guffawed. His middle shook and spilled over his belt. His shirt exposed his Fruit of the Looms between the buttons. Effective business negotiator? She strained to imagine DeMarko in that light, although he'd come through in unexpected spades.

"Great job, Roger." She smiled at him, then up at Dalton. "Yes, Trip, the terms are satisfactory."

Dalton looked disappointed. "Careful not to gush, Sally, I might rescind my offer." Then, a tight-lipped smile spread across his face. He leaned toward her. "Relax. A deal's a deal. Cheer if you want to."

She mimicked jazz hands and cheered, "Woohoo."

Dalton clapped. "That's my girl."

Sally bristled at his arrogant notion that sleeping with her once implied he owned her. In light of his generosity, she decided to let it go.

"We need to get the sale approved at the board meeting, but it's just a formality. Sally, I'd like you to do the presentation on Selexikote."

DeMarko frowned. "You said I could do it."

Dalton gave him a supercilious sneer. "Come on, Roger. Your talents are suited behind the scenes. Sally's the marketer."

"Roger, I'll make it clear that Selexikote was your baby," Sally said.

"Alright, then." DeMarko replaced his glasses.

Sally's cell phone sang, *Here Comes the Sun*. She'd missed Noah's earlier calls, so she'd kept the phone on despite the meeting. She fished it from her briefcase and hurried toward the door. "I need to take this."

"No." DeMarko shouted.

Sally tottered in her heels. "What on earth, Roger?"

"You shouldn't jump every time Noah calls. You're emasculating him." DeMarko's face turned the red of sunset. "Let's finish this deal."

Sally had no patience for DeMarko's psychiatric mumbo-jumbo. Recently, he'd warned her to keep an eye on Noah. Now, he wanted her to give him space. Who was he to lecture her on how to parent? "He's my son, not yours."

DeMarko perched his glasses on the end of his nose and peered through them. "He needs independence, not your interference."

"I don't have time or patience to listen to the two of you bicker." Dalton drummed his fingers. "None of us should be distracted by anything other than this deal. Sally, leave your phone on that étagère right where you're standing. Roger, how about you do the same? You both want the deal or not?"

Dalton's request approached absurd and demeaning, but Sally thought it best to comply and get this over with. Once the deal was concluded and she presented at the board meeting, she'd have no reason to be in his orbit. She'd call Noah back as soon as their meeting ended.

She pressed the off button and placed her phone, as commanded, next to the door. "Roger?"

He glared at Sally and passed his cell over to her. She placed it next to hers on the étagère's glass top.

She smirked at Trip, who looked like he was relishing his silly display of domination. "How about yours? Or are you exempt?"

"Fine. All's fair." Trip shrugged, to Sally's surprise, located the cell on his desktop, and handed it to her. "Here you go. We're all at attention."

She added his phone to the grouping and returned to her chair. "You were saying..."

Dalton's smile reappeared. "I'd like your presentation to focus on the success of Selexikote. Tell stories about the kids in the control group and how the drug turned their lives around. Talk about Noah. I want Duschene to give back to the world. I want to be remembered as a C.E.O. who contributed more than just a bottom line. Will you do that for me, Sally?"

Dalton's softer side surprised her. "Of course. Trip, it's good that you're doing this."

"Contrary to popular belief, I'm a nice guy."

A delicate musical strain—a Russian folk song from the past—sounded from her briefcase.

Dalton's eyes widened. "Where have I heard that tune before?"

"For God's sake, Sally," DeMarko blurted. "Turn off your cell."

Sally fumbled in her bag. "I did. It's not—"

Dalton's expression darkened. "Roger, I think we're finished here. Would you leave us alone? I'll call you later." He stood.

DeMarko threw Sally a nasty look and shook his head. "Fine." He heaved himself out of the leather chair and lumbered to the door. "Trip, we're still doing dinner, right?"

"I'll call you," Dalton snapped.

Sally felt a chill suck all the joy out of her. What the hell had just happened?

DeMarko paused briefly at the door. Then, Sally heard it open and shut behind him.

The Russian lullaby faded, and the room fell silent.

Dalton stood and made his way around the desk. He pulled the stuffed chair closer to Sally, smoothed out Roger's imprint in the leather with his fingertips, and sank onto the seat. "I heard that song when I last met with Bernard. What are you doing with Goldberg's watch?"

Her throat went dry. "He left it in my office by mistake. I'm returning it."

His eyes narrowed as he searched her face. "Really? When would that be?"

Sally's cheeks heated under his glare, but she stood her ground. She would befriend whomever the hell she pleased. "I'm having dinner with Bernard tonight."

"I sent him to St. Louis to make a deal." Dalton shook his head, tssking. "No, you'll dine with me tonight to consummate this transaction. I suppose you know he quit."

She refused to be intimidated by Dalton's macho bullshit. "I know."

"After I'd saved his ass. Oh well, no good deed goes unpunished. I'll bet you ten million dollars, he didn't share his story with you. Double or nothing?"

She frowned.

"I didn't think so." Dalton rose and walked to the bar. He poured chilled Chard into two Baccarat crystal goblets, strolled back, and handed one of the stems to Sally. His six-foot plus frame towered over her. "Here.

You'll need this." He sat down, his predator's gaze slicing through her.

"Once upon a time, Bernard Goldberg headed operations. I trusted him. Gave him free rein. He built a plant in China and, under his watch, contaminated drugs slipped into the United States. Nineteen people died within six months." Dalton clinked the crystal with the nail of his index finger and paused, listening to the chime. "Bernard begged and pleaded. Help me. Mea culpa. The little shit fell apart. Duschene paid millions in remunerations. We settled all of the lawsuits, we settled with the F.D.A., and I bartered to guarantee Bernard wasn't prosecuted."

Sally felt a sweat break out. "Horrible accidents happen in our business. Why would he be prosecuted?"

Dalton took a sip of his wine and swished it in his mouth. "Ah. Far Niente, Two-thousand-two. The best." He smiled at her. "Because, my dear, of his motive. Money. Goldberg risked missing a huge target bonus. He eliminated critical procedures to increase profits and ensure his stake. There was no horrible accident. Bernard murdered for profit."

"Oh, my God." She prayed Dalton was lying. She couldn't picture Bernard as a bad guy. He'd made a point of sharing that he'd inherited nothing but a watch. Had he been desperate for money? What did she really know about him?

"I didn't fire his ass. I should have, of course, but I kept him on. He pays me back by quitting in the middle of a deal." His eyes roamed over her. "You look pale, Sally. Take a sip of wine. It's really very good."

She felt nauseous. "I'm fine."

"Now, let me guess. He recommended you not sell Friedman Pharmaceutical."

Sally stared at her Manolos.

"That's funny." He shrugged. "He told me I shouldn't buy it. He said... how did he put it? We're not a good fit. But I don't agree."

She studied his dark features, his sneering excuse for a smile, and she felt total revulsion.

"He convinced you he's found someone to manage the company, right?" Dalton placed his hand on her knee, just below her skirt. "Well, you're a smart business woman. I'm sure you've guessed who that is."

She lifted his hand, depositing it on the arm of his chair. "Don't, Trip."

"It's Bernard, of course. He's done this before." He laughed and returned his hand to her thigh, stroking beneath her hem with two fingers. "You look sad. Well, I'm not surprised he didn't tell you the truth."

Dalton's tone and touch frightened her. Sally stood, her head spinning. She placed the crystal stem on the desk, grabbed her brief and purse, and moved across the room. "I need to return some calls. Noah tried to reach me. I need...to go." She hurried to the étagère to retrieve her phone, but it was missing. Had Roger moved it?

"Sally, come back here."

"Do you see my phone anywhere?"

Dalton stood.

My God, why would Roger take her phone? Was this his sick way of teaching her a lesson in parenting? Or had she somehow, without realizing it, returned her phone to her brief or purse? No, of course not, she distinctly remembered placing it on the étagère. Sally heard crystal break. She froze.

Dalton came up behind her. "Where do you think you're going?" he growled. "We're not finished with this meeting."

She looked at him, defiance blazing in her eyes. "Yes, we are."

He slammed her against the door. Her brief and purse tumbled to the carpet. "Who do you think you're fucking with? Did you think you could just collect ten million dollars and move on to the next guy?" He forced his hips against her, pinning her in place as he took her mouth in a display of total dominance.

She pushed at him, trying to force him back. He didn't budge. She bucked against him, straining to free her head. Her scream sounded muffled as it emerged.

He jerked back his head. "Go ahead. Scream. No one's going to come."

"You fucking bas—-"

He gripped her throat, his other hand snaking up her skirt a heartbeat before he ripped her bikini panties.

Gasping for air, Sally tried to claw at Dalton's face.

He seized her shoulders and again slammed her into the solid door, stunning her. Stars danced madly behind her eyelids.

"You fucking tease. Do you screw everyone you do business with? You think Bernard's better? Is that it?" he demanded, his rage apparent in the hissed words.

She struggled for air. He used his knee to spread her legs.

The doorknob jammed the side of her hip, and she

yelped in pain. His hand found her, his cufflinks scoring her thighs as he shoved his fingers into her. She heard the clank of his belt buckle, the grate of his zipper.

"Stop." she hoarsely screamed into his shoulder.

"Oh, was Bernard gentle? I doubt you could even feel him, he's such a little shit."

Tears streamed down her cheeks. His mouth covered hers again, cutting off her oxygen.

Bernard. She reeled at the thought of him. She felt betrayed. Fury claimed her, fury against all men. She couldn't let Dalton, the son of a bitch, own her, not without a fight.

She gasped for air, pushed, and thrashed. She freed her head and her teeth found his cheek. She tasted blood. His blood.

"You bitch." His crushing grip on her throat tightened even more. She felt faint. He penetrated her, his rage and strength shocking her.

Sally longed to leave her body and float elsewhere. Anywhere far from the pain splintering her and the humiliation of being victimized by this animal.

"God, I love a flat stomach," Dalton muttered.

She thought about Noah—how lucky she was to mother him, and how he deserved to have a nurturing mother he could cherish, instead of a woman that men treated like a whore. She'd failed her son, and that self-knowledge devastated her.

Dalton released her throat and groped her breasts.

Sally drew in a ragged breath just as Bernard's pitiful inheritance sang out across the room. She wondered then if anyone could ever really rely on anyone else. She wondered, too, if she could ever rely on herself.

Dalton rammed against her, hard and fast. "You made me do this, you fucking cunt."

Noah jostled his way forward to board American flight two-three-five to Minneapolis. Sticky. Airless. Sweat trickled down the sides of his face. A wave of claustrophobia flooded through him, and he elbowed for a small piece of turf.

He shuffled to avoid stepping on the petite sandaled feet in front of him—tender heels, hot-pink toenails, an ankle bracelet with a heart.

The man behind him sneezed. A loud, wet spray of microscopic bacteria nose-dived in his direction. Noah could already feel his cilia surrendering to the foreign invasion. Great. He'd be hacking and coughing, his alveoli puffed and swollen by the time he spiraled into full-blown mania on the twenty-third. Tomorrow.

He found his spot, row twenty-three, seat B. In the middle, of course. What else? He slipped into his seat, relieved to gain distance from the germ mass-producer.

A woman sat in the window seat, staring out at the tarmac. A bald spot peeked from the middle of her gray, curly bob. Snowflakes of dandruff dusted her black blouse.

Noah tried not to disturb her as he stowed his back-pack on the floor in front of him, shoving it to one side. There wasn't much in it: *The Elegant Universe* by Brian Green, "The Cosmic Life Cycle" (a special, just-received edition of *Scientific American*), a tooth brush, paste, floss, and "Synchronicities II."

He felt agitated, and cramped. He hoped to calm down, catch a nap. He fastened his seat belt, leaned back, closed his eyes and visualized himself safe in his apartment.

A sweet smell hit his nostrils.

Cinnamon.

Hadassah. A jolt of fear coursed through him. His eyes flew open. He gripped the arms of his seat.

The woman beside him poked his left arm. "Would you like some?" Her voice was Southern soft and charming. "I don't know how they expect anyone to eat all this." She motioned to a cinnamon roll almost as large as the tray table before her.

Noah recognized the pink and brown cardboard Cinnabon container, a whimsical advertisement for franchising obesity in America. He'd always marveled at the snaking lines of people securing their flight to-go box of artery-clogging cream cheese frosting and eleven hundred useless calories.

"Please, have some," she said.

He laughed to himself at his cinnamon paranoia and heightened imagination. No danger. No ghost on board. His neck muscles unclenched.

He shook his head. "No, thank you."

"Well, if you change your mind. It's not like you'd owe me."

Her dark eyes pierced him. His skin prickled with alarm. What's wrong with you? Chillax. She's nice. Friendly. Lonely.

"You're kind. Thanks." He forced a smile and stiffened as the plane shimmied away from the gate.

He needed to rid himself of his nerves and this feeling of impending doom by focusing on something else. He took a deep breath, turned away from his seatmate and pulled out two loose sheets of paper, an envelope and a pen from his pack. He reviewed the two letters he'd written.

```
To Whomever Finds This Note:

My name is Noah Friedman. If I'm wandering
around and look lost or confused, please
contact Fleck McNulty at 314-993-8574.
Give him the sealed envelope in my pants
pocket. Please don't open it.
The world is populated by wonderful and
awful people. I know, since you found me,
you're one of the good guys.
If not, what a bummer.
Thanks for your kindness.
Gratefully,
Noah Friedman
```

Taking the other sheet of paper, Noah reviewed the second letter.

```
Fleck,
Selexikote causes Alzheimer's in long-term
users. I've been on the drug for fourteen years,
and my brain cells might make a spontaneous run
for the exit without any warning. If you got
a call, I guess they've checked out. Sorry,
dude.
Roger DeMarko discovered that this drug
promotes brain cell growth in the pre-frontal
```

lobe. In layman's terms, it transforms people from stupidos into off-the-chart brainiacs. Who wouldn't want that? (You thought I was a natural-born genius. Oh, well. Life is filled with small disappointments.)

DeMarko and the head of Duschene International, Charles Dalton III, plan to market Selexikote to the general public. Huge profits and buyer be damned.

Sally knows nothing about this. If these bastards try to implicate her, she's innocent. She may need your help. Her worst crime is wishing I were different than I am. As the Chinese say, 'Be careful what you wish for.'

So, Dude, I need your help:

Take care of Kitsala. I know you're not crazy about cats, but she's really a sweetheart. If you can't do it, ask Jean-Paul. Find her a good home.

Nail DeMarko and Dalton.

Help Sally. She'll be a mess. I'm her only family.

Believe in yourself. You're a kick-ass journalist.

Forgive me for not telling you and Jean-Paul what I learned in the warehouse. I couldn't take a chance you'd miss the deadline of the UNAIDS conference.

Fleck, you're the best friend anyone could have. Please tell Jean-Paul I wish I'd had more time with him. Like you, he is my brother.

Thanks, buddy.

Noah

Noah tri-folded the letter, stuffed it into the envelope, licked the flap and pressed, then scribbled *Fleck McNulty* on the front. He shoved it and the Samaritan note deep into his left jeans pocket.

The plane taxied.

Suddenly, the cabin temperature plummeted. Noah shuddered. He reached up to twist the air-conditioning vents, but they were already closed.

"On behalf of your flight crew, I'd like to welcome you on board today." A flight attendant's voice crackled through the air. "I'm Cheryl. I apologize for the heat, but the air conditioner will turn on as soon as we're airborne. Thank you for your patience, and enjoy your flight to Yompola, Russia."

Russia? His ears played a cosmic joke. He'd heard wrong.

"Chilly?" His seatmate's raspy voice, heavy with a Yiddish accent, froze his heart.

Hadassah touched Noah's hand, and he felt the burn of frostbite. He felt compelled to look at her despite his trembling.

Her eyes were deep chasms. "You owe me," she hissed.

Holy Einstein. He pulled his hand away and searched for the call button.

The engine revved. Crap.

Get away, get away from her.

The plane trembled. He jabbed the light button. No. He stabbed overhead. Any button. There, the call button. Punch, punch, punch. He unhooked his seatbelt. He stood in the aisle.

The aircraft's nose tilted upward, throwing Noah

off balance. He staggered, but leaned forward, stretching his legs to climb toward the forward cabin.

Over the drone of engines, he heard something cut through the air. A body thudded against him from behind. Arms clamped around his legs. His knees buckled. He collapsed, his face slamming into the stiff carpet and burning his cheek.

He heard a woman's high-pitched scream.

"Shit." a man shouted. "We're all going to die."

Another voice howled, "Fucking terrorist assholes."

He tried to kick free, but weight rooted him to the cabin floor.

Someone strong yanked Noah's hands behind his back and crossed them. Hot breath steamed the back of his neck. He smelled onions. He felt metal dig into his wrists. His skin pinched as handcuffs clicked shut.

He was thrust up and back onto his feet. Someone dragged him backward, past a stream of fearful faces. Accusing eyes glared. Hands covered mouths. Fingers pointed. Heads shook back and forth like lawn sprinklers. From the window seat in row twenty-three, Hadassah's eyes stabbed him with icicles, her shoulders tremoring with delight.

Noah landed in a jump seat in the plane's rear galley. A solid, stocky man in his early forties hunkered down next to him. His face glowed redder than Fleck's, and he panted. "Who are you working with?" A vein near the man's temple bulged, pulsing dark blue.

"Wha—What?" Noah stammered.

The clench-fisted predator demanded, "How many in your group? Who heads your cell?"

Fear flooded Noah, making his muscles weak. He'd

reacted instinctively when he'd jumped into the aisle to escape Hadassah and warn the pilots. He'd really fucked up. His heart galloped. "Wh—who are you?"

The man slipped his hand into his jacket, revealing a holstered gun. He took a small wallet from his inside pocket and flashed a gold badge in Noah's face. "No one you want to screw with. Federal Air Marshal Woods." Woods' eyes darted up and down the length of Noah's body. "Were you trying to get all of us killed, or just yourself?"

Noah slumped further down in his seat. "I wanted to warn the pilots."

"About what?"

"About the ghost who's highjacking us to Yompola."

Woods cocked his head. "Great. Another druggy." He patted Noah's t-shirt, even though it had no pockets. "I spotted you the moment you boarded the plane," he said. "Sweaty, wild-eyed, jerky movements...classic symptoms. What are you high on, kid?"

Noah felt the trembling of Woods' hands. It surprised him that the marshal might be scared, too.

"Carrying illegal substances?" Woods dug into Noah's pants pockets. He removed the envelope for Fleck and the Samaritan note. He searched further, groping the sides of Noah's crotch.

"Jesus. Do you have to do that?" Noah couldn't catch his breath. Sweat poured down his face.

A blond, thirty-something flight attendant sat in the jump seat opposite. A brass nametag on her blue uniform read, "Cheryl." She smiled at him. Big teeth.

Noah searched her face. Open. Kind. He pleaded with his eyes. Help me. Please.

Suddenly, Jean-Paul's blessing flooded his mind. "May the Ancestors be with you. Heed their counsel, and they will guide you." If Hadassah had found Noah, maybe Great-Grandma Sara could find him, too.

Please. I'm ready to listen. Help me.

Help with what? He didn't know what to want. He'd felt compelled to get off the plane, away from Hadassah. He needed to warn Sally. Now, he yearned for freedom. Too many ideas bombarded him at once. His brain felt like the Internet. His head throbbed.

Cheryl beamed at him. Something in her eyes seemed familiar and comforting, like chicken soup and roses. She sent a thought message that Noah received loud and clear. "You can have it all, *bubala*. You can get off the plane. You can get to Sally. You can keep your freedom. The impossible is possible, *boychick*. Relax."

Noah took a breath. Great-Grandma Sara had found him.

Cheryl leaned toward Woods. "Perhaps this is just a misunderstanding, Officer."

The marshal combed his hair with one hand. "Another nut-case. I got to get out of this job." He looked at Noah, his eyes softening for a brief flicker. "Your screws need to be torqued down tighter, huh, kid?"

Woods held Noah's written notes within reach, and Noah thought about grabbing them with his cuffed hands. Cheryl shook her head. He heard Sara's voice. "Don't."

"Can I have those back?" Noah asked. "They're private."

Woods' eyes morphed to shiny bullets. He twisted away from Noah and tore open the envelope. He read the letter, shaking his head. "Crazy bastards everywhere you go. I'll keep these as evidence." He shoved the papers into his pants pocket. "So, Noah, the plane's being highjacked to Yompola, wherever that is, and there's a corporate plot in Minneapolis. Going to create trouble there, too?"

Noah stared up at him. If he told Woods about Hadassah, Selexikote, and DeMarko and Dalton, it wouldn't make any difference. Woods wouldn't believe him. Noah retreated to the safety of silence.

He heard Great-Grandma's voice. "That's right. Don't fight. Just listen and breathe."

Noah inhaled deeply and sent a mental message to Woods. *Please, I mean no harm. Please, let me go.*

"Officer," Cheryl said. "You can see he means no harm."

Woods shrugged. "Doesn't matter. He ran the aisle during take-off. That's all the reason I need to arrest him." Woods pulled a PDA from his pocket and thumbed it. "I'll text a message to your pilot to return to St. Louis. My cover's blown. I can't risk that some other loony on board might think it'd be fun to join this party." His hands shook, and he settled the PDA in his lap. "Jesus, this fucking career is killing me."

Noah focused his thoughts like a laser beam on the air marshal. *I know you're hurting. You can talk to me. I want to help you.* He shifted toward Woods so their shoulders touched.

Woods flinched, but didn't move away. "I'm sorry. I can tell you're an okay kid. Crazy, not evil. Doesn't matter."

A red light pulsed. Cheryl picked up the intercom

and put it to her ear. "Yes, sir." Then she punched a button. "Ladies and gentleman, we're returning to the St. Louis airport. There's no reason for concern. As soon as we're on the ground, we'll update you on a new departure time. Thank you for your patience."

A groan, unintelligible words, built and rolled to the rear of the 737.

Noah felt the plane bank to the left and start its descent. He wondered what was in store for him when they landed. How long would they hold him? Hours? Days? Tomorrow was the twenty-third. How would he get to his mom in time?

Woods leaned toward Cheryl. "Remember the guy who got killed in the Miami airport a while back?" he said. "The FAMs thought he had a bomb? Turned out he was just a harmless bastard who hadn't taken his medication." Sweat soaked through Woods' shirt and dark stains spread around his collar. "I knew the FAM who took him out. He fell apart after. Started back drinking. His wife finally left him." Woods pulled at his fingers. His knuckles popped one at a time. "I hate this career. I've never helped anyone." He blew out his breath. "Cheryl, you got a scotch?"

She gave him a questioning look.

"Sorry," he said. "You're right. I'm on duty."

Noah fixed his mind on Woods. He concentrated, blocked out the rest of the world, and threw his energy.

That's right, mine Noah. Help him.

Noah radiated comforting thoughts. I'm sorry for your stress. I'm sorry for your sadness. You'll be alright. You'll find your destiny.

Suddenly, Noah felt a small shift, imperceptible at

first, then, palpable. Like a portal in the universe had cracked open. Noah could feel consciousness rise out of him, and he saw seeds of joy on Woods' face. His soul and Woods' soul crossed the door's threshold from opposite sides. Two misty shadows blended, mingling compassion and purpose.

Woods' eyes watered. He silently took a key out of his pocket, and he unlatched the cuffs on Noah's wrist. He bent his head, whispering, "Listen, kid. When we land, I'll walk you up to the front before anyone deplanes. When they open the gangway, we'll walk out. Then you run. You run faster than you've ever run before."

Woods laughed, and it shook his whole body. He slapped Noah on the back. "Hell, I've wanted to quit this fucking job, anyway. We'll run for our lives, kid. We'll both run."

Noah looked over his shoulder. Woods waved and turned in the opposite direction. Noah shot him a thank-you jolt of energy for good luck as the air marshal disappeared into the throngs of people in the airport. Then, Noah sprinted. Past crowded gates, past the smell of hot dogs and pizza, past the chaos of passengers queuing up and chatting on cell phones, past threads of conversation and travelers wandering aimlessly. He was surprised his body still manufactured enough adrenaline to run, but it did despite his energy transfers and the draining fear of the plane ordeal he'd endured.

He darted and weaved, escaping the terminal. Emerging outside into the bright sunlight, he inhaled the familiar, muggy air of St. Louis.

What a relief to be free. What a feeling of renewed zing.

He slipped into the line to grab a taxi and thought through his next steps. He didn't dare take another plane (a laugh-out-loud ridiculous thought). Instead, he would drive to Minneapolis. Only, it'd been three years since he'd last been behind the wheel. Since his last manic episode when he'd been slapped with a D.U.I. Since then he'd vowed never to put himself or anyone else at risk again. Three years since he'd given up owning a car. Since he'd decided not to pollute the planet with his own fuel consumption. Two years since he'd allowed his driver's license to expire.

What choice did he have? This was an emergency. He'd forgive himself this one infraction.

He had to admit, the idea of driving appealed to him. His internal motor commanded him to move and to keep moving. Maybe it was that last squirt of adrenaline, or maybe his chemistry was a little off. So what? The buzz felt great, and his thinking clear.

His plan crystallized.

Fleck had given Noah spare car keys, in case Fleck ever lost the original set. A stroke of McNulty brilliance, since Fleck had trouble tracking his wallet, his credit cards and everything else that wasn't attached by Velcro. Noah had bailed him out at least three times that he could remember.

With Jean-Paul and Fleck at the UNAIDs conference, Noah doubted his friend would mind if he borrowed his wheels for his impromptu trip.

Noah would cab it to his apartment to snatch the keys, and take the cab over to Fleck's to pick up the car. Then he'd drive the car back over to his place and load up.

There was one minor flaw in this paragon of plans. A small nit. Fleck's car was a piece of crap. A real hooptie.

Now, Noah wished he'd supported Fleck's desire to buy or lease a new one, despite his total lack of funds. He knew he couldn't rent a ride without a driver's license, so he'd pray for the best. May the Ancestors be with him. It'd be good if they knew a thing or two about auto mechanics.

His cell phone blinked 10:07 a.m. Enough time to retrieve Fleck's car, get to his apartment, pack up, plan his route, snag cash, buy snacks, and be on his way. Noon at the latest. Minneapolis must be an eleven-hour trip, give or take, and he'd arrive around midnight.

Noah would see Sally first thing tomorrow morning before she went into the nine o'clock board meeting. Close, but enough time. He'd make this work. He would.

A Yellow Cab rolled up to the curb, and he hopped in. "Hanley and Clayton," he said to the back of the driver's head. "I'll guide you from there."

"You got it, boss." His jet-black hair glowed shiny like a bowling ball, and his accent indicated Indian, Pakistani, or Pashtun. A clear vision of the cabbie's childhood home in the patchy hills of Afghanistan sprang out of Noah's neocortex, and he smelled lamb cooking over an open flame.

His hand stroked the taxi's scratched leather back seat, and he saw a black and white cow grazing in a

Chinese pasture, chewing its cud. He heard the bleat of a newborn calf. The seat beneath him pulsed, animate with a bovine beat.

Information bombarded Noah's senses. He felt like a machine on overdrive. It was as if his brain was a computer that normally processed five gigabytes a second, and now, it amped up to process fifty. Hell, maybe more.

He'd never reach overload. Bring it on.

He felt euphoric, like he'd touched the face of God, like he accessed the whole universe. Einstein must have felt like this when he channeled inklings of his relativity theory.

Noah felt a compelling urge to jump where time slowed down, and where he could float in an elongated present moment. Vibrant and alive. Intoxicating and dangerous. Nonetheless, he willed himself to focus on the task at hand.

He keyed in Sally's number. One ring, and he heard her recorded voice. "Hey, Mom. Call—" Crap. He forgot he shouldn't leave a message.

He'd resisted her hovering over him, and he'd fought hard to win his independence. Ironic. Now, he chased her.

Where the hell was she?

Sally lay atop a massage table, eyes closed and under a warmed sheet in her suite at the Ritz Carlton, Minneapolis. Paid for courtesy of Duschene International.

Don't get mad, get even, had always been her motto.

She intended to get extremely even. Oh, yes, she would.

"Put it on my tab," she'd said when she'd arranged for the massage. "Two hours. Female." Now the woman's healing hands helped to ease her bruised body.

"My God, honey, what happened to you?" Erica, the masseuse, asked.

Sally welcomed the chance to tell her story. Rumor struck her as far more effective than filing a police report. If she filed a report, who would believe her? Even with DNA evidence, of which there was plenty. "Consensual," he'd claim. He'd dredge up all kinds of witnesses to their earlier tryst.

Her face burned with shame. God knew her reputation. Duschene had legions of lawyers. They'd never settle. She couldn't bear the thought of exposing herself in court and enduring that public spectacle.

Money proved the sweetest revenge. Her share of twenty million dollars remained the clearest path forward.

She embraced an opportunity to spread the truth about Dalton. Who knew where a rumor might creep around, settle in, and bite him on his over-sexed *shmuck*? "I was raped by Charles Dalton, III, C.E.O of Duschene International," she told Erica. "Do you know him?"

Erica gasped. "Honey, you all right?"

"I intend to be." That was the truth. Sally's truth.

Earlier, she'd taken the proverbial rape shower. She'd crumpled to the bottom of the glass enclosure and wept, then scrubbed herself raw, thus doing all of the cliché'd crap she'd seen portrayed in film. For an hour, she'd allowed herself to grieve. But being a victim wasn't her style. Spending Dalton's money suited her best.

"By the way," Sally added. "He has a tiny penis."

Sally signed Erica's ticket, adding a two-hundred-dollar tip.

The suite phone rang and rang. "Do you want me to get it, honey?"

"No. Take it off the hook."

After Erica's departure, Sally ordered room service. Although not that hungry, she needed to fill the hole gouged out of her soul. She ordered both sides of the menu. Steak with béarnaise sauce, Duck a l'orange, Caesar salad, leg of lamb, cheeseburger, onion soup, shrimp scampi, vegetable panini.

"Ms. Friedman, how many people will be dining?"

"Just me. I'm a little hungry. I was raped and beaten by Charles Dalton III, C.E.O. of Duschene International. Do you know him?"

Silence. Then, "We'll bring this right away, Madam."

Erica had told Sally of a great shop in the hotel arcade. Sally called and learned they'd just received two Escada suits, size two. She ordered both, charging them to her suite. The saleswoman suggested a pair of Jimmy Choo's. She ordered them in every available color. Why not?

"I need a scarf," Sally said, gently fingering her bruised neck. "Do you carry Hermès?" So, she added several, one thousand dollars each, to the bill.

Ten dozen roses— *One for every million*, said the note—had arrived during her massage. *Sorry I didn't get to buy you dinner. Looking forward to your pres-*

entation at the board meeting. Trip.

Sally deserved ten million dollars. (She'd earned it the old-fashioned way, ha.) Wasn't life perfect? She'd still retain her ownership of Friedman Pharmaceutical. The widespread distribution of Selexikote would help millions of children, and after the deal closed, she'd stay the hell away from that schizoid-sociopath, Dalton. No reason to ever see him again. As well as De-Marko, that crazy bastard. He still had her cell.

She dialed the front desk. "Any messages for Sally Friedman?"

"No, Ms. Friedman."

She sighed and tried Noah's number. No answer. Again. "Where are you? I can't answer the room phone, so leave a message at the front desk. I'll check with them periodically and call you back. Are you out of juice?" On the second or third try she'd left Noah the hotel's main number, as she couldn't bear the thought of picking up the room extension only to discover Dalton or DeMarko on the line. Or Bernard.

She wouldn't talk to or see him, either. Dalton had probably lied about Bernard, but too much of the story rang true. She no longer trusted her judgment in men. Too many times she'd been wrong. Enough.

The doorbell rang. Perhaps room service had forgotten the truffle honey? Her aching muscles protested as she stood. Underneath the fluffy hotel bathrobe, her naked thighs rubbed together in the worst places. That sorry son of a bitch. Perhaps she'd call the shop again and order a few Hermès handbags.

She kept the chain on the door, opening it enough to peek out.

The concierge stood in the hall, a sheepish look on his face. "Ms. Friedman, I have a note for you."

"Oh, finally," she said, relieved that Noah had called after all.

She accepted the card and read it. *Sally, I'm worried about you. You didn't show up for dinner. You're not answering the phone. Please let me know you're okay. I'm in the lobby. Bernard.*

Sally blew out her breath. "Would you wait a moment, please?" She hobbled to the bed. Christ, she hurt. Opening her handbag, she reached inside and found what she was looking for. She fished out a large bill from her wallet and labored back across the suite to the door. "Would you take this to the gentleman who gave you the note?"

She passed him the bill and dropped the gold watch into the concierge's open hand.

"Is there a message?" he asked.

She'd had it with all men, including Bernard. He'd only disappoint. "No. No message."

She closed the door.

She'd spend the rest of the evening working on her Selexikote presentation. She'd be flawless, the queen of compartmentalization. The board would weep, champion the drug, and bless the day they'd heard of this chance to help humanity. She'd stand pristine and strong before them, making it clear to Dalton that he hadn't won, would never win. She would reclaim the piece of herself she'd lost in his office. She'd leave no lingering ghost, no totem he might treasure.

The doorbell rang again. Thank God, she already stood close by. She opened it.

"Sorry for the delay, Madam. It took a bit to find thirty bottles of Cristal. Where would you like me to set up the cart?"

"In the bathroom."

"The bathroom?" The server looked astounded, shrugged, and rolled the cart across the thick wool carpet to the marbled bath.

"Would you open them, please?"

"All of them?"

"Please."

She rested on the bed and listened to the release of corks, the gush of air, waiting until she counted thirty pops. She signed the ticket. Another huge tip.

She ushered him out the door, closed it, threw the deadbolt, and slid the chain into place. Then, carefully, oh so carefully, she walked bowlegged into the bathroom and plugged the tub. She emptied the champagne one bottle at a time.

She had to be sharp in the morning. She couldn't afford to screw up the performance of her life. She filled one glass—that's all she'd have—and she raised it in front of her.

Facing the full-length mirror, she eyed her reflection. A strong woman, bruised, but full of resolve stared back at her. "A toast to Charles Dalton III. Fuck you."

She took a sip, swished it in her mouth, and then swallowed. "Ah, Cristal, two-thousand-two. The best."

She dipped her toe into the effervescence.

"You can find me in the club,
Bottle full of bub.
Look mami I got the X
If you into taking drugs..."

Noah sang along at the top of his lungs, blasting Fifty Cent from Fleck's Toyota Corolla's rigged-out speakers. He'd rolled down the windows, and the wind gusted against his face.

He'd forgotten how bitchin' it felt to be out on the road. He sped past open fields. Corn, corn and more corn. He played "I spy." I spy a farmer on a combine. His eyes picked up the checkered red and yellow pattern of the farmer's shirt. It matched the color of a cardinal flying low overhead—all red with a yellow beak. Synchronous. A sign he headed the right way. He smelled silos of grain, and someone frying chicken in a nearby farmhouse. Jesus, he was hungry.

He'd already eaten through his snacks, a sixty-four-ounce blue slushy, and a bag of M & M's. His stomach still screamed at him, "Hey, asshole. Feed me."

"Okay, okay, shut your yap."

He heard people in passing cars and saw their lips move.

"I'll stay at your mother's for one day. No more."

"You never tell me you love me."

"Billy, will you shut the fuck up for one minute?"

Why can't the world get along? Noah wondered. He drove north for what felt like hours. An eleven-hour trip, a straight shot up the Avenue of the Saints, and he thought he'd been on the road for half of it by now.

The sun held its position high at two o'clock. How could that be? He'd left his apartment at noon.

At the next highway sign offering *Food, Rest-stop, Shopping,* he'd stop and refuel himself and the car.

Overhead, a flock of mallard ducks flew in a V formation, guiding him onward. The V turned and pointed to the right. When Noah spotted the next exit in that direction, he pulled off the highway. Bingo, he hit the jackpot. A Barnes and Noble and an all-you-can-eat chicken place. He'd give them a run for their money. Maybe they had buttermilk biscuits.

Man, a cold beer would go great.

"You want a topper before we close?"

Noah felt disoriented. He'd been lost in the flow, his head bent over his research. He looked up and saw Crystal holding a coffee pot, poised to pour.

"Is it time to close already?" he said.

In a natural way, void of make-up, Crystal was a babe. Even in that goofy, pink uniform with her name embroidered on the left breast pocket above a bizarre logo—a chicken with a spiky halo over its head. *Avenue of the Saints Martyred Chicken Restaurant* suffered a twisted sense of marketing.

Her aqua eyes crinkled to slits. "You've been here like forever." She giggled.

"Really?" He grabbed his phone off the speckled Formica table and saw his confused reflection in the cell's blank screen. He'd thought about buying a dual jack to juice his mobile in Fleck's car before he'd hit the road. In his hurry to tool on up the highway, he'd forgotten. The cell lay dead and useless in his palm.

No way to know the time, or call Sally, or reach out to anyone else if he needed help. He'd been careless and stupid. Now, he was behind schedule. A surge of heat burned his cheeks. "What time is it?"

"Quittin' time." With her free hand, she swept flaxen strands from her eyes. "Nine o'clock."

Crap. He rested his head in his hands and tried to piece together how he'd lost seven hours.

This was the second time he'd been in the restaurant today. Earlier, he'd consumed a mass of sacrificed chicken and a few beers. He would've had a fourth or fifth bottle, but Crystal had suggested he might want to slow it down if he had a long drive ahead of him. He liked her, so he'd listened.

He'd drunk enough just to take the edge off, and he'd felt relaxed and in control, as though he could speed up and slow down time at his whim. Fresh concepts and images had zipped all around him, and all he'd needed to do was pluck them from the air. He'd flowed with the cosmos.

He'd paid his bill and marched into the Barnes and Noble across the road. They stocked the coolest physics section with all his favorites. What synchronicity. He replaced his copy of <u>The Elegant Universe</u> by Brian Greene, the tome lost when he'd abandoned his backpack in row twenty-three on the plane.

The math section sported a hot-off-the-presses book on fractals. He'd also bought a new journal—Synchronicities II had been jettisoned on the flight—before returning to the restaurant to start filling it in.

Crystal had taken her dinner break. After she'd poured him a coffee, she sat down and listened while he'd lectured on the peak oil crisis, the world's disappearing resources, the collapse of the economy, the extinction of species, and the dissolution of society. She hadn't laughed. She'd gotten it.

When she went back to work, he'd felt bombarded with research ideas. Fragments of thoughts and coincidences had streamed from his head, through his veins, and onto paper.

Now, he thumbed through his Synchronicities III notebook and read the pages dense with ink.

It was a coincidence that he was traveling up the Avenue of the Saints, guided by the Ancestors—two groups of dead people.

It was a coincidence that his bill totaled twenty-three dollars exactly, and tomorrow was the twenty-third. It was a coincidence that he'd motored exactly two hundred thirty miles so far. It was a coincidence that twenty-three birds—he'd counted—had steered him to Crystal, who'd kept him on point. Her birthday was the same day as his, October twenty-third, and they liked the same politics. Remarkable.

He didn't judge himself to be a twenty-three obsessor, but wasn't it curious that this lowest of the consecutively digited prime numbers, the atoms of mathematics, kept popping up?

It was more than serendipity that every parent contributed twenty-three chromosomes to the start of human life, and that the average physical biorhythm cycled in twenty-three days.

He craved to chronicle more of these connections, computing and contemplating while his brain was crystal clear. Hah. Crystal. Another coincidence.

Time slipped silently away from him. A seven-hour drive from the restaurant to Minneapolis loomed ahead. Still workable if nothing unforeseen showed up. He'd arrive at four in the morning and find his mom in time.

While he puzzled over his predicament, he'd failed to notice that Crystal still stood by his booth, tossing her corn silk hair. Was she flirting?

He wanted to reciprocate, but lacked the courage. Anyway, minutes marched forward. "What do I owe you for coffee?"

"It's on me." Her gaze spoke volumes. Warm, inviting volumes.

The ventral tegmental area of Noah's brain lit up, and his body flooded with dopamine. He'd forgotten that warm rush of arousal that now coursed through him. It had been forever since a babe had noticed him. He wanted to thank her for it. Instead, he pulled out a twenty and three singles, slipped them under his coffee cup, and slid out of the booth. "Nice meeting you."

Her brightness dimmed. "If you pass through here again, come see me. Okay?"

Could he chance it on the return trip? After his mission went well? "You never know," he said. "The universe is filled with coincidence."

"Huh?" She gave him a funny look.

The tingling feeling dissipated. He hurried out into the warm, cloudless night. The brilliant stars illuminated the lonely silhouette of Fleck's car. It was a perfect night for spirits to be out and about.

Suddenly, a chill went through him. He quickened his pace across the deserted lot. Gravel crunched under his shoes, and he kicked up clouds of dust. He bolted toward his destiny. Away from thoughts of Crystal.

He rushed to unlock the car door, jerked it open, and slid onto the ripped seat of Fleck's dingy, road-worn Toyota. The car chugged to life when he turned the ignition. He lowered the windows, threw the gear into drive, and the car lurched forward a few feet before it sputtered and died.

Crap. He turned the key, and he heard a cranking noise. He tried again. Same sound. And again, but no dice.

What should he do? He knew nothing about cars, didn't own a AAA card, didn't possess a working cell, and was floundering in the middle of nowhere.

Across the lot, the restaurant had faded into the black backdrop. Only a neon, haloed chicken blinked and crackled in the dark.

Someone tapped the car hood. Noah's heart skipped a beat. He looked up to see Crystal, and he filled with relief and something more.

"You need a jump?" She pranced to his side of the car.

"I don't know."

She laughed and shook her amber waves of grain. "Yeah, you need one. You're smart, but you don't know cars, do you?"

He smiled up at her and shrugged.

"My brother's an auto mechanic."

"See. What are the chances of that? The universe is filled with coincidence. Like I said."

She examined him for a minute. The moon illuminated her wrinkled brow and slight frown. "You're different."

Suddenly, he regretted seeing her again. It was a better memory to have escaped thinking she'd liked him. Noah sighed. "Most people think I'm weird. It's okay."

She beamed at him, leaning in through the window. "I like different."

The car bumped along the winding country road. Even with the brights on, it was hard to see the twists and turns in the dark. Noah gripped the wheel tight with both hands in an attempt to steady Fleck's old tin can, precariously balanced on bald tires.

Funny, he should have felt anxious to get back on the Avenue of the Saints and onward to Minneapolis. But he liked having Crystal in the car. It felt like a date, like he'd known her a long time, and suddenly, it didn't seem to matter if he delayed the journey. Just for a little while.

Crystal chewed on her index finger. Moonlight flooded through the windshield, and Noah saw she'd bitten her nail down to the quick. "Thanks for saving my brother a trip," she said. "He hates when my ride home has the night off."

"Are you kidding? He fixed my car."

"No big deal. Just a jump." She pointed over the

dashboard. "Keep right at the fork. We're almost there."

Noah turned the wheel, and the road narrowed to a lane canopied thick with trees. Through breaks in the overhead branches, the constellations glowed bright in the pitch-black sky. Out here in the middle of nowhere, he could even see the faint glimmer of the Milky Way. Crickets played frenzied love songs, and fireflies flashed bioluminescent mating dances in the warm summer night.

She gestured to a house on the right. "We're here."

Noah eased the car onto a gravel crescent drive.

"Don't kill the motor," she said. "You'd better not turn off the ignition 'til you get all the way to where you're going."

"Good call." He threw the car into park and let the engine idle. He couldn't make out her parents' two-story in the dark, but the lawn looked clipped and the hedges shaped.

"Well..." she said, then hesitated. "I guess this is goodbye." She smiled at him, and her lower lip trembled. She looked like she wanted to say something. Or maybe she wanted something from him.

"What is it?" he asked finally.

"I can tell you're going to be somebody."

Noah just looked at her and shrugged. Her face, a natural wonder, mirrored the beautiful curves of the countryside. He wanted to touch her cheek.

"My friends and I are so lost." Her eyes misted. "None of us do anything. None of us make a difference." She clenched her fists. "Life can't be just slinging chicken. It's so pointless."

He wished he could help her, but he didn't know how. If he could take away her hurt, he would. He placed his hand on hers, the one with the chewed fingernail. "What do you want, Crystal?"

Silent tears fell down her face. "I like little kids. I want to teach. I'm saving up, but there's no money to finish school. It's not happening."

Her tears fell freely now, and her body shook with sobs. Noah wanted to hold her, but he didn't have the right. He just kept his hand on hers, and tried to focus his energy, like he'd done before with Woods.

"God, this is embarrassing." She twisted away from him.

"Do you ever watch hummingbirds?" he asked.

She dug a Kleenex from her purse and dabbed her nose. "What?"

"Hummingbirds are like miniature machines that instantaneously convert energy from sucrose to wing power. I love to watch them fight over a sugar-water feeder outside my kitchen window. They battle with each other like every drop is their last meal. When the feeder runs out, I refill it with bird brew, and replace it."

Crystal gazed at him, perplexed, her head tilted toward him.

"Sometimes, if a hummingbird buzzes over to eat while the feeder is missing, the bird will hang suspended in air, trying to figure out what happened. It seems dumbfounded, as though its world has irreparably changed. It's only for a minute or two that the feeder is missing, but to them, it must seem like days, or weeks, or maybe, forever."

Crystal's eyebrows furrowed. No longer crying, she

squeezed Noah's hand.

"Maybe your sugar feeder has temporarily disappeared. One day, all of a sudden, out of the clear blue sky, it will materialize within reach. Replenished with endless resources. You just have to wait and you'll have everything you need. It may seem like forever. It's not."

Her eyes brightened, and her mouth curled up slightly. "You really think so?"

He nodded. "I do."

She sat up straighter, gripping his hand. "Can I come with you?"

"What?"

"I've got an aunt who lives in Saint Paul. I can stay with her and go back to school. Give me a ride? You shouldn't turn off the ignition anyway, you know, or you might not be able to start it again. I could stay in the car for bathroom and coffee breaks, okay? We can take turns driving." Her words burbled out in one long stream.

Noah laughed. What a wonderful synchronicity. She wanted to go where he was headed. He didn't want to leave her. "Okay."

She put her hand on his knee. "I trust you," she said. "I meet lots of people who come through town. Most of them are full of shit. They make promises and disappear. You're different. You're the kind of person who does what he says he'll do." She leaned over and kissed him. Her lips felt soft and fluttery, as sweet as an answered prayer.

She pulled away, yanking on the door handle. "I'll pack my bag. Won't take me five minutes." She threw open the door and ran up the walk to her parents' home.

Noah watched her disappear into the house. He felt something he hadn't remembered. It made him smile. Maybe it was normalcy. Maybe it was hope. Or it just might be happiness.

The wind picked up and whistled through the trees. A weeping willow swayed in the breeze, its drying leaves swirling through the starred sky.

The passenger door slammed shut. Suddenly, the car's air conditioner kicked on. He'd thought it was broken. The inside temperature of the car chilled. Noah reached to switch the control, but it was already in the off position. Cinnamon scented air blew through the jets.

Not Hadassah. No. Please. Not now.

He heard the snap of locks. He pushed down on the door handle, but it jammed. A motor whirred and the car windows raised shut.

Pellets of hail, bullet sized shards of ice, ricocheted from all angles, bouncing around the car interior like neurons in an atom mixer. Sideways. From the ceiling. Off the floorboards. Noah shielded his face from the sharp, hard BBs. He shivered with fear.

A frozen hand touched his shoulder. He yelped. Hadassah pinned him with her awful eyes. He sat paralyzed behind the wheel.

"Kumen," said the ghost. Come.

The hail stopped. The Toyota's gear shifted by itself into drive, and the car lurched forward on the half-circle driveway.

"Noah, wait." Crystal's scream pierced the car windows.

In the rear-view mirror, he saw her run toward the

car with her suitcase, one arm flailing in an attempt to flag him down.

The car screeched on the gravel and sped faster. His body jerked forward.

"Noah, Why? Why?" Crystal's wails reverberated in his ears.

Noah pressed his face and hands to the driver's side window. He mouthed, "I'll be back."

The car, driven by some phantom being, hurtled away from Crystal's house. Through the rear-view mirror, Noah watched Crystal's futile efforts to halt the car. He felt powerless to stop his abduction by Hadassah. Crystal's image shrank from sight.

Hadassah sat on the passenger side of the car and fixed one black hole of an eye on him. The other dark void stared straight ahead. Her fury was contagious, and Noah caught her anger.

A cavalcade of emotions churned in him. Fear of what Hadassah had in store for him. Fear that he would fail to complete his journey, warn his mother, and stop the sale of Selexikote. Fear for millions of susceptible people, who would take the purported miracle drug and slide into a state of oblivion. All because of Noah's complete and utter incompetence to stop it.

Although it should seem like his least important concern, he felt acute hurt from this missed opportunity with Crystal. He'd never be able to explain his abandonment of her in a way that made logical sense.

Suddenly, snow flurries cascaded from a clear, star-lit August sky. Thick blankets of clouds amassed and cloaked the moon and the stars. The flurries plumped to mature flakes.

In a matter of seconds, a full-blown blizzard raged outside the car. The once gentle canopied country lane transformed into a death trap. Thick icicles hung from the branches like Cossack broadswords, threatening to detach and slice through the roof of the car.

Bald tires provided poor traction. Noah gripped the sides of his seat in anticipation of an inevitable hydroplane and crash into a tree.

Some invisible entity maneuvered the steering wheel, corrected slides, and turned again. Hadassah proved a damn good driver. One bony finger pointed over the hood of the car to command it forward.

The trees thinned, receding from view as the vehicle glided over the increasingly deeper snow like a horse-drawn troika. They passed a sign that read, *Yompola*. Beyond the sign, as far as the eye could see, emerged desolate Russian nothingness. A few decayed remnants of once ramshackle huts that looked like tombstones and crosses stuck haphazardly in deep powder.

The car slid to a dead stop against a snow bank.

Hadassah stood before a hovel, raised her arms and the doors opened. "Kumen," she rasped.

Noah's first instinct was to bolt, but his past attempts to flee had proven pointless. She would find him. Whether it was day or night. Whether he journeyed by plane, train, or automobile. Whether the Ancestors protected him or not.

He closed his eyes and tried to calm himself. Maybe Hadassah wasn't real. Maybe she was merely an entropic thought. He sucked in a deep breath to clear his brain. Through the muddle in his head he heard a voice. At first, he thought it was Great-Grandma Sara, but the husky, German accent sounded masculine.

Holy Einstein, it was the man himself. "True religion is to know that what is impenetrable to us really exists, manifesting itself as the highest wisdom and the most radiant beauty."

"She's real?" Noah asked.

"How should I know? I haven't seen her. You must decide what's real," Einstein said. "Use Physics. Copenhagen Interpretation. Schrodinger's equations. Stop avoiding your destiny and *tink*."

Good advice. What did it mean? He took another deep breath and thoughts coalesced in his head.

The Copenhagen Interpretation stated nothing is real until you look at it. Noah examined Hadassah, who was all too real. According to Schrodinger, for every present moment we experience, a positive wave flows into the future and a negative wave flows into the past, like ripples on a pond. Noah's energy flowed to Hadassah, and her energy flowed to him. She manifested spirit like Woods, or Crystal, or anyone else. All of them connected to the same source.

Perhaps Noah could help Hadassah, too.

That's right, boychik. Help her, Great-Grandma Sara cooed in his ear.

He took one more cleansing breath, stepped out of the car, and approached the ghost.

She raised her vapor-like arm, pointing at him as she bellowed in rage. "If you don't make things right with me, four losses you will suffer."

She spewed the hex she'd imposed on him before. This time, Noah felt no fear.

"First, loss of freedom," she hissed. "Second, loss of

memory. Third, loss of family. Last of all, loss of life. *A broch tsu dayn lebn.*"

Visions of Hadassah streamed into Noah's consciousness. He saw her as she had been in life. Alone in her house, locked away in a self-imposed prison. She'd prayed to God for help, but none had come. Her memory had faded from stress, age, and longing. She'd lost her husband. At last, she'd died alone, unloved and isolated from the rest of the world.

The curse she'd prescribed for Noah matched the fate Hadassah had suffered herself. This was all she knew.

Noah beamed his energy to her. "Tell me how to help."

Hadassah's form spun like a tornado, kicking up a serpentine swath of snow. "Oooooooooh," she moaned.

In her wail, Noah heard the despair of a tortured animal, the weight of the shadowed soul, and the last gasp of the dying sun. He heard the sound of hunger, felt the suffering of the outcast. The collective grief pushed him to his knees. He felt pulled into her wake of misery. She hurt, and he hurt.

He yearned to comfort Hadassah. Her anger would never dissipate until someone rescued her. His Ancestors, the generations before him, had added to her pain. Now, it was Noah's responsibility to correct the past. Weren't we all responsible for one another, flesh or spirit?

Hadassah's shape stood before him once more. A gush of frozen icicles broke from her hollow eyes and shattered to the ground. "Bring Chaim back to me," she groaned.

Noah had no idea how, but knew he must find Chaim. If not Noah, then who? Jean-Paul seemed expert in the matters of dead people. Perhaps he'd have the answers as to how to perform this quest. "I'll bring Chaim back, but I need to fix something else first. Please. Help me."

Hadassah's gaping mouth curved into a moon shaped crescent. Her bony finger touched his forehead, only this time, her touch felt warm.

Fleck's Toyota idled on the shoulder of the highway. Fading stars dotted the dawning sky, and a robin chirped its morning chorus. A marker sign read "Avenue of the Saints. Minneapolis, Three Hundred Miles."

"Good morning, Minneapolis and Saint Paul," a female disc jockey's voice blared from the car radio. "It's five a.m. on August twenty-third. This is KDWB in the Twin Cities, bringing you commercial-free hits for the next twenty-three minutes."

Noah felt exhausted and wired. Four and a half hours of driving to go. No matter how hard he pushed through the rest of the drive, he'd reach his mom after the start of the nine o'clock meeting. Provided he didn't encounter another debacle. Crap. What else could possibly go wrong?

He'd have to pull some stunt to get Sally's attention. He'd have to break into the boardroom. He'd have to do something outrageous to halt the meeting. What?

He didn't have anything with him but the clothes on his back.

Then, the idea found him. Simple. Crazy. But it would work. Did he have the nerve?

As he'd heard them say in the Twin Cities, "You betcha."

Chapter Ten

"It's twenty minutes after nine on this beautiful morning of August twenty-third. This is KUSD in the Twin Cities, and that was 'What Hurts the Most' by Rascal Flatts."

Since inadvertently abandoning Crystal, Noah had developed a strange affection for sappy country music. But he forced himself to push dreams of her to the back of his head. This was no time for self-indulgence. Later, maybe. Not now.

He kept the car glued to the Avenue of the Saints. The same highway meandered all the way from St. Louis to Saint Paul, and now the landscape of corn-fields, pastures, and lakes had been replaced by asphalt, concrete, and brick. He'd arrived in Minneapolis.

A few more miles, and he'd reach his goal, Duschene International Headquarters. The board meeting would've started, but surely no transaction could have gone down since nine o'clock. Adrenaline coursed through his body—well, technically, eighty percent adrenaline and twenty percent norepinephrine. Or was it the other way around? Twenty percent adrenaline... crap. Another lost brain cell.

Details continued to evade him. Facts, dates, formulas that had been poised on the tip of his tongue yesterday, all had vanished, as though hard files had been deleted from his hippocampus. This scared him shitless.

Focus. Pull it together, he chanted to himself. He braced for the task ahead, rehearsing his plan. He'd barge into the boardroom, disrupt the meeting, and explain DeMarko and Dalton's scheme to his mother. Not only would he convince Sally to stop the sale of Selexikote to Duschene, he'd gain her support to end the manufacture of this hellish drug. Forever.

She'd help him. Together, they'd save the world. They could do this. Only Noah couldn't remember why this would save the world. His brain moved through viscous liquid, like molasses or tar. The resistance measured 6.56×10^{23} centipoise. Was that right? Oh, crap. He no longer knew.

Thank God, he received help from the Ancestors. They escorted him, providing a comforting entourage.

Birds flew in front and alongside the Toyota. Dozens of robins clung to the car hood. A flock of pearl-gray doves hung on the ledge of the open car windows. A red-tailed hawk sailed ahead to scout the route, periodically flying back to land on the roof and peck out navigational instructions. Noah had deciphered that one tap of the beak meant turn right, and two taps meant turn left.

Passing motorists stared in surprise and pointed. In the next lane, a guy almost rear-ended the car in front of him. A rainbow cloud of plumes danced in the car's wake.

Noah wondered if anyone could see his backseat passengers.

In the rear-view mirror, he caught a glimpse of Hadassah and Great-Grandma Sara seated together. Sara leaned forward and thumped his shoulder. "*Boychik*, slow down. You'll attract attention. Drive slow and make an old woman happy."

"Grandma, you're not old. You're dead."

She slapped the back of his head.

"Ouch."

"Another *zetz* you'll get if you're not respectful."

"Don't listen to her, you *schmendrik*." Hadassah hissed. "The sooner you finish this *facocta* errand, you can find Chaim,"

"*Facocta* means shitty," Grandma said.

"I know, Grandma."

A car changed lanes, swerved in front of the Toyota, and slowed to a crawl. Noah slammed on the brake to hold his distance.

Hadassah stuck her vapor-like torso out the window, upended a few doves, and shook a fist at the motorist in front of them. "*A broch tsu dayn lebn*," she screamed.

"That means, 'May your life be worthless,'" Grandma said.

"Thanks. I've heard it before."

A tap on the car roof caught Noah's attention. Then he saw the upside-down head of the hawk bob in front of his windshield. "Thanks, buddy. Got it."

The hawk nodded and flew off.

Noah jerked the wheel to the right. There it was, a block ahead. In front of a sprawling office campus, a monument sign read, "Duschene International Head-quarters."

A gleaming steel and glass, sixteen-story structure soared over five or six lower-slung properties that bordered it. The sprawling tower reminded Noah of a clipped, precise voice he'd heard along with De-Marko's that morning in the warehouse. An appropriate headquarters for the likes of...what was his name? Oh, yeah. Charles Dalton, III.

Noah veered into the parking lot in front of the building and found a spot marked for visitors. He threw the car into park and for the first time in twelve hours turned off the engine. The car chugged, shuddered, and died.

"Hurry up, you *meshuganeh*," Hadassah howled. "Find mine Chaim. Or...*a choleryeh ahf dir*."

"That means, 'a plague on you,'" Sara said helpfully.

Noah sighed. Great, just great. He opened the car door and jumped out, stubbing his left toe on the concrete walk. Ouch. Crap. It started to bleed. He should've kept shoes on.

Hell, naked was naked, regardless of whether or not he wore shoes. Too late to think of that now. What a genius.

Earlier, he'd pulled off on the shoulder of a desolate section of Interstate Thirty-Five to strip off his t-shirt, jeans, briefs, shoes and socks. He figured streaking ought to break up the board meeting. Just to make sure he'd follow through with this scheme, he'd left his clothes in a heap somewhere on the side of the Avenue of the Saints.

So far, no one had seemed to notice. He'd stopped

for birdseed soon after, forgetting he was naked. Another one of those details eluding him. The birds had chirped, and pecked and he'd felt guilty for not feeding them. After all, they were doing their part. He needed to do his.

Fortunately, no one had been shopping at the small grocery at seven a.m. Noah had tossed three bags of seed and his credit card on the counter. The pimply-faced clerk had searched him with vacant eyes and said, "Paper or plastic?"

"Uh, paper, I guess."

Now, on the snaking landscaped walk, Noah picked up his feet, quickening his pace. At last, he arrived at the glass entry of Douchebag International Headquarters. A whir of motors and the doors slithered open on invisible tracks. He stepped over the threshold, a marathoner crossing the finish line, and felt cool marble beneath his feet.

"What the fuck?" a muffled voice volleyed.

Noah looked across the lobby and saw a security guard wedged behind the front desk. He held a doughnut mid-bite, apparently unable to decide if he should put it down or shove it in. He struggled to stand.

Noah ran toward the elevators on the opposite side of the lobby.

"Hey, you. Stop."

He reached the elevator bank and scanned the directory posted on the center of the granite wall. "Executive Board Room, sixteen hundred." He jabbed the UP button.

Come on, hurry, hurry. He glanced behind him, noting the chubby guard wobbling forward on stubby legs but gaining ground. Dark stains spread under the arms of his blue uniform shirt.

Ding. The doors whooshed open. Noah jumped into the cab and punched sixteen.

The guard neared the opening. Noah scooted against the back panel of the elevator cab. Close, damn you, close.

The watchman reached out and his fingers scratched, but he failed to block the door from closing. Their eyes locked, and in the guard's wide glare, Noah saw fear.

"Sorry, man," he said. "I have no choice."

The bronzed doors eclipsed the guard from view. Noah felt a surge of relief as the elevator rose. An orchestral version of John Lennon's "Imagine" floated in through hidden speakers.

The polished metal reflected Noah's starkness, though he imagined himself wearing bronze-plated armor. He felt prepared for battle. He invoked David. He embodied Odysseus the Cunning. He, Noah Friedman the Extraordinary, would ensure that he protected the world from....oh, crap. Why was he here? Think, think. Selexikote. Stop the sale of Selexikote. Go to the boardroom. Find Mom.

When Sally witnessed his willingness to sacrifice himself for the world's sake, she'd stop dead in her tracks and leave with him. This would work.

Ding. The elevator emptied him out on the sixteenth floor. Thick cream carpet. Granite walls. A glass receptionist banquet.

"Can I help...Oh. My. God."

A feminine squeak skipped through the air. Noah saw a blond head float above the raised-glass countertop. Designer-cut hair framed a bright pink face of a woman about his age.

He used his hands like fig leaves. "Sorry. Not my fault. Which way to the board room?"

She ducked behind the counter. Noah heard the digital singsong of punched phone keys. "A naked guy just walked in here," she whispered, but Noah heard her loud and clear.

"Sorry to have bothered you." He sprinted to the right, praying he'd find the meeting on his own.

Noah entered an expanse of open cubicles. It looked like a beehive, drones buzzing in their separate cells. At the far end, he spotted large chestnut doors. Bingo. The Executive Board Room must be secreted behind them.

He barreled across the floor, his muscles stretching, arms pumping, penis bobbing, balls slapping—Jesus, the pain. He passed shocked facial expressions, gasps of surprise, and a flurry of dropped papers.

He shoved open the heavy doors. Thirty members of the cognoscenti swiveled their heads in unison and gawked.

"What in the world...?"

"Whoa."

"Is he one of ours?"

"Call Security."

"Our company culture sucks."

He scanned the room for Sally. There she was. She stood at the end of the table in front of a PowerPoint slide. "The Miracle of Selexikote: A Cure For Bipolar Disorder In Children."

She froze when she saw him. One hand pointed toward the projection, the other hand in mid-gesture to her audience. She looked paralyzed.

Noah watched her professional exterior slowly crumble. Her mouth fell open, her eyes widened in horror. "Oh no," she moaned.

Sirens whined in through the windows and grew louder. Through the floor to ceiling window, he saw two squad cars and an ambulance. Shit. The boardroom doors flew open. Walkie-talkies crackled, spewing commands.

"Mom. Don't sell." Noah ran around the table to reach her. "Leave with me. They're the anti-Christ. They'll destroy humanity. Selexikote is evil." He vomited the words in one stream before he could forget his purpose.

Someone grabbed his right arm. He swung with the other, but someone else cut short his upward swing.

He focused on Sally, throwing his energy to her, to help her stay calm and listen. Interference assaulted him. "Mom, believe me. Let me explain."

Her face flushed as red as her power suit. She had a look of bewilderment, despair and hopelessness all rolled together in her tortured gaze. Her body quaked. She shielded her face. "You stopped your shots. How could you do this to me?"

Noah struggled to break free, but the security guard and a policeman restrained him.

"Sally, I'll take care of this," Roger DeMarko said.

Noah jerked his head in the direction of his doc and stared in disbelief. If Noah's brain cells hadn't been popping like soap bubbles, he'd have remembered sooner that DeMarko owned fifty percent of Selexikote, and, of course, he'd be at this meeting.

A new revelation struck Noah that he'd failed to consider. DeMarko had anticipated Noah making this entrance. He and Dalton had orchestrated this inevitability so Noah would have no credibility with Sally. So they could lock him up. He'd walked into the devils' snare.

Two other police officers joined in to control Noah.

"Charles, where should we take him?" DeMarko asked.

"I'm on the board of Abbott Psychiatric. You can treat him there." Charles Dalton said, unfazed.

At last, Noah put a face to the voice. Dalton's precise speech fit his features: his patrician, square jaw jutted at a patronizing angle, his steel blue eyes disdainfully skimmed the surface of others.

The men dragged Noah away from Sally.

"Mom, don't let them take me. You don't understand."

Sally stood mute, cradling her face in her hands.

"There, there." Dalton placed a hand on her shoulder.

Noah pushed against the men, but Jesus, they were strong. He felt so tired, so inadequate. "Mom, don't sell. Don't-"

Someone's hand covered his mouth. He wanted to bite that hand, but he managed to control the impulse.

"Get him out of here," Dalton barked.

"I'll go with him in the ambulance," DeMarko said.

Sally nodded.

An ambulance. Alone with DeMarko. No witnesses.

The hand slipped from his mouth. "Mom, you come, too," he pleaded. "Don't let him take me."

DeMarko smiled at Noah. Such a cold smile. "I'll sedate him. Don't worry about a thing, Sally."

Four men each gripped a limb and carried him.

"Mom."

The doors swung open.

"Mom, no."

The doors swung shut.

❋

Sally shut her eyes tight. She heard grunting, the scuffle of feet, the sound of doors swinging wide and thudding against walls.

"Mom. No."

The doors slammed shut, Noah's lunatic voice fading away.

She remained frozen, her face buried in her hands. She struggled to block out the burn of strangers' stares and the hum of voices around the boardroom table.

"Dalton puts on a great show, don't you think?" someone commented.

"Far more interesting than last month's meeting," another said.

"Where'd they find this loony?" some insensitive buffoon murmured.

The words reached Sally's ears. She'd heard people whisper about Noah before—in the kid-crowded corridors of his grade school, at the derelict-infested police station, in the nutso-bursting, psychiatric emergency room.

She refused to listen or to see or to deal.

"Members of the Board," she heard Dalton boom. "While this may have been an unfortunate interruption, it's a perfect example of the power of Selexikote."

She craved numbness. How could Noah have done this to her? All she'd ever asked was that he stay on the damn meds. Was that so difficult? She'd spent her life ensuring his mental health, striving to control the situation. She'd schlepped him to a thousand and one doctor appointments and paid for the development of Selexikote, doing her damnedest to reshape her square peg. She'd agonized over him and willed herself to see past his baggage.

"This young man took Selexikote successfully for fourteen years," Dalton calmly addressed his minions.

She'd accepted Noah, hadn't she? She'd endured his obsessions over coincidence and awareness and all his other bullshit. She'd adjusted to his idiosyncrasies: his preference for making prolific notes in that stupid journal, as opposed to making friends. She'd looked past his inability to embrace business. God knew she'd tried to bear his flaws. How could he have done this to her? Today of all days.

"This young man operated at a high level," Dalton said, "but he missed one injection of this drug, and the results...as you've all observed...are catastrophic."

Sally hurt inside and out. Her love for Noah would destroy her. She could withstand being raped and beaten—a walk in the park compared to the pain of losing the child for whom she'd held so many hopes and dreams. She'd mustered every ounce of strength to make it through standing in front of Dalton and his board, pretending to be so fucking tough. Her bruises throbbed, but she'd done it, damn it. Now, her Noah... brilliant, capable, so full of promise. She saw and felt nothing but the loss of his potential. Another dead dream. What would become of him? What would become of him?

"Two weeks off the drug," Dalton announced in a clear voice. "That's all it took. We can save millions of families from the heartbreak you've just witnessed."

Two weeks? Sally glanced at Dalton. Had she heard him correctly? How could he know? Why did he seem so prepared and unflustered by Noah's intrusion into the boardroom?

She needed a drink, and a quiet place to think as far from this boardroom and Dalton as possible.

Noah lay as rigid as the stretcher strapped tight to his back. Fear gripped him, stiffening his sore muscles like rigor mortis. Scant light filtered in through paneled doors of the ambulance cab, and the paramedic ("Name's Tom") had dimmed the overheads. "More soothing," he'd explained.

Noah had abandoned his attempt to escape. He'd jerked his limbs, flailed, and screamed like a toddler, but the security guards had subdued him in short order. In the end, they'd tossed his naked body into the ambulance as if he were a piece of bruised fruit.

"You doing okay, buddy?" Tom, early thirties, bent over him, pressing a cold stethoscope to his chest.

His muscles throbbed and his head ached. Noah shivered beneath a thin sheet. The ambulance felt like a cold meat locker, or worse, a morgue. Hadassah? No cinnamon.

"I'm going to give you something to help you relax."

Noah nodded, closing his eyes. His disjointed thoughts raced in circles, and he tried to make sense out of his situation. How had he gotten into this mess? The last two days seemed like a blur. He tried to remember his path, replaying snippets of conversation in his head.

"You must figure out how to make things right."

"You're the one who will save the world."

"You carry important messages the world needs to hear."

"You're the kind of person who does what he says."

"Find mine Chaim."

Save the world, my ass. He should never have listened to Great-Grandma Sara, Fleck, Jean-Paul, Crystal, or Hadassah. He'd failed everyone. The only thing he could save the world from was Noah. Now, he resigned himself to the inevitability of what lay ahead.

An ambulance. Alone with DeMarko. No witnesses. He sucked in his breath.

"Nothing to be afraid of, buddy," Tom said with a smile. "I'm going to give you a shot, and you'll sleep for a while, okay?" He rummaged through a supply shelf above the stretcher. "Hey, here's a spare pair of scrubs." He gestured to a pile of hospital-green fabric. "You want me to help you get dressed?"

Noah shook his head. Why bother? He'd failed his mission. Exhaustion overwhelmed him.

"What happened to your clothes?" Tom asked.

"Long story."

"Bet it's a good one." Tom frowned and searched another supply drawer, probably looking for the shot. *Hurry up and find it.*

Noah didn't understand what had gone wrong. He'd felt certain Mom would listen. He'd counted on that. When she'd looked at him, all she'd seen was a deranged loser. He felt hurt by her attempt to distance herself. He'd searched her face, and what he hadn't found shook him. No acceptance. No love.

He longed to sleep, to float away from everything and everyone. He shut his eyes again, praying for release and that shot.

"*Boychik.* There's work to do," Great-Grandma Sara shouted in his ear.

Noah's eyelids twitched open.

Sara hovered above him, clinging to the ambulance ceiling. Her cinched-bag lips and two long chin hairs stood out against her misty form. "Get up."

"Go away," Noah groaned.

"Don't speak to me like that. Show respect." Sara zetzed his nose good.

"Ow." Noah tried to rub it, but his hands remained strapped to his side.

The smell of cinnamon hit Noah's nostrils like a double assault of pepper spray. He sneezed. Hadassah's vapory form appeared at his feet. Tears gushed through her hollow eyes like waterfalls. "Find mine Chaim."

Noah shook his head. "I can't."

"*M'darf im vi a finfter rud tzum vog'n.*" Hadassah clenched a vapory fist.

"That means, 'You're as useful as a fifth wheel on a wagon,'" Sara said.

"I don't care."

Sara scowled. "Fight, you *nudnik*."

Hello? Restraints? What was he supposed to do? Grandma was a freakin' genius.

"I heard that." Sara pinched his arm.

Crap. Noah wished they'd leave him alone. "Stop it."

Sara shook a finger in his face. "Trouble brews, *bubala*." She placed her hand on his shoulder, and a surge of energy bolstered him.

Hope. Maybe all wasn't lost. Okay, okay, he got it. He needed to get out of the ambulance. How? He needed a plan and protection. He looked up at Tom, who held a syringe in one hand. "Please, no shot. I'll be calm. Just stay with me."

"Got some friends in your head? You're talking pretty good to someone." He looked down at Noah. Kind eyes.

"Just a dream. Please, I'm fine. No shot." Noah thought he glimpsed compassion beneath a black swoosh of hair.

"Okay." Tom nodded. "No shot." He returned the syringe to the supply shelf.

Relief flooded Noah, and his muscles loosened.

"I'll be up front with the driver. I'll see you at the hospital. Your doc's going to ride with you."

An ambulance. Alone with DeMarko. No witnesses.

Fear jolted Noah. A fifty amper. He thrashed. "No. You stay."

"Relax, buddy, or I'll have to give you that shot." Tom waddled, bent in the shape of a C, his back brushing against the low ceiling of the vehicle. He opened the ambulance doors and jumped to the ground.

"He's all yours," Tom called out.

Noah heard labored grunting as someone heaved his body into the ambulance cab. The sound of panting grew nearer.

DeMarko's sweaty face appeared above Noah's. His breath smelled medicinal and stale. He set a black doctor's bag on the floor and sat down, huffing as he peered through his thick glasses. "Well, if it isn't the Master of the Universe. It would appear our destinies are linked. Or is it merely coincidence?" He laughed.

The ambulance engine came to life. The driver shifted into drive, and the vehicle accelerated, lurching to the left.

"You should have taken your shots." DeMarko waved his index finger close to Noah's face. "You should have spent your time doing important research. Instead of stealing my file. Instead of snooping around warehouses. You've created a problem." He shook his head, clicking his tongue. "What to do? What to do? Extreme psychosis calls for extreme measures." DeMarko dug into his black bag. "I travel prepared for all occasions. You never know who might need a little something."

Noah jerked at the restraints, but they didn't budge. "Tom, help." He twisted toward the front of the ambulance. "Help." The double-leaded window separating the paramedics from the cab was closed. Noah stared at the back of Tom's head, white ear buds in place, dark hair bobbing to the music streaming from his iPod.

DeMarko waved a syringe filled with thick purple goo. He pushed the plunger to test it, squirting a stream into the air. It landed on the sheet, burning a slithery hole in the shape of a death adder. A curl of ash, a rubbery smell, wafted through the air. Noah's stomach flipped.

"I hope this drug doesn't have side-effects." De-Marko shrugged. "Oh, well. Depression is inevitable after mania. Suicide is always a risk. How tragic it would be if you were unsupervised. Good thing I'm here to help." He leaned closer.

Sally didn't care about the ten million dollars. She operated on autopilot, picking up her purse and her briefcase, and hurrying through the conference room door.

The elevator doors yawned. She stepped into the empty cab. The doors clamped tight. She felt isolated and utterly alone. This was what life had in store for her. The padded walls closed in. A wave of claustrophobia swept through her. Muzak pounded her ears, a symphonic arrangement of "Dancing Queen." Christ, there was no end to the cruelty.

The elevator doors opened onto the lobby. She stepped onto the crème swirled marble floor, the color of a tasteful Kahlúa and Cream or a Dirty Martini.

She rushed outside, closer to the numerous drinks she intended to enjoy. The prospect of numbness propelled her forward.

"Sally," Bernard called out.

Not now. Stay the fuck away from me.

"Sally, wait." He rushed toward her.

"Leave me alone." She released her grip on her purse and briefcase. They crashed to the asphalt. Spinning around, she shoved Bernard with both hands.

He stumbled backward, looking stunned.

She swung at him. She'd kill him for not telling her his story. She'd kill him for not warning her about Dalton. Bernard must have known the truth about him.

He caught her arm. "Sally, please."

She pulled away. "I don't trust you. I don't want you. I..." She stopped. Then, she collapsed inside, her body going slack. Tears broke free in a torrent. Her face crumpled. "Oh, God...."

Bernard pulled her to him, wrapping his arms around her. She sagged against him. He rocked her back and forth, back and forth.

"Noah. Noah's sick. I can't go through this again. I can't." Her words hiccupped between sobs.

"Yes, you can. You're strong." He lifted her face and gazed into her eyes. "You've always been strong. You're Sally Friedman." He kissed the top of her head, her forehead, and her chin. He kissed the tears wetting each cheek. "Sally, Sally," he murmured.

She buried her face against his shoulder and wept. She felt Bernard's strength flow into her. Suddenly, she didn't care if Dalton's story about him was true. He already knew her faults, and yet he stood here, holding her, trying to comfort her.

"Noah's in trouble," he said. "We're here to help."

Sally looked up. A chiseled-looking black man, wearing traditional African dress, towered over her and Bernard. Fleck stood beside him, the two of them looking slightly embarrassed.

Sally couldn't make sense of this picture. Why was Noah's best friend standing in the parking lot of Duschene International Headquarters?

"Fleck, what are you doing here?"

"Hi, Sally. Surprise, surprise." Fleck shrugged, a goofy grin on his face. "I'd like you to meet my friend, Jean-Paul Amon.

Fleck's friend offered a strong hand and bowed. "It is a pleasure to meet the mother of such a great man."

Jean-Paul's touch was surprisingly gentle. He smiled, beaming sincerity and respect.

"What's going on?" she asked, looking from man to man to man for the truth. Heat vapors rose from the asphalt parking lot, bouncing off car mirrors and chrome. Sally felt light-headed. Nothing made sense. Had she heard Bernard correctly? He hadn't witnessed Noah's performance in the boardroom. How did he know Noah was in trouble? All of Sally's alarm bells rang. She pulled back from Bernard's embrace, searching his face for answers. "What do you mean, Noah's in trouble?"

Bernard squeezed her hand. "Has he been here? Have you seen him?"

She'd seen more of Noah than any mother of an adult son ever cared to see. "He barged into the board meeting, stark naked and screaming nonsense. His doctor, Roger DeMarko, took him by ambulance to Abbott Psychiatric."

Fleck, looked panicked. "He's with that bastard?"

"No," Sally protested. "DeMarko's a good…" Then, she saw Bernard's look of horror, and her blood went cold.

DeMarko. How long had she blinded herself, believing what she wanted to believe? All the signs had been there. His suspicions about Noah. DeMarko's increased paranoia. His theft of her cell phone. Her heart sank as the pieces of the puzzle assembled. DeMarko had deliberately tried to keep mother and son apart. He operated with a harmful agenda, and Noah was his target. She should have known. What kind of a mother was she?

A wave of urgency to rescue her son washed over her. She snatched her purse off the asphalt. "I've got to find Noah."

She sifted blindly through the mess in her bag for the rental car keys. Then, she froze. A deeper revelation seeped through her, stilling her fingers and scorching her cheeks.

Dalton and DeMarko had orchestrated everything, spreading chaos like a malignant tag team. DeMarko's job had been to keep her separated from Noah. Dalton's job: break her down, numb her. What better way to achieve the goal than to rape her? Why? Greed? Power? Thrills? No time to worry about that now. Later, with her son at her side, she'd plot her revenge.

She faced Bernard. "If DeMarko hurts my son, I'll kill him."

His eyes widened in surprise. "I believe you. Come on," he said. "We'll take my car."

"Wait." Jean-Paul raised a steady hand as he moved closer to Bernard. "We must go slow to go fast."

Jean-Paul presented a calm contrast—the eye of a hurricane versus Sally's sheer panic and rage. Why not? He wasn't the one who'd screwed up. He wasn't the one who'd allowed DeMarko to take Noah. What did he mean, *go slow to go fast*? Tick tock. She must reach Noah before something catastrophic happened.

"Bernard," Jean-Paul said, "we will not make it to Noah in time without help."

"What?" Sally's legs went weak, and her heart fluttered. She swayed against Bernard.

Jean-Paul's chiseled face showed no trace of fear. "We must invoke the Ancestors to protect Noah against dark forces. It will be swifter than looking for him. Perhaps, he will find us."

"Invoke the Ancestors?" Sally's tone rose shrilly, even to her own ears. "What are you talking about? I'm not waiting for whatever the hell that is."

Jean-Paul placed his hands on her shoulders. She felt the coolness of his palms through her suit jacket. "Please trust me, Ms. Friedman. You do not know the kind of evil we are dealing with."

"Evil?"

"Fleck and I will invoke the Ancestors while Bernard explains everything." This perplexing yet regal mystic gave Sally another slight bow. He shielded his eyes, scanning the horizon like a hunter, and he motioned to Fleck. "Come, my friend," Jean-Paul commanded, as he glided toward a thicket of trees at the far end of the parking lot.

Fleck jogged to catch up, his expression a mixture of anger and purpose.

Bernard appeared unruffled by Jean-Paul's peculiar suggestion, as though the man had recommended stopping to fill the gas tank on the way, instead of invoking ancestors. He stretched an arm around her. "Try not to worry. I trust Jean-Paul. He's a wise man."

The enigma reached a row of trees. He sidled close to a sturdy trunk, pressed his ear against the bark, and wrapped his arms around it.

Noah was in danger, and this apparent savior had slowed down to make love to an oak. "Bernard? Your Wiseman's hugging a tree."

He shrugged. "That's interesting."

"I'm leaving." She dug into the tangle of debris in her purse, fumbled upon the key ring and pulled it free. The tag description—Silver Taurus, four-door—seemed vague, and she couldn't remember what the rental looked like.

The patchwork of cars blanched in the blinding sun, appearing similar. Where had she parked the damn thing? She pointed the smart key and pressed the button, hoping to hear a high-pitched sound. Nothing. She aimed again in a different direction. Nothing.

"I'm not letting you go alone," Bernard said.

"Fine. Come with me."

"Do you even know where you're going?"

"Abbott Psychiatric. I'll get directions."

"We need to wait for Jean-Paul."

She shot Bernard an angry look. "You're going to have to hit me over the head to stop me."

"If that's what you want." He grabbed her hand and marched ahead, dragging her with him across the steamy lot.

They weaved in, out and between the parked cars, navigating a sea of metal and heat as he searched for the spot where he'd parked. He stopped at last, pressed his key fob, and a car beeped. A Prius. Small. Nothing flashy.

He opened the passenger door. "Get in. When you get hit over the head, I'd like you to be seated."

She glared at him. "Gee, thanks." Against her better judgment, she settled into the front passenger seat.

Bernard ran to the driver's side of the car and slid in. He turned on the ignition, and a blessed blast of chilled air hit Sally's face.

"Go slow to go fast. Take a deep breath." Bernard lifted two sheets of paper off the dash and handed them to her. They looked like they'd been torn from one of Noah's journals.

Her son's careful handwriting covered both lined pages. One was addressed "To whomever finds this note." The other salutation at the top read, "Dear Fleck."

Bernard placed his hand on her arm. "Fleck got a call from a federal air marshal by the name of John Woods. He arranged to meet Fleck at the airport and gave him these."

The pages shook in her trembling hands. She closed her eyes for a moment, letting the air conditioning soothe her burning cheeks.

"Slow down, Sally. Slow down to go fast," Bernard said.

Sally fixed her gaze on Noah's words.

They slugged her. A right hook to her psyche and her senses.

A wave of nausea overtook Noah. He'd need to push through his fear so he could fight DeMarko. How?

DeMarko leaned closer.

A medicinal odor slammed Noah's nose, striking him as oddly familiar. The same smell sometimes soured his own breath when he woke up in the morning, or clung to his body if he didn't shower after the gym.

DeMarko reeked of the odor. Potent. Funky. Selex-ikote. DeMarko must be popping massive doses of his own designer meds.

The revelation shocked Noah. "You're on the drug," he blurted out.

DeMarko narrowed his eyes, black painted slits on a plastic piggy bank. "You're not the only one who has a right to genius," DeMarko snarled. "I've surpassed you. My brain cell growth is exponential." He grabbed a corner of the sheet and pulled it back, exposing Noah's restrained left arm. He angled the syringe against it.

Noah flinched. Terror flooded him.

Sweat covered DeMarko's brow, and his panting resumed. "It's a shame," he snorted, searching for a vein. "I actually think I might miss you."

Noah's adrenaline pumped at high gear now. Logic sliced through his fear. Fight. Play for time. Play for your life.

"Yes, mine Noah. Fight." Great-Grandma Sara smiled serenely from overhead. "Help is coming."

Hadassah lunged at DeMarko. "*Chazer,*" she screamed. "Pig." She pummeled him with her vapory fists. He blew through his puffed-out lower lip and swatted her away, as though he were troubled by a mosquito. She glowered at the doctor with her empty, hooded eyes, trying to mesmerize him. He blinked, waving the air in front of him with the hand that held the syringe. She retreated up to the ceiling and whispered in Sara's ear.

Holy Einstein. Noah prayed Hadassah wasn't the promised help. He'd have to figure this out on his own. Play for time. Noah tried to feign nonchalance. "Roger, let's make a deal."

DeMarko laughed, his mirth tinged with malevolence. "What can you possibly offer me?"

From overhead, Sara nodded, still smiling down at Noah. She pointed to the ambulance doors behind DeMarko. Thin trails of smoke sifted through the cracks at the threshold and the doorjamb. A gray haze rose.

"I'll be your dog and pony show," Noah urged DeMarko. "You can show me off to pitch the drug. I'll recite the Encyclopedia backwards and forwards. I'll explain String theory. You'll be famous. Brains courtesy of Doctor Roger DeMarko."

The smoke billowed, forming a large gray mass and filling the back of the ambulance from floor to ceiling.

"Shut up," DeMarko grunted. "You're a ticking time bomb. I can't trust you."

Noah forced a smile. "Roger, we've been together for years. We're a team. I look up to you."

The smoke started to sculpt itself into a body. Long limbs, lanky arms. A specter took shape, like the one Noah remembered seeing on the morning he, Fleck, and Jean-Paul had broken into the warehouse. The head of the spook shot through the roof, and Noah could only see its filmy form from the neck down. Then, the creature shrank, adjusting to shorten its seven-foot frame.

Its head dropped into view. A hazy bone protruded through its fog nose. The creature put a smoky finger to its plate-sized lips, tapping them silently, shaking its head, sending a message to Noah. *Shh. Don't tell.* A sooty smell filtered through the ambulance cab. Noah's eyes watered.

DeMarko coughed and seemed puzzled. "I will miss the opportunity to have intellectual debates with you." He cleared his throat. "I can't risk..." He coughed again, made a choking noise. "What's that smell?" DeMarko looked up and his eyes widened. He jerked back in surprise.

The creature's head plunged toward DeMarko's. Its features morphed into a fanged mouth, wider than the doc's skull. The mouth spewed a stream of sparks and ash.

DeMarko squealed and dropped the syringe. It landed on the sheet, resting atop Noah's left arm restraint.

The smoky creature roared a howl so loud and deep it reverberated off the tin-can walls, vibrating the metal supply shelves, clattering the instruments, and shifting the oxygen stand.

The ghoul's smoke vapors disappeared into De-Marko, melding with his corpulent flesh and bones.

DeMarko tried to stand, but his body was racked with coughs. Smoke poured from his mouth. His face turned purple. He staggered backward, twisting, gagging, bouncing off the sidewall of the ambulance. He yanked at his tie, scrabbling to unbutton his shirt collar. The buttons broke and rattled across the floor. He lumbered for the oxygen tank still scooting on its wheels, fumbled, but found it. Twisting the nozzle, he pulled the rubber piece over his mouth. Smoke seeped from the sides of the mask in billows. Vapor trails flowed out his nostrils and ears.

DeMarko's eyes widened in panic. His eyeballs glowed blood red. He wheezed a whistling, high-pitched gurgle, stumbled nowhere, groping, clawing. His leg caught against the stretcher and he fell forward, his mass landing sideways on top of Noah.

DeMarko lay deathly still. His body had hit the syringe plunger, depressing it, squirting liquid onto Noah's sheet. The chemical sizzle of burnt fabric melded with the smell of smoke. Burnt cotton sheet. Better yet, burnt polyester arm restraint.

The sweet smell of freedom.

Noah's wrist blistered, but so what. The strap loosened.

DeMarko rested prone across Noah. Under his weight, Noah felt the in and out of DeMarko's labored breathing, in between arrhythmic coughing spasms. Unconscious. Not dead.

Noah twisted free his left arm. He shoved, inching DeMarko's body aside until it fell in a fleshy heap onto the floor of the ambulance.

Noah unfastened the buckle on his right arm and his legs, then jumped off the stretcher. He grabbed the puke green scrubs from the supply shelf, dressing quickly.

Should he take DeMarko's shoes? He bent down and raised a leaden foot to compare the size and decided they would be more hindrance than help.

He rushed to the ambulance doors and peeked through the window. The vehicle sped along a busy highway. No way could he open the doors and jump out. He stepped over DeMarko's bulk and tapped on the window behind Tom's bobbing head. No reaction. Noah slammed both fists against the glass, making it shudder. Tom flinched and turned around. A shocked look formed on his face. He mouthed, "What the fuck?" Tom shouted something to the ambulance driver, and the driver's head jerked sideways to look.

A screech of tires. The van shifted lanes, weaving over to the right. A slam of brakes, and the vehicle jarred to a stop. Tom threw open his door, jumped from his seat, and disappeared from view.

The back doors of the ambulance popped open.

"My doc's had a heart attack," Noah shouted. "Hurry."

The paramedics hoisted themselves into the cab, rushed to DeMarko, and knelt at his side.

"He's still breathing," Tom said.

"Jesus, no wonder he had a heart attack." The driver fluttered his hand, wafting the air away from his face. "This guy must smoke more than a barbeque on the fourth."

Tom stared at Noah while the driver attended to the unconscious doc. "How did you...? You're out of the restraints."

Noah shrugged his shoulders, giving Tom a sheepish grin. "Adrenaline kicked in, I guess."

The two paramedics bent over DeMarko, conferring on how to save him.

Noah slipped out the ambulance doors and eased down to the asphalt shoulder. Federal Air Marshal Woods' advice hammered in Noah's ears. "Run for your life, kid. Run."

The asphalt scorched his bare feet, but Noah pushed through the sting, pumping his legs. Faster, faster, faster.

"...Selexikote causes Alzheimer's in long-term users. I've been on the drug for fourteen years, and my brain cells might make a spontaneous run for the exit without any warning. If you got a call, I guess they've checked out. Sorry, dude..."

Sally released her grip, and the letter drifted to the floorboards.

Bernard patted her arm. "You okay?"

She sensed the sides and roof of the car closing in, trapping her like a butterfly in a glass jar. How could she possibly be okay? It was her fault her son might have early onset Alzheimer's. Her failing that she'd trusted crazy-assed DeMarko and allowed him free rein with Noah. Her culpability that she'd provided no layers of Selexikote's oversight.

Her head throbbed, and she rubbed her temples. My God, the truth hurt. She was selfish and self-obsessed. She'd welcomed the drug as a quick fix, a roadmap to move Noah through school and life without the messiness of tantrums and her own involvement. She'd been hell bent to engineer a normal son.

She could kill DeMarko and expose Dalton, but neither act would change the blindingly obvious. She was to blame when Noah's mind disintegrated. "I'll never be okay again." She refused to meet Bernard's eyes.

"Don't fall apart on me, Sally. Noah needs you."

She shook her head. Noah had needed her when he was little, and she'd failed him miserably. She'd handed him over to DeMarko then, and she'd just done it again.

Bernard lifted her chin, forcing her to make eye contact. "This is no time for a pity party. You with me?"

The rear car doors flew open. Sally's heart jumped, shaking her out of her numbness. Jean-Paul and Fleck climbed into the back seat.

"Bernard, get on the highway and go north," Jean-Paul said. "Now."

Bernard guided the car out of the parking lot and made a left turn, heading for the freeway.

Sally guessed they were done going slow to go fast. Now they were hurrying, which suited her fine.

"Do not worry, Ms. Friedman." The top of Jean-Paul's head barely cleared the car ceiling. "Noah is well."

"How can you be so sure?"

"I talked to the Ancestors. They are with him now, and he is strong."

The Ancestors again? Who was he talking about, his dead relatives? Who was this guy? Why was he even here?

"Jean-Paul, what is your relationship to my son?"

"The Ancestors led me to Noah to find help for my people."

Fleck leaned over the top of her seatback. "I was investigating a story about AIDS drugs in Africa, and I met Jean-Paul. Noah's helping both of us," he said.

Sally tried to follow the thread. "Duschene distributes Telaxiphentol to African countries. Is that the connection?"

"Yes." Jean-Paul nodded, making a swishing noise as his head brushed the upholstered top of the car's ceiling. "We believe Duschene is shipping diluted drugs."

Questions flooded Sally's head. "You're helping them, Bernard?"

Eyes glued to the road, he nodded. "I'm responsible for Dalton learning to make money from distributing drugs that kill. Because of Noah, I have a chance to redeem myself."

Sally's breath caught. "So, it's true? Dalton told me you purposely shipped tainted drugs to increase profits. It's true?"

"He told you that?" Bernard looked at her in surprise, then shifted his focus back to the road.

"That bastard," Fleck shouted from the backseat. "Don't believe anything Dalton says."

"It wasn't like that," Bernard said. "I'll explain later."

Sally had a lot of explaining to do, as well. Perhaps she, too, could redeem herself.

The four sat in silence as the car raced up and down hills that were once a section of Minnesota's north woods. Forests of pine on either side of the highway stood majestic in the sunlight. They passed a lake surrounded by pink and white lady slippers, resilient to the high temperature despite their delicate appearance.

"Pull over," Jean-Paul cried out.

Sally almost jumped out of her seat. "Why? There's nothing here," she said. "We've got to get to Abbott Psychiatric."

"Stop," Jean-Paul insisted, pointing to the right.

Bernard pulled onto the shoulder and slowed the Prius to a stop.

"Bernard, don't listen to him," Sally demanded.

Jean-Paul shoved open his door before the car came to a complete stop. He jumped out and ran toward a tall pine tree, once again wrapping his arms around the trunk. He leaned his ear against it.

Bernard and Fleck got out of the car, following him. Sally stormed after them.

Jean-Paul retraced his steps, a calm expression on his face as he spoke. "Noah will arrive any minute."

"What?" Sally shouted. "I thought we were hurrying. I thought we were finished going slow. We need to find him now."

"He will find us." Jean-Paul crossed his arms over his chest.

Sally's anger spiked. "How do you know?"

"The tree told me."

"The tree told you?" She stared at them. Three whack-jobs and Jean-Paul was the leader.

She closed in on him. When it came to her son, she would not be intimidated by anyone. Not anymore. She jabbed Jean-Paul in the chest. "I don't know who you are and what you think you know, but this is my son, and we're going to Abbott Psychiatric. Now." She turned to Bernard. "I don't believe this mumbo-jumbo bullshit. I don't trust this man."

"He is coming," Jean-Paul insisted.

"It's insane to wait in the middle of the highway, hoping for visions to appear. Please, Bernard."

"There." Jean-Paul pointed above her head.

Sally pivoted. In the distance, a form crested the hill. It was hard to make out. The figure wore green, blending against the grassy hills and trees. Someone ran toward them, sure enough. Yes, she could see a boy—no, a man—loping down the hill.

She moved in his direction, straining her eyes to see. Could it be possible? Could it be her Noah?

"Mom."

The word wafted toward her on a wisp of warm breeze.

"Mom."

She kicked free from her Manolos and took off. "Noah." Now, she was yelling and laughing, and my God, it really was her Noah. It really was him. "Noah, Noah." She saw him clearly, his copper hair flying, his lean arms pumping as he ran. Her love for him powered her legs.

They reached out for each other. At last, she wrapped her arms around her son.

GOOD MEDICINE

Chapter Eleven

Hadassah hovered above the boy while he slept, her anger simmering like a strong soup. She'd waited long enough for him to follow through on his promise. Perhaps he never would. Liar. Descended from a family full of *ganefs*. Thieves.

She blew cinnamon up his nose. He rubbed at it, then rolled over onto his side and pressed his face into a pillow.

She'd prayed for God to send her someone who would bring Chaim to her. This is who he came up with?

In the dark hotel bedroom, she studied the snoozing shape, as still as the dead, more boy than man, the one God had chosen for her. Surely, he'd cursed her again with such a *schlemiel*, such an inept hero.

The boy's family owed her. Now, he must make things right. "I'll bring Chaim back," he'd pledged. "I need to fix something else first. Please. Help me."

She'd been patient as he waged his battle to fix the something. Enough was enough. He must find her Chaim.

Suddenly, Sara floated into the bedroom, shaking her finger at Hadassah and wedging a protective barrier in front of her lazy great-grandson.

Hadassah shot her the evil eye. Sara simply smiled in return. Oh, to be like Sara, free from longing and anger, vibrating high and light.

Hadassah drifted away from Sara and the boy, into the adjoining bright room where his mother talked and ate with Pincus' great-grandson, Bernard.

If Hadassah had been able to deliver the eggs to Pincus as Chaim had asked, Bernard would have been a rich man. Instead, the idle boy's mother enjoyed stolen wealth.

Hadassah could tell that Bernard liked this woman, who paraded around all dressed up in vinegar and honey. He nodded and laughed when she talked. He looked at this woman with the same spark Chaim had flashed at Hadassah on Friday nights.

This *fatootsed* woman was pretty enough, with hair the color of pennies just like her sluggish boy.

She, too, owed Hadassah and could pay her debt through marriage. Then, the egg fortune would be returned to its rightful place.

Yunge hob'n khasene fun hits, alte fun kelt. The young marry because they are hot, the old because they are cold. Hadassah imagined Bernard and the woman felt somewhere in between, which would work fine for a marriage. Weddings were all funerals with music, anyway.

Hadassah pictured her wedding to Chaim—lace veil, candles, and fresh strudel—and thought that saying really wasn't true. He'd given her a pair of pearl earrings. She'd given him a gold watch that played music sung by angels.

Bernard laughed and dug the wedding present she'd gifted Chaim from his pocket. "Third time it's chimed today."

Yes, Hadassah loved that sound.

The tootsie lifted her teacup. "What time do you have?"

"Almost two. Should we wake Noah?"

Hadassah brushed by the woman's unblemished hand, rattling the china cup against the saucer and spilling hot liquid.

"Ow," the woman cried.

Hadassah shook with glee.

"You all right?" Bernard helped to steady her cup.

"We must not wake Noah," the tall black man said.

"Yes, let him sleep," Bernard's maybe-bride, said. "I've never seen him so tired."

"No, we gotta wake him." Another young man, a big-footed *shlemazl* the same age as the sleeping boy, paced the living room. "He said for us to be back at Duschene by three."

"We promised we'd follow his plan," Bernard said.

"It's only fifteen minutes from the hotel to Duschene." She mopped her scalded hand with fine linen. "We have time."

"If he wakes when he is dreaming, he will get caught in the other world and not return," the dark man warned. "He will wake himself when the time is right."

The someday-bride-to-be nodded. She looked with reverence toward the black man. "If you say we should wait, we'll wait."

Bernard reached for her bejeweled fingers.

Hadassah riled at watching this contented scene. She grew gloomy and dense, a threatening storm. She'd take the good-for-nothing *schlemiel* in his sleep. She'd force him to follow through on his promise. If he didn't find her Chaim, she'd curse him anew. To hell with him. May he suffer and remember. May he have pain in his belly and a cramp in his back. May he swell up yellow and green. May he turn into a *blintze*, and may his mother, who didn't deserve the likes of Hadassah's great-great-great nephew, change into a cat. Then, may she eat up her son and choke on him, so the world can be rid of them both.

The black man caught her eye, surprising Hadassah. He stood, pointed his finger at her, and advanced, his eyes flashing the command, "Do not take him. Let him fulfill his quest."

She'd given the boy enough time. No more. Her soup boiled over. *Ooooh.* She spun like a whirling dervish, slaloming in, out, and around the furniture and all the living souls. Her fury exploded, weighting the room and squeezing past the windows to the wider world.

The redhead cried, "My God. What the hell?"

That one always cursed and blasphemed. Bernard would never get used to her. One after another of life's disappointments would shroud him, and he'd be destined to remain penniless.

"How's it possible?" this *chalaria*, this crass mother of the worthless boy, shouted. "Snow flurries in August."

Everyone ran to the window and peered outside.

Ha. Snow was easy, a piece of strudel, only the beginning of the magic she'd perform. Hadassah would trick Sara and remove the boy's protection. Then, she'd take him.

She thundered back into the dark bedroom where he slumbered unaware, and she floated over to Sara. "Your granddaughter is happy," she cooed to the lighter specter. "Go see if you can make a *ksube*, a marriage contract."

Sara kissed the boy on his forehead, and the lazy bum sighed in his sleep. Sara flitted out of the room.

"Jean-Paul, where are you going?" Bernard asked. "You said not to wake Noah."

The black man stormed into the bedroom and planted himself between Hadassah and the boy. His eyes flashed anger.

Hadassah thrust backward, rustling the damask draperies that hung in thick folds over the windows.

"I said do not take him," he commanded. "He will come on his own."

Sally stood at Bernard's side mesmerized as snowflakes zigzagged against the hotel suite's living room windows.

"Insane. I gotta catch this up close." Fleck raced to the couch, searching beneath pillows and scanning the room. "Anybody see my camera?"

"I stuck everything behind the bar," Sally called out.

"This is just like that movie, _The Day After Tomorrow_," Fleck burbled, racing to the counter and disappearing behind it. "Jake Gyllenhaal? Anyway, the world's all crapped up and it snows in the middle of summer." Fleck found his camera and hurried to the door. "Text me when Noah wakes up, okay?" He slammed the door behind him.

Bernard nudged Sally. "I think we might finally be alone."

"Where's Jean-Paul?"

Bernard gestured toward the bedroom. "With Noah." He moved to the couch, sank into the pillows, and patted the cushion next to him. "We need to talk."

Sally joined him. "Whenever anyone says that, it's rarely good."

Bernard smiled, but it faded quickly. "I promised to tell you my story."

The last forty-eight hours had been exhausting and frightening. Finally, Sally had enjoyed a momentary feeling of calm. Noah, napping in the next room. Bernard within arm's reach. "I don't want to hear it unless there's a happy ending." She flopped down at his side.

He shrugged. "I'm hopeful it might have. I'd like that."

Sally poured hot water over her tea bag, needing to do something with her hands. "Ready or not."

Bernard closed his eyes and exhaled. "After my son and wife were killed, I was depressed for a long time. I filled every minute with work, so I wouldn't think about what I'd lost."

"Sounds like a healthy escape."

Bernard looked at her, and his eyes blazed. "It was criminal. I need you to understand this. No escape is healthy. Not mine, not yours..."

Sally felt stung to hear his accusation of her as well as himself, but she deserved it and appreciated his honesty, failed escape artist that she was. She settled her cup and placed a hand on his knee. "You're awfully hard on yourself."

He stood and crossed the room. "I'd sleep two, maybe three hours a night. So, I got a little help from my friends. Pills to fall asleep. Pills to wake up. Pills to relax. The drug business was convenient." He laughed nervously. "I started making mistakes...small ones at first, and then...." Bernard paused before the picture window. White streaks careened around his silhouette.

Sally resisted an urge to rush to him. "You did the best you could."

"Please let me finish this." He paced back and forth while he talked, wearing a path into the carpet. "One day, Dalton sent a directive to curb oversight costs. I sarcastically told him the only way to run a tighter ship was to fire a few inspectors in China. They ensured drug formulas were meticulously followed, and hell, I could do that myself. 'Fine,' he said. 'Do it.'"

"Oh, Bernard."

"I never gave the order. I didn't fire the inspectors, despite his directive to do so." His neck flamed red.

"I believe you."

"Six months later nineteen people died on my watch."

Sally's breath caught. "That's horrible. But it wasn't your fault—"

"Try telling that to the families of the nineteen people." He shook his head. "I went through my files, and there it was for anyone to find, a memo I'd apparently signed eliminating twenty Chinese inspectors. I couldn't remember writing it, but there it was. My signature." He brought his hands to his face. "I've never taken a pill since. Not even aspirin."

"I'm sorry, so sorry."

"I immediately offered my resignation. Only Dalton wouldn't take it. He found a role for me as head of his due diligence team...a job that kept me swamped in detail outside of Duschene and away from internal reports."

Sally knew Dalton didn't possess altruistic motives. "Why did he keep you on?"

"A better question is why did I stay? Why in hell did I stay?" Bernard returned to the couch and sat. "I was so numb I didn't know or care for a long time why he insisted on keeping me. But now, because of Noah, I have an answer."

"What does Noah have to do with it?"

"He asked me to help him investigate whether Duschene was shipping tainted Telaxiphentol to African nations. The light clicked on."

Sally took his hand, and he let her.

"Once I took my head out of my ass, it became obvious. If you wanted to increase profits and leave no trail, why not do it with a drug and a market where no one expects survival rates to increase? Why not do it in countries where people are disadvantaged and weakened? Or where marginalized people don't have a world voice? Perfect target."

A wave of anger rushed through Sally. "Dalton framed you for the murder of innocent people."

"My former secretary had developed quite an art of

copying my signature onto all kinds of documents I'd never written. Good news is, she's willing to testify. She quit after her affair with Dalton ended."

Sally wondered if Dalton had raped the secretary as well. "Even if Dalton's crimes are exposed, he's got you waiting in the wings."

He nodded. "The perfect stooge with an established track record of incompetence. What an idiot I've been."

Me, too, Bernard. Me, too. "So, what do we do now?"

"Help Jean-Paul's people. Bring Dalton's crimes to the light of day. I've got a file full of evidence. It turns out, I'm pretty good at due diligence."

"I'll help."

"This isn't your battle."

"Yes, it is. You're not the only one who's been hurt by that bastard." Sally removed her scarf, exposing her necklace of raw bruises.

Bernard sucked in a sharp breath. "He hurt you, that asshole." He gently touched her cheek. "I should have warned you. Did he...?"

She flushed, ducking away from his fingertips. "Did you know what he was like?"

"No proof. Only suspicion. But I should have said something. I should have protected you." He hissed through clenched teeth, "I'll kill the son of a bitch."

She started to retie the scarf around her neck, but Bernard turned her to him. The silk fluttered to the floor.

"Sally." He pulled her close. "There's so much about myself I regret. I'm a coward, and I failed you. I don't know if you could ever love me. I don't deserve it, but—"

"I have regrets, too. The reasons and circumstances may be different, but my story is the same as yours." She gazed into his eyes.

"Sally, is it possible you could ever—"

"Too late, Bernard. I already do."

She lifted her chin, and his lips met hers. She could have sworn she tasted a hint of cinnamon.

The bedroom door opened, and Jean-Paul stuck out his head. "Pardon me."

Sally broke from Bernard's embrace.

"I apologize," the shaman said. "Ms. Friedman, we will need warm clothes and coats. Hurry."

"No problem."

The shaman bowed and closed the door.

"I'll go shopping with you," Bernard said.

"No need." Sally floated to the bar and picked up the house phone. "This is Sally Friedman. I need to buy a few more things. Yes. Charge it all to Charles Dalton, III."

Noah awoke to muffled voices and the faint high-pitch of Mom's laughter sounding from the next room. He felt groggy and spent, his brain still clinging to fragments of a vivid dream. A dank prison cell, bone-shaking cold, muscle-shriveling hunger. He rattled barred windows and stared out across an endless expanse of Siberian snow. As the full measure of his fate sank in, he slumped against a stone wall, sliding down listlessly to a puddled floor.

All the while, Hadassah's curse mocked him. "Four losses you will suffer. First, loss of freedom. Next, loss of memory. Third, loss of family. Last of all, loss of life."

Only a dream. He pinched himself, felt it, sat up in the bed, and tried to collect his wits. Where was he? He was supposed to do something, but what? He searched his memory for answers.

Diffused light inched its way into the room through gaps in thick drapes. A night table stood beside the overstuffed bed. A multi-button telephone. A digital clock glared 2:23. A.M. or P.M.? he wondered. A bottle of Ambien. He picked it up, squinting at it through the dim. *Sally Friedman. Take one nightly as needed.* He'd taken a nap in Mom's suite at the Ritz Carlton.

"I thank the Ancestors for bringing you back from the other world," Jean-Paul's voice boomed from somewhere nearby.

Noah startled and scoped the corners of the room, unable to pinpoint the shaman. "Where are you?"

"Look up." Jean-Paul sat cross-legged, suspended in mid-air above the bed, his head brushing the ceiling. He'd shed his traditional dashiki and hat in favor of a t-shirt and jeans.

Noah stared in shock. "I'm still manic, right?"

"Watch your head." Jean-Paul stretched out his legs and swam past the four-poster to the carpeted floor.

"Will you teach me how to do that?"

Jean-Paul scooted a chair close to the bed and sat down on it. "You are not ready. Also, I do not know how to teach it. It does not like the language of English." Jean-Paul laughed and slapped his thighs.

Noah didn't understand what was so funny, but the shaman seemed quite tickled. He couldn't stop laughing. He grabbed his stomach and wrested his giggles.

"Never mind." Jean-Paul waved a hand. "You have other things to learn. You must go on a quest."

Noah's head throbbed, and the smallest gesture made his bruised body ache. The thought of doing anything felt overwhelming. He needed food and more rest. Holy Einstein, he'd barely slept for three days. "I'm so tired. If I could just—"

Jean-Paul crossed his arms. "Too many people stay engaged in endless sleepiness. Meanwhile, dark times happen. Get up."

"I'm no good at superhero bullshit. I can't help—"

"Why? Because you tried once?" The shaman shook his head. "Do you think treasure is buried beneath a tent with a sign pointing to it? No. It is hidden deep in the heart of the mountains. You must keep searching."

Noah sighed. "Why me?"

"You know the amount of healing that needs to be done in the world. Are you willing to ignore it?"

"There are better people—"

"Redefine yourself. The capacity to survive requires that you are willing to do things you have never done before. Stop—what is your word—bitching. Get up."

"Where are we going?"

"You must appease this angry spirit who follows you. The one with powerful medicine."

"Hadassah."

Jean-Paul nodded. "We need her help before we can help my people."

"I'm not sure we should count on her. She's difficult."

"Good. A militant attitude is needed to be effective." Jean-Paul stood and settled his hands on his hips. "The relationship with the Ancestors is reciprocal. You help her. She helps you. She is tired of waiting for you to fulfill your promise."

"Well, excuse me. It's not like I don't have other things to deal with right now."

Jean-Paul appeared unsympathetic. "Learn to multi-task."

"I don't know how to do what she wants. I can't help her."

"You can't? What does that mean, you can't? Who, then? You want someone else to do the dishes for you?"

"She wants me to go back in time and find her dead husband."

"So?" Not even a nerve twitched on Jean-Paul's face.

"So?" Noah rose to his knees in exasperation. "Why can't she do this herself if she's so powerful?"

"Something must have happened in her relationship with her husband. It stops her. Perhaps, they were separated when she died. Or, no one ever grieved for her. She needs someone to intervene and sacrifice. You must honor her, and help her move on to the next world."

"This is crazy."

Jean-Paul placed his hand on Noah's shoulder and looked deep into his eyes. "When the majority does not see something, does that mean it is not true? This theory that you research—this fifth dimension of awareness and measuring coincidence—is this not the truth you seek?"

He had a point. Perhaps this wasn't so different from Noah's theory. He had proven he possessed the ability to focus on places and transport himself there. "Maybe it's the same thing," Noah conceded.

Jean-Paul nodded. "When energies are in alignment, you can achieve things without a logical explanation of how they happen."

Maybe Noah could treat this quest as a research experiment. Was this his destiny? "What if I fail? What if I can't get back?"

"You must be driven toward things that are overwhelming and yet find yourself still banging at that door." Jean-Paul found a shopping bag near the door of the suite and pulled items from it. A pair of jeans, underwear, a sweater, a ski jacket and boots. "Get dressed."

Noah stared in bewilderment at the gear. "Aren't these duds a little heavy for the height of summer? Even in Minneapolis?"

Jean-Paul marched to the window and drew open the drapes. Snow fell outside, blanketing the hotel grounds in tall mounds of white. "The spirit who haunts you is powerful. Now, get out of that useless green cloth. Hurry."

Noah hands shook as he hurriedly dressed and tried to make sense of the blizzard beyond the window. "Hadassah made it snow? Or did I sleep through autumn and you're afraid to tell me?"

"Your ghost is quite expressive."

"Where are we going?"

"You. You are going," Jean-Paul said. "To the threshold of infinity. I will help you. But only you can jump off."

The crack of snapping oak branches echoed through the forest that surrounded Duschene International Headquarters. Clusters of pine trees buckled under the weight of Hadassah's ongoing white vengeance, as the snowstorm grew fiercer by the minute.

Flakes whipped against Noah's face, numbing his cheeks and stinging his eyes. He sweated beneath his heavy ski jacket, a result of worry as well as his effort to trudge through deep snow pack. He lifted his knees high, his muscles burning as his thoughts avalanched, burying his psyche under a substance more solid than snow.

His ability to appease Hadassah seemed improbable, but a more profound fear gripped him. What if this journey was a figment of his imagination? Perhaps he still napped in the hotel suite or, Holy Einstein, lay drugged in the ambulance.

He struggled to bury his freakiest thoughts, but they kept clawing their way to the surface. Would he have any warning when Selexikote erased his memory? Would he be able to complete his mission? Mother of all creepy thoughts...would he remember who he was?

Noah concentrated on the sound of Jean-Paul's even breathing. The shaman's medicine bag swished against his nylon ski jacket. The hypnotic rhythm of these sounds seemed oddly comforting, lulling Noah further into the woodlands.

He rested his shovel in a snowdrift and turned to

sight the others, his unlikely soldiers in this daunting quest.

Fleck slogged next in line, about twenty yards back. His red ski cap tassels, waggling above an even redder face, made him easy to spot against the white. He lugged a *kuor*, a ritual drum. Strapped around his neck, it swayed behind him like a U-Haul trailer.

Further back, Noah made out the figures of Bernard and Sally. Bernard guided Sally, his gloved hand in hers, urging her onward. They toiled a few steps and stopped. Noah counted one, two, three, four...and Bernard pulled her forward again.

"I think we're losing them," Noah said.

Jean-Paul glanced back and nodded. "We have journeyed far enough. This spot will do. We are sufficiently hidden." He tromped away from a row of trees and pointed. "This is where we must dig the fire pit."

Noah plowed his shovel into dense powder, scooping mounds of snow up and over his shoulder. He marveled anew that it was, after all, the end of August.

Before they'd all abandoned the car in a drift on the side of the highway, about a mile from the Duschene Office Park, they'd listened in awed silence to the radio. Nonplussed broadcasters blamed global warming for the bizarre front, condemning outdated meteorological equipment for their failure to predict the storm in advance. "This weather event is unparalleled," one forecaster wailed. "The sky is truly falling."

No, thought Noah, simply a woman scorned. Hadassah wreaked havoc when she was pissed.

Noah had been surprised to discover that Duschene's parking lot teemed with snow-covered cars.

Board members and employees had apparently been forced to wait inside until the storm abated.

Hadassah would blizzard the world nonstop until Noah found Chaim. If he succeeded, her help in battling Dalton and DeMarko could prove to be literally out of this world. If he failed, the spooktress wouldn't let him live.

He continued to dig, pausing when he heard the crunch of footsteps and panting behind him. A few feet away, his mom collapsed in a heap.

"I'm too out of shape for this shit." Her breath escaped in high-pitched whistles.

"Nonsense. You did great," Bernard assured her.

She looked at him in exasperation, and rocked onto her back to make a snow angel.

Fleck wheezed, dropping to his knees beside Sally. "This..." he gasped, "...is just like the movie..." He gave up mid-sentence. "I'm fried. Can't think of a single title."

"Never mind," said Jean-Paul. "Fleck, gather fallen branches and twigs for a ritual fire."

"I'm coming." He struggled to his feet.

"I'll help," Bernard headed toward the trees.

Sally whimpered. "I'll join you if you want."

Bernard smiled down at her. "I want you to rest, sweetheart."

Noah rolled his eyes. Bernard and his mom had apparently gotten it on, and that was cool. Still, weren't they a little too old to gush?

"Hello," someone called from a distance. A figure waved and poled forward on cross-country skis.

"You found us." Jean-Paul shouted.

A man caught some downhill movement, gliding forward to catch up to the group. "Is that you, kid?" he yelled. "Noah Friedman?"

"Do I know you?" Noah shielded his eyes from the snow and tried to identify the padded frame.

"It's Woods." He reached Noah, dropped his poles, and offered an arm. "Federal Air Marshal John Woods. Well, no longer an air marshal, just Woods."

Noah stilled, dumbstruck. He grabbed Woods' outstretched mitt and tottered, almost losing his balance as Woods shook hard. "What are you doing here?"

"Jean-Paul needed another pair of hands."

"But how did you hook up with—

Fleck chimed in, "You wrote a note with my contact info, stuck it in your pocket, and John found it. He called me."

"And we need his assistance," Jean-Paul said. "It is fortuitous the Ancestors have provided such a strong man to aid in your quest.

Woods slapped Noah on the back. "Hey kid, I quit that job and my stress disappeared overnight. I'm happy for a chance to return the favor."

Jean-Paul stood before the fire pit, brushing snow off his medicine bag. He removed his ceremonial tree branch, rotating the wand end with the red feather attached in a broad, circular motion.

Noah watched in amazement as Jean-Paul defied physics, commanding wet wood to burn. Sparks ricocheted and caught hold. Fire crackled. Sputtering licks of color soared into the air.

The group sat on logs, feeling grateful for the heat thawing their hands and feet. When the fire would begin to ebb, Jean-Paul shook his wand, and a surge of flame howled higher. The blaze turned cobalt, then violet. Tendrils formed the shape of faces. Great-Grandma Sara's chin hairs and cinched bag smile undulated against the forest backdrop, creating a peaceful presence. A twin spire formed platter-sized lips and a nose bone.

Suddenly, the fire hissed. Crimson flames shot above their heads. Great-Grandma Sara's form disappeared. Wildfire took the shape of Hadassah's deep hollow eyes. Noah shivered.

Jean-Paul flourished his wand. The fire died down, returning to violet. "It is time for the ritual to begin," he announced. "Listen carefully. Everyone has an important role to play. Fleck, you will drum."

Fleck cradled the *kuor* between his legs, a blank expression on his face. "I'm not real musical."

"Let your spirit drum," Jean-Paul said. "Stare into the fire and the Ancestors will command you. Do not stop drumming until I say. This is critical. Do you understand?"

Fleck chewed on his lower lip. "Can I stop to snap a few shots?" He lifted a camera slung around his neck.

"The drum sends Noah to another world, and the drum brings him back."

"So, if I stop drumming...." Fleck's eyes widened, nearly bugging out of his head. "Oh. I get it."

Noah reeled from the revelation that his return to

this world depended on McNulty's ability to concentrate on one thing at a time for more than five minutes. Crap.

Jean-Paul walked in front of Bernard and Woods, gesturing to a zebra hide draped over the snow. "The two of you will hold the animal skin. You must hold it tight. When I tell you to pull up, pull up with all your strength."

Bernard nodded. "Got it."

"Not to worry. We're a team." Woods slapped Bernard on the back, making him pitch forward.

Noah envisioned both men pulling up, with Woods flinging Bernard in the air and the zebra skin with him. Double crap.

"*Ashe.*" Jean-Paul faced the fire, and the group fell silent.

Sally sat beside Noah, and she leaned close. "What does '*ashe*' mean?" she whispered.

"Kind of like, 'amen', or 'that's all.' Something like that."

"That's all?" Looking from face to face, Sally raised her voice. "You forgot me. How do I help?"

The shaman walked over and squatted before her. "Your job is the most important of all." He spoke deliberately, his expression grave as he placed his hand on her shoulder. "You must dispense with all logic. Discard all rationality. You must believe Noah can go to another world. You must believe he will return. Do not stop summoning him back to us. Can you do that for him, Ms. Friedman?"

Despite the fire's heat, Sally's face blanched as white as the surrounding drifts. Jean-Paul might as well have asked her to rewire her brain, Noah thought. Mom's analytical—all business and balance sheets. What if, no matter how hard she tried to believe, Noah didn't return? She'd never stop blaming herself.

"Jean-Paul, that's not fair," Noah said.

Jean-Paul folded his arms across his chest and stared straight ahead. "You have your journey. She has hers."

Sally shot Noah a look of calm resolve. "Don't worry. I can do this."

The shaman nodded to her and knelt before Noah. "We did not come into this world to put ourselves on hold. Are you ready?"

Noah blew out a breath. He didn't know if he'd ever be ready. Hell, he didn't even know if this was really happening. "Jean-Paul, what if this isn't..."

"Real?"

Noah stared in disbelief that the shaman had read his thoughts.

"What is the difference between reality and fiction?" Jean-Paul poked Noah's shoulder. "What if I can touch you and you're not real? If you are aware..."

"Then, it's real," Noah finished for him.

"Yes." The shaman stared into Noah's eyes. "Listen to me. There is another purpose to this quest. Aside from pleasing the ghost. Can you guess what it is?"

Noah shook his head.

"The piece of you that's dying must be reclaimed."

Noah's throat went dry. "My memory?"

Jean-Paul nodded. "You must heal yourself."

Noah felt a stirring, a small seed of hope as it tried to take root. Could he really be cured of the negative effects of Selexikote? "How? The drug erases—"

"Few of us possess the only memory that is truly important. We come into this world to deliver our gifts, and then we forget what they are. You must remember who you are meant to be."

"My true purpose?"

"There is an old African battle cry, 'Go forward and die.' You must be willing to risk all and be reborn in order to be healed. Are you ready?"

Noah didn't comprehend what lay ahead for him, but he felt certain of one thing. He wanted to remember the beauty of this world. He looked around in awe—the majestic pines swaying, their limbs heavy with powder, the magical snow icing the landscape into an endless birthday cake—and he longed to stay aware. If a plan existed to ensure that, he felt hope. His body quaked. "I think so," he whispered.

"No." Jean-Paul jabbed Noah's shoulder with his wand, the end with the animal tail attached. "Even when you are not sure of the outcome, you must be bold enough to walk into the darkness. Say, hell yes," he cried, jabbing Noah again.

Suddenly, Noah felt a jolt. A surge of courage flowed through him, warming his muscles. He slapped Jean-Paul's shoulder. "Hell yes," he said, his voice booming and steadier than ever.

Jean-Paul smiled. "Do what you are compelled to do, and you will discover you are never alone." He patted Noah's back. "Come. You are ready." The shaman stood and made his way to a copse of trees.

Noah started to follow, then hesitated. He returned to Sally and took both her hands in his. She tried to smile, but her face looked strained in an attempt to control her tears.

"Don't worry, Mom. I'll be back." He threw his arms around her. "I promise."

She hugged him, burying her face in his jacket. Then she pulled back, gazing into his eyes. "I'm so proud of you, Noah. I always have been."

They smiled at each other. Noah felt he might already be remembering his true self. "Me too, Mom."

He stood and turned to join the shaman. The wind picked up with a fresh fury, blowing snow up from the ground and mixing it with a renewed downfall to create a whiteout.

The howling wind screamed, "You owe me," drowning out Jean-Paul's crunching footsteps. Ice stung Noah's cheeks like needles. He shielded his face, straining through the fog to spot the shaman's tracks in the drift.

Noah's throat refused to swallow. His heart buzzed like a hummingbird's, but he forced himself forward, feeling an urgency to get this show on the road. Tilting his body against the wind, he trudged one foot at a time and chanted strong and clear, "Go forward and die. Go forward..."

Fleck started drumming. The steady banging pierced the wailing gusts. Noah exhaled through his nose, trying to slow his heartbeat to match the rhythm of the *kour*. Calm. Steady.

He bumped into Jean-Paul.

The shaman radiated a serene presence. He gestured to a nearby tree wildly oscillating in the wind. "Your ghost tires of waiting. It is time."

Noah felt as ready as he'd ever be. He just needed to hear the plan. "What do I do?"

"Bernard and Woods have dug a path. Can you see it?"

Noah detected the shoveled outline ahead of him, but fresh downfall was filling it back up. Another few minutes and they'd have to dig the path again. "Yes."

"When I tell you, run as fast as you can down the path. Your friends are at the other end, holding the animal skin. Jump high into it."

"You mean onto it?" Noah asked. "I jump on top of the animal skin."

"No. Do as I say. Jump into the animal skin."

Noah felt too terrified to be amused by the quaintness of Jean-Paul's translation into English. This was no time to debate the fine points of language. He'd jump up on the animal skin. Same difference. "Then, what?"

"Think about your ghost. Picture her. Conjure her world."

"Got it. Then, what?"

Jean-Paul shrugged. "Find her dead husband."

Noah stared at him in disbelief. "That's all you got?"

Jean-Paul folded his arms across his chest and stared back. "Then, you come back. We hope."

"We hope?" Holy Einstein, the hits kept on coming. Noah's resolve faltered.

Jean-Paul patted his shoulder. "Think positively."

He fought a desire to upchuck.

"Oh, I almost forgot." Jean-Paul slapped himself. "Take off your clothes. You do not need them in the other world."

Jesus, did he have to get naked again? He'd barely worn clothes in the last twenty-four hours. "All of them? It's a little cold out here."

Jean-Paul dismissed him with a wave of his gloved hand, and strode along the path dug by Bernard and Woods. The mist folded in, shielding the shaman from view. Noah heard him give the men the signal to lift up the animal skin and hold it tight. Fleck's drumming quickened.

"Por a saminay. Por a saminayo," Jean-Paul intoned, his voice penetrating the wind.

Noah pulled off his gloves, unzipped his jacket, and slid out of it. With numb fingers, he struggled to shed the rest of his clothes. A violent shiver shook him as he stood in his birthday suit, every inch of his body exposed to frigid blasts.

"Come, Father, this is your son, Jean-Paul. Come, Mother, this is your sister, Jean-Paul. This is your uncle, Jean-Paul... your grandfather, Jean-Paul...your daughter, Jean-Paul."

The wind stopped shrieking, the shaman's voice filling the forest. "Ancestors, come. Help Noah on this journey. Guide him to deliver his gifts. Give him courage in the other world. Help him find his way back."

The snowfall ceased. A startled Noah felt warmth begin to flow through his body. His hands thawed, his skin glowed with sweat as though the sun bathed his limbs. His muscles unclenched.

"Run, Noah. Run."

Noah pumped his legs, his head bent so he could see his way on the path. Would he sense when to jump? He looked up. In the distance he spotted a green luminescence, eerily compelling. The light was close to the ground, maybe on the ground. He was almost upon it, could see the glowing green clearly now, but he had trouble making sense of what it was. His eyes played tricks on him in the fog.

Bernard and Woods gripped the animal skin. Iridescent green ooze dripped from the bottom of the zebra hide, making a round hole in the snow. The hole seemed to possess no depth, as though it dropped forever, carving a tunnel into the earth.

Noah gained ground, his terror and excitement building.

He heard Bernard and Woods panting as Jean-Paul chanted, "Por a saminay."

Noah glided across the snow, the green glow beckoning him forward. His blood hammered in his head. He pushed through his nausea.

Now, Noah. Now. Jump. He leapt up into the air, targeting the top of the animal skin. He held his arms stiff at his side, his legs together and straight.

Bernard grunted. Woods muttered, "Hold steady," as the two men readied to take his weight. Noah let gravity pull him down to the top of the animal skin. He braced to feel the tough hide against his bare soles. But, no. He fell through it. Then, down. He'd jumped into the animal skin.

Falling, spinning, he hurtled deeper, deeper through the green hole in the earth. The cold and the snow disappeared. The sounds of Bernard, Woods, and Jean-Paul faded away. The green glow melted into pitch dark.

Black.

Silence.

Pinpoints of light filtered into the darkness from every direction. Red, blue, purple and gold streaks danced like comet tails.

Noah's fear dissolved. He felt as though he'd melded with every particle of the cosmos, inseparable from swarms of orbiting electrons. He was the blackness yet he was the light.

He raised his hand in front of him. Floating atoms where fingers should be swished in the wake of his thoughts. Like the clothes he'd shed in the storm, his body wasn't needed in this other world.

Freed from his corporeal prison, his energy exploded. All the doors and windows, any barrier to universal consciousness, blasted wide open. Images. Events. Ideas bombarded him: The wheel, penicillin, the hula-hoop. The printing press, the vegetable peeler, the World Wide Web. Ideas whirled around and through him, and all he'd need to do was pluck one, focus, remember, and create it into existence.

Navigating this new world would be a ball. A random thought struck him and took hold. "I want to be one with the zebra hide."

Suddenly, the streaks of light formed solid beams that stretched like highway lanes. One of the lines blinked rapidly. Noah willed himself to it, grabbing onto the light band.

He zoomed forward.

Grassy plains appeared. The hills of the Serengeti bobbed up and down as he galloped. He shook his Mohawk mane, brayed soft snorts, unbridled from complex thought.

Noah whooped, a zebra living in the moment. No problems, no fretting about tomorrow or yesterday. It savored the breeze, the sun on its back, and the rush of running wild. How magnificent to live as the zebra.

A jerk of fear surprised him. He smelled his animal sweat. In the distance, a lion crouched in the brush. The zebra reared on its legs and bolted, racing in the opposite direction. Crap. It sucked to live as the zebra.

Flee. Remember your mission. Stop messing around.

He recalled Jean-Paul's instructions, ignoring all other thoughts. "Think about your ghost. Picture her. Conjure her world."

Images of Hadassah crystallized. The deep wells of her eyes and black babushka. Snow and ice. Loneliness, anger and grief. Cinnamon.

The scene of the Serengeti faded to black. The bands of light stretched ahead to infinity. A red line blinked furiously. Noah floated toward it. He latched on. It raced, hurtling him forward and down.

He tumbled, spinning, but hanging tight to the band of light as it pulled him through the nothingness.

Noah tried to calm himself. He focused on his quest and imagined Chaim: beaver hat, topcoat, and knee-high boots. A gold pocket-watch with a chime. He remembered the aching fatigue in Chaim's worn body. He pictured the Czar's St. Petersburg palace decked out in red, and the brilliance of the jeweled egg.

In the distance, Noah saw blinding white. The band of light sped him toward it. Was it a snow-covered peak or a planet? The mound grew larger. Suddenly, the endless white surrounded him. The band shook violently. Noah lost his grip.

Please, Ancestors, help me. Help me find Chaim. He somersaulted. Ancestors. Falling. Twisting. Help me. Down, down, crash landing into something solid.

He shook himself, adjusting his jostled senses.

A full moon peeked through clouds in a starless sky. Bare trees swayed in a damp breeze, casting scary silhouettes over a muddy road. The clip clop of horses' hoofs grew louder. The flick of a whip. Noah looked up. A man steered his horse and wagon around a puddle and past Noah, who stood invisible at the side of the road.

A sign jutted up from the mud, and he drifted over to it. *Ekaterinburg.*

Noah snatched a detail from the cosmos library. Ekaterinberg, Russia. The town made infamous by death. The town where the Bolsheviks had executed Czar Nicholas II, his family, and servants on July 17, 1918.

Noah felt a surge of fear as he flashed back to his experience in Chaim's body and rewound the rest of the scene. Soldiers storming the palace. Ramming the doors. Encircling Chaim and the Czar.

Wrong time, wrong place. Chaim had been caught in history's web and taken with the Czar's family to Ekaterinberg.

Across the road at the end of a muddy drive, Noah spotted a shadowy house. Lanterns glinted from its second story windows. Sentries stood at the front door and the fence perimeter, their caps pulled low over their eyes, rifles slung over *gimnasterkas*, soldier's shirts.

Somewhere in this house, Chaim and the others were held captive, Noah could feel it. Somewhere in the village of Yompola, Hadassah marked time, baking pastries Chaim would never eat.

Noah needed to reach Chaim before the Czar's execution. When he found him...then what? What miracle could he perform? Was he really even there? He didn't possess a body. He seemed to be just a jumble of neurons—pure energy and thought. No match for guns.

It started to drizzle.

A young woman screamed.

The killing had begun.

Grief seeped through the house's doorframes, joints, and cracked stones like a festering wound. Screams shot from the upstairs window. Silhouettes of a woman and a soldier tussled. She tried to run. He caught her by her hair. Their shadows disappeared from view.

Noah's phantom heart pounded. He floated past a sentry guard and into the death house. He heard the stomp of boots on the stairs above, a rustling of skirts, the hushed whimpers of the resigned.

The Czar rounded the staircase, wearing a cap and soldier's shirt. He carried a young boy, his head nuzzled into the Czar's shoulder. He whispered to the child in Russian, "Shh. We're playing a game. Just like chess."

"Will we win, Father?"

The soldiers poked the Czar and the others with their rifles, herding the family out of the house and into the courtyard. Next, they'd bring the servants.

Time was ticking away.

Noah pictured the Czar's tutor—his short beard and mustache, his long, curled sideburns, the age lines carved into his face. He felt Chaim's energy swim toward him from a locked room beside the kitchen.

A sentry blocked the door. Noah would have to float through him to reach Chaim. He imagined himself inside the soldier. Then, he jumped in.

Sergei. From Minsk. Twenty. His stomach rumbled. Noon, yesterday. A tin of sardines. A stale cracker. The last of his rations. Damn this revolution. His legs tingled from standing guard over an old, weak man— an assignment a baby could perform. His shoulders numbed from the weight of the rifle in the wrong position. He burned to lie next to Svetlana. When the killing ended and the people were freed, he'd marry her. He'd find the money somehow. They'd eat meat and drink milk and someday have children.

A timepiece chimed behind the door. Maybe he could filch his prisoner's watch unnoticed. No. He didn't dare.

Noah jumped out of Sergei's body, through the wooden door and its swarm of devouring termites, and into the room.

Moonlight shone through a small window. Chaim sat slumped on the floor, his back pressed against a colorless wall. He kissed his gold watch and returned it to his pants pocket. Glancing at the door, he dug into his coat and removed the egg, his latest present from the Czar. Shielding it with one hand, he fingered the emerald bulrushes, the ruby roses, the sapphire laurel leaves. He sighed, his shoulders shaking.

Shots blasted from the courtyard.

Chaim cradled his head.

Noah jumped inside Chaim's body. *Don't give up*, he urged, hoping Chaim would heed Noah's voice in his head.

I'm finished.

You can figure this out.

Fools figure out nothing. Only death awaits.

Hadassah waits.

No. She knew grief would be my reward. She begged me not to go to St. Petersburg.

You will lose your freedom, Hadassah had scolded.

Don't listen to the rumors. I'll be safe.

You will lose your family.

Don't jinx me. I'll return to you, Chaim promised.

You will lose your memory of our good life together.

Nonsense. How can I forget what is built into my bones?

You will lose your life.

You worry too much, my Hadassah. We just need a little more. To make our time in America easy.

She cursed me. Four losses. Now, I'm finished, and so is she.

Try, Noah urged, for *her sake.*

How? I'm a weak, old man.

You have wits. You have a treasure. Bargain. Hurry.

The bolt on the door scraped.

Chaim secreted the egg in his coat.

Sergei stood in the open doorway. "Let's go. On your feet."

"Is killing an old man so important to the success of

the revolution?"

"Following orders is important."

"I thought the revolution was about not needing to follow orders."

Sergei pointed his rifle. "Stand up."

"I have something." Chaim stood. "For Svetlana."

Sergei gasped. "Svetlana? How could you know about her?"

Chaim fished the egg from his pants pocket, holding it high to catch the moonlight. "A present for her."

The jewels glimmered, splashing prismatic color against the pale walls.

Sergei looked bewildered and frightened, but his eyes lit up. "You're the devil."

"The egg is yours if you let me go."

The soldier laughed. "It's mine anyway when you're dead."

"When they shoot me, they'll strip me clean. You'll have to share this with the others. If you let me go, you can hide the egg. No one will ever be the wiser."

Noah jumped inside Sergei's head. He bolstered his energy to shift Sergei's thoughts.

A fortune within his reach. He could afford to keep Svetlana in milk for life. Could he risk it? If they caught him stealing from the people, he'd be shot. If he let the man go and hid the egg, perhaps, yes, he could keep it for himself. With so many to slaughter, would anyone realize they had missed one more servant?

No one stood between them and the front door. The other soldiers gathered in the courtyard for the killing. He could rush the old man out of the house. Then, he'd run to the courtyard and discharge his gun. In the chaos, the others would forget this old man. Yes, this way would be safer. He'd have to act quickly. "Give me the egg."

Chaim stood frozen. He looked confused. "Why would I do that?"

Crap. Noah jumped back into Chaim's body.

Chaim handed Sergei the egg.

"The watch. I want that, too," Sergei said.

Chaim shook his head. If he gave up the watch, he'd lose part of his soul. He'd never find his way back to Hadassah.

Holy Einstein. Noah felt drained, his energy dissipating. He couldn't give in to exhaustion. He jumped back into Sergei's head.

"No. Keep the damn thing." Sergei motioned with his gun. "Let's go. Quietly."

Noah jumped out of Sergei's body. He felt dizzy and weak. How long he could keep this up? He felt as though he, Noah, was disappearing.

The prisoner and his guard slunk to the front door.

Noah followed, trying to float, but he bumped along like a deflated balloon, skittering against the floorboards and bouncing up.

The two men bolted from the house.

Sergei raced to the courtyard.

Chaim ran to the muddy road.

Noah trailed behind.

The road forked. No signs. Chaim turned around and around, looking confused.

Noah remembered the wagon he'd passed on his way into the death house. He'd watched it make its way down the road to the right.

He bolstered himself, leaping back into Chaim's head—please, let this be the last time. He hoped he possessed enough energy to return the old man to Yompola.

Turn to the right, Chaim.

Chaim ran on stiff legs, his arthritic knees wobbling. There stood the hay wagon.

The driver snoozed in the moonlight, loosely holding the reins while his horse nibbled at a small pile of hay.

"Good evening," Chaim said to the driver. "Are you for hire?"

The driver's eyes opened, and he wiped at a string of spittle. "Can you pay?"

Chaim dug into his pocket. A look of despair came over him. Not one ruble to his name. Nothing. Only his watch.

Suddenly, Noah felt a force pull him like a magnet, yanking him out of Chaim's body. He struggled to stay inside the old man and give Chaim his answer, but this power, like a black hole, wrenched him from the flesh and bones.

No, not yet. The mission remained incomplete. What if Chaim couldn't make his way back to Hadassah?

Noah tried to hang on, but he weakened, spinning away, up, up into the darkness.

HADASSAH
AUGUST 1919
YOMPOLA, RUSSIA

Sun streamed across Hadassah's face, signaling another day of hunger and pointless waiting. Bad luck followed her every step, preventing her from dying in the night.

She dragged herself off the bed, panting, teetering in stockinged feet across the one-room hut. She paused to rest against her baking table, gathering strength to make her way to the empty pantry shelves. Habit, not desire, compelled her to search for something to eat.

A sprinkle of cinnamon dusted the bottom of her spice tin. She tapped the contents onto a spoon. Not even half a spoonful. She swallowed it, gagging on the spice. Her body wracked with coughs. She doubled over, struggling to catch her breath.

She should drag herself to the nearby stream and refill her jug of water. No. No more useless striving. Today, she determined to die. Maybe this was it.

The coughing subsided. Her lungs grasped for air and found it, returning her breath. Her anger rose. Tears threatened, but she pushed them back. She stood defiant, raised her eyes, and shook a gnarled fist at the ceiling. "God, what did I do to you? Why do you insist on cursing me?"

No answer. Silence. The sound of death.

Noise had always floated into her house. A child playing on the street. A vendor rolling his cart. The gossiping of *yentas*. She stared out her window at the forsaken landscape.

Even the birds had deserted Yompola. She used to feed them bits and pieces left from her baking. Now, they'd flown off in search of the living.

She hobbled back to her bed, lay down, pulled the knitted woolen over her body and waited to die.

A horse clopped. A steady beat. Hallucination must be a sign that death stood near. She smiled, closing her eyes. At last, peace.

The clopping sound grew louder. Wheels ground the dirt road. A wagon creaked. The Cossacks had returned. They'd search the village for anything they'd missed during last night's looting. Perhaps, this time they would slice her from end to end. The sword would be quick.

She must make sure they found her. Smoke. A signal. She'd set fire to the house, and they'd come running, sabers flashing.

Hadassah gathered her strength and hauled herself off the thin mattress. She scurried to the bookshelf, seizing the last remaining volume of Chaim's collection and her tin of matches. She struck the phosphorous tip. It grabbed the vellum. The brittle pages flamed and curled. She threw the book on the bed. The wool ignited.

She fanned the blaze. "Come get me you *mamzers*, you bastards. Kill me, too."

A Cossack banged on the door.

Flames shot toward the ceiling.

The door burst open.

"Hadassah." Chaim stood in the doorframe, looking bewildered. He must have lost thirty pounds. His dust-covered beaver hat and his spotted black coat hung loose. His boots were muddy. His hair and his beard needed trimming. The lines in his face had etched deeper.

Hadassah had never seen anything so beautiful. She fell to her knees.

Chaim rushed to her, lifting her to her feet, gathering her in his arms. "Hadassah, Hadassah. *Got tsu danken*. Thank God."

He rushed her out of the hut, away from the smoke and flame. Into the brilliant summer sunshine.

Chapter Twelve

Sally meant it when she promised Jean-Paul she'd "dispense with all logic." No way she'd any idea that willing Noah to another world and back would be this damn hard. She felt as if she were in a fog, which ordinarily might be funny considering she stood in one, but she felt too anxious to enjoy the irony.

Watching Jean-Paul's magic fire with its licks of iridescent color, Sally could almost believe the inconceivable. The blaze shot up through the snowfall as though the blizzard fueled the flames higher. Incredible.

Miracles swirled around this shaman. She'd witnessed him say something he couldn't possibly know, and then it happened. Surely, she could keep faith with him now.

But it was more daunting than she'd thought. She felt vulnerable standing alone in the snow, willing herself to ignore her logical brain and believe Jean-Paul.

The whiteout blinded her. She couldn't see Fleck, but she heard his steady drumming. He must be exhausted by now. The others were hidden a good twenty feet away. For all she knew, Jean-Paul, Noah, Bernard, and Woods sat in a circle passing a bong. What was taking so long?

She tried picturing Noah completing his mission, but negative thoughts intruded. Something horrible had happened. He'd lost his memory. He couldn't find his way home because she'd failed. What if her lack of belief stopped him dead in his tracks?

She'd never been religious. Her Grandmother Sara had schlepped her to temple and schooled her to say blessings over the candles, bread, and wine. Sally never found solace in prayer. Business meetings and acquisitions—now that was religion. When she closed a deal, she shook hands with God. A great orgasm—definitely, God.

She fell on her knees before the fire, pressed her hands together, and rocked back and forth like Grandma Sara. "Please, God, if you bring Noah back I'll give more to charity," she whispered, feeling unnatural to be praying aloud and thankful Fleck couldn't hear her through his banging. "Please, God, if you bring Noah back, I'll never drink again." Well, no need to get carried away. "I'll drink less, how's that? I'll think good thoughts about other people. I'll give my employees raises. I'll stay faithful to Bernard. I'll cook dinner once a week, volunteer my time, clean out my closets. Please, God, please." She hoped God had a sense of humor.

She tried creating a positive vision—that *facocta* S̲e̲c̲r̲e̲t̲ how-to that had enjoyed fifteen minutes of fame. A well-meaning employee had given her a DVD, and Sally had actually viewed it. What a bunch of crap, but she'd try.

She closed her eyes and pictured Noah as successful.

He has problems.
Completing his research.
He's made little progress.
With a wife.
He's odd. He'll never have a romantic relationship.
With children.
He could never handle that responsibility.

Her thoughts spun out of control. She envisioned Noah's wife and children over for Sunday dinners and the holidays. Happy. Successful. She prayed again. "Shema Yisroel. Hear, O Israel."

Snow pummeled her face, but the heat of the fire turned it to mist. The wind moaned shrilly, like a baby crying—the ghosts of future grandchildren not meant to be.

"Pull up." Jean-Paul's voice cut through the wind, his tone oddly strained. "Pull up with all your might."

Something had gone wrong. She felt it. Noah needed to come back now and it was her fault she couldn't will him to her. "What's happened?" She moved toward the shaman's strained voice.

"Pull again. Now." Jean-Paul sounded frantic.

She stumbled, ate a mouthful of snow, and dragged herself to her feet. Twenty feet seemed like a mile. She slogged, falling again. "Please, God, please."

Jean-Paul's arms appeared through the fog, lifting her up by her shoulders. "Sally." His face crusted over with snow, he looked deathly white. "Go back to the fire."

"I'm trying to will him back, but I failed. God knows I'm lying to myself. The Ancestors know I'm a fake."

"Go back. Will him here. Follow my instructions."

"Don't depend on me. Please, do something."

Jean-Paul turned away, his rising breath melding with the fog as he disappeared into it.

Sally heard him speak in low tones to Bernard and Woods, but she couldn't decipher his words. Maybe Bernard could will Noah back. Someone needed to intervene. "Bernard? I need you. Where are you?"

The mournful Russian lullaby sang from his watch, beckoning her to it like a foghorn. She put one foot in front of the other, aiming for the sound and bumped into Bernard, who looked as grave as Jean-Paul. He gripped the animal hide, balancing the strength of a grim-looking Woods on the opposite end.

Sally felt sick with fear. "Any sign of Noah?"

Bernard shook his head. "Jean-Paul's trying to bring him back. You need to help."

Her stomach clenched. She felt a wave of nausea. "I don't know how."

"Stop. For Noah's sake, do your part." Bernard turned to Jean-Paul, who appeared out of the fog.

The shaman chanted, "Por a saminay. Por a saminayo." He waved the animal tail end of his wand over the hide, hitting it with his other hand.

Sally went numb. She backed away from the men, into the solitude of the mist. She was failing Noah. Again. His life depended on her willing him back, and she didn't know how to do it. But she loved him. Please, God, let love be enough.

She closed her eyes. Focused her thoughts. Stilled herself to feel her son. A warmth flowed through her, tingling her body. She felt his true essence, and her eyes welled with tears. A gentle soul. Intense. Sensitive.

Wise. Eager to help anyone. Trying so hard to please. Different. Yes, odd, but wonderful because of it. She loved him exactly the way he was. Already successful. Complete and perfect.

Tears streamed down her face, forming icicles on her cheeks. "Noah, if you can hear me, listen for a Russian lullaby. I'm standing right here, baby. Come back."

Suddenly, the wind died. The forest fell silent, except for Fleck's hypnotic drumming, and the chime of Bernard's watch.

The snow stopped. Sally opened her eyes, surprised to see that the fog had lifted.

"Pull up." Jean-Paul sounded excited.

Bernard and Woods strained to lift the animal skin. Nothing happened.

Sally panicked. She wanted her son, and she damned well wasn't going to stay here and wait any longer. She saw the deep trench, the path Noah had run. She trudged through the drifts of snow to reach it. If Noah could jump to the other world, then she could, too. She pumped her legs, gaining ground.

"Pull up." Jean-Paul yelled.

"Sally, what are you doing?" Bernard cried.

She jumped.

The ground rumbled.

A large ball of purple flame about the size of an armchair shot out of the zebra hide above Sally's head.

The animal skin slackened, tumbling Bernard and Woods backward. Sally fell onto Bernard.

The purple ball catapulted straight up into the air, sparking violet as it arced over the trees. It landed in a snow bank a few yards away. A geyser of crystals exploded from the ground. Snow sprayed, making a *pffft* sound as it hit the drifts.

"Hurry." Jean-Paul raced toward the meteorite, motioning them to follow. "Quickly. Cover him with snow."

Him? That ball of flames? "Noah." Sally scrambled to her feet. She felt a sharp pain in her left ankle, fell to her knees, and crawled.

The three men reached Noah first. They threw fistfuls of snow onto the burning ball. They kicked at the drift, spraying it to cover him.

Sally's blood banged in her ears as she strained through the snow. "Noah." Almost there.

Jean-Paul stepped before her, blocking her advance. He smiled as he lifted her to her feet.

Sally winced and raised her left leg.

"Are you all right?" Jean-Paul asked.

"Yes. Noah?"

"Fine. A little shook up, but no damage. Give him a minute. Until he is dressed."

Sally wanted to push her way forward, to see for herself, but she thought better of it and would listen to the shaman.

"You're sure he's okay?"

"Oh, yes. Look." He gestured to the blue sky, shaking a triumphant fist and laughing, his teeth glinting in the brilliant sunlight. "He has pleased the ghost."

COMING
TOGETHER

Hadassah
August 1919
Yompola, Russia

Trails of smoke rose from the burnt cinders of Hadassah and Chaim's home. The two sat side by side on the wagon seat, staring in silence. She clutched his hand. He patted her knee.

A crippled, swaybacked mare—a real *schlepperdicka* animal—for which Chaim had paid dearly and had been swindled blind, sniffed at the dirt. She snorted, her nostrils flaring in protest at the barren ground.

Ramshackle huts on either side of their smoldering pile of rubble stood bereft. Discarded items littered the road. A hand-sewn doll. A man's leather dress shoe. A rusted pot. A broken baby carriage.

The looters had assessed these pitiful remains of village life as not worth the bead of sweat it cost to throw it into a wagon and haul it away. *Chazeray*. Trash.

The town of Yompola stood no more.

The old mare whinnied, stamping the ground with one hoof.

Chaim sighed. "We should get going before we lose the horse, too."

Yes, they must protect the sum total of their fortune—a creaky wagon and a near-death horse.

While they'd watched their house burn, Chaim had told Hadassah the story of his time away and of how he'd earned his way back to her. After escaping from the house in Ekaterinberg penniless, Chaim refused to sell his watch. No matter. In the wake of the revolution, there'd been no wagon for hire to *schlep* him over three hundred miles to Yompola, nor any means to send Hadassah a message.

Nevertheless, God had provided. Chaim found a horse with a wagon wandering aimlessly across a field. He couldn't find the owner so he fed the hungry animal what he could find, and turned its nose toward Yompola. Now, Hadassah gazed at the ghost town, etching Yompola into her memory. It was true, she'd never loved the town, but even the loss of leaky roofs, meager fields, and empty chicken coops seemed worth mourning.

Life was about learning to live with loss. The murder of all these people clenched her heart. Yossef-the-tailor. Nissin-the-candlemaker. Rabbi Makovsky. Rivka, Rebekkah, Shifra, Zlotah. Why? Why them, while she and Chaim had been spared?

As this thought sank in, something inside her cracked open, like a crocus on the dawn of spring, escaping its tight bulb. Her anger melted away. She felt soft. God had blessed her. Oh, *gotenyu*, dear God, how he had blessed her. Had Chaim not traveled to St. Petersburg, he wouldn't have been imprisoned. Had Chaim not been in prison, she wouldn't have gone crazy. Had she not been gossiped about as the town's crazy person the Cossacks would have entered her house to murder her. Had Chaim not been miles away, he, too, would have been slaughtered. Merciful God had answered her prayers.

Chaim seized her chin, turning her face to his. "What's this? You're crying? Now, now. We'll make a new life."

Her tears became deep sobs. She lacked the strength or desire to stop. "Please forgive me, Chaim. I sinned. I should never have lost my faith in God. I should never have given away the eggs."

"Greed is a worse sin than loss of faith. I shouldn't have left you. I shouldn't have gone back for another egg. But..." He thumbed a tear off of her cheek. "I see you have forgiven me. So, I'm forced to forgive you." His mouth spread into a smile.

She inched closer to him on the wagon seat, and he put his arms around her. She continued to cry, her shoulders heaving, her head supported by his chest, releasing herself to him, at last freeing what seemed like eons of bitterness and grief. She grieved for Yompola, for her stillborn child, for all this pointless loss.

Chaim rocked her, whispering, "Shh, now. Shh."

"God blessed us when you went back for the egg," she said as her weeping abated.

Chaim nodded. "God has blessed us many times. When I was in prison, I prepared to die. Guards were rounding up the Czar's family and the servants, and I knew that I, too, would be executed that night. I'd resigned myself to never seeing you again. Then, God sent an angel to me. I felt this presence fill me, telling me to give away the egg. The egg had gotten me into trouble, and the egg would get me out of it. This angel told me secrets about the guard, so I would know how to convince him to free me. Suddenly, I knew I could escape." He kissed her cheek, his eyes wet and soft. "I wanted nothing more than to see your sweet face."

"Hunh," she grunted. "Sweet like an onion."

He laughed, shaking his head, his eyes narrowing to slits. "That's better. That's my Hadassah. Oh, how I've missed my Hadassah." He squeezed her.

She laughed, too.

The old mare groaned and pawed at the ground. The sun stood high in the sky to warm them as they sat in silence, thinking of the dead they'd leave behind. Chaim chanted the *Kaddish*. He removed his watch from his vest pocket and pressed the pushpin. "Time to start over," he said. He kissed the watch and replaced it, patting it gently into place. Then, he collected the reins, snapping them to urge the broken-down horse forward.

"What do we do now?" Hadassah asked.

"We join Pincus in America. You'll bake *rugalach*. I'll teach. We'll make our way."

"We'll have money from the eggs."

"Maybe. If the family makes it. If they follow through with their promise. Maybe not. It's in God's hands."

Yes, God would provide, she thought as she jostled on the seat. What did it matter? They were together. Hadassah thought about Leja's cute family. Faigie, Jossel, and adorable little Sara. She prayed with all her might they would enjoy a good life. Just a day ago, Hadassah would have cursed them, she would have haunted them from her grave if they didn't deliver the eggs.

Now, she simply prayed for their safety. She envisioned little Sara as an old woman, happy and light, surrounded by great-grandchildren. Oh, she wanted little Sara to be blessed.

Once they reunited, they'd tell each other stories about their contented lives. Their families would be friends and allies.

"There's something else we will do in America," Hadassah said.

"Yes?" "You will teach me to read."

Chaim looked at her in surprise. He nodded, again fixing his eyes on the road. "We'll start tonight."

The horse picked up her pace, perhaps sensing a cool stream with green banks up ahead. A good watering. Grass to eat.

The old mare had some fight left in her, after all. She trotted at a brisk pace, head high, hurrying toward the prospect of nourishment.

Onward, hoof by hoof.

One foot in front of the other.

Toward life.

Chapter Fourteen

Noah had felt a g-force vacuum him up and up, compressing and incinerating his body like a lump of coal transmuting to a diamond. Then, a bone-shaking burst hurled him like a cannon shot, transforming him into ice, dust and fire.

All the while, he heard drumming—Fleck's steady boom, boom—and his mother's faint voice urging him home.

Finally, he rammed into something hard and shockingly cold. Total blackness.

Eight repeating measures of a Russian lullaby floated from Chaim's pocket watch and echoed in Noah's ears. His brain seemed a dizzying jumble, his nerve endings felt ablaze. He must have crash landed somewhere next to Chaim. The force that had pulled him had dumped him back onto the muddy road to Ekaterinburg. Good. Another chance to finish his mission.

Only, this world felt different. His back felt stiff. His neck muscles knotted into a kink. He wiggled his toes to life.

He perceived Jean-Paul kneeling next to him, patting him, and waving his wand.

"Wow, kid, what a ride." Noah heard John Woods' voice. "Wish you could've seen it."

A shower of cold and wet burned Noah's skin.

"Noah, can you hear me?" Bernard asked.

Noah felt as frozen as a fish packed in ice, and his teeth clacked like loose-fitting dentures. "Barter with the wagon driver," he groaned. "Don't give away your watch."

"What? Noah, you okay?" Bernard poked him in the shoulder. "Can you move?"

"Wake up, *bubala*," Great-Grandma Sara cooed. "There's work to do."

Okay, okay. Noah opened one eye. Blinding light. Crap, he'd be slammed with an epic headache. Bernard and Woods peered over him with worried expressions. Noah opened the other eye.

The sky had cleared to robin's egg blue. The sun was thawing the snow on the trees. Water dripped from their boughs, making splooshing sounds as trickles hit the drifts.

Hadassah's storm had ended. Perhaps he'd fulfilled his mission to her satisfaction, after all. Or, had she simply spent her venom?

The sound of Chaim's watch drifting from Bernard's pocket seemed oddly out of place.

"You look confused," Bernard said. "I'm sure it'll take a while to come 'round."

"The music..." Noah said dreamily.

"My watch won't shut up. You want to see?" Bernard pulled off his mittens and unzipped his ski jacket pocket. He pulled out a gold timepiece; a diamond Star of David surrounded by six falling comets adorned the flip cover. Bernard displayed Chaim's watch like a magician who'd performed some kind of time-travel trick where the watch landed in Bernard's possession.

"Where'd you get that?" Noah asked, his voice stronger.

"I inherited it from my great-great uncle."

Noah jolted awake. "Your ancestor is Chaim?"

"Chaim Goldberg." Bernard looked puzzled. "I don't remember telling you his name."

"Here, kid." Woods piled Noah's clothes next to him. "Your fire's out. Better put these on before you freeze to death. Besides..." He cocked his head in the direction where Sally stood huddled with Jean-Paul. "Your mom's anxious."

Noah freed his arms from under the snow and scooted into a sitting position. A scarlet, crescent-shaped burn on his left bicep, about the size of a silver dollar, had already begun to scab. Noah examined the wound, the shape oddly reminiscent of the falling comet design on the gold watch. He hoped it would scar into a permanent remembrance of his initiation. His arms and chest were singed, but those marks would fade and be forgotten.

He pulled a t-shirt and sweater over his head, stepped into jeans, and slipped on a jacket. "Tell me," he said to Bernard. "How did Chaim die?"

"In his sleep. He lived to a ripe old age."

"Alone?"

"No. His wife, Hadassah, sat by his side."

Holy Einstein, Noah marveled. The universe held

such mysteries. He smiled, his muscles warming with contentment. He'd traveled to another dimension where time had warped, and he, Noah Friedman, had played an integral part in changing past and current events.

He'd found Chaim for Hadassah, hopefully removing his family's curse and gaining Hadassah's support to help Jean-Paul's people.

He shook free of the remnants of Hadassah's wrath. He felt lighter. The throbbing in his head dissipated. Every atom in his body danced with the knowledge that he could do or be anything. He remembered who he was meant to be: an energetic life force, a conduit for cosmic order, an enabler of synchronicities. Simple. Thrilling.

Noah stood and waved to Sally, who looked as if she, too, had experienced an ordeal. She'd pulled off her ski cap, and her damp hair stuck out in copper clumps. Her eyes were puffy and red, and black mascara painted her cheeks. She must have injured herself, because she favored her left foot and peg legged toward him. Unstoppable.

Noah closed the gap. He put his arms around her, and she let him support her. "I heard you calling to me," he said. "Thanks, Mom."

She smiled up at him. "Next time I call you, come running." She punched his arm hard, "You hear me?"

"Look." Jean-Paul called, rushing to them with ease through slushy snow. "Your ghost has gathered the Ancestors." He pointed behind Noah.

Sally gasped and pulled back. "Oh, my God. I see them. What's happening?"

Noah pivoted, shielding his eyes, and squinting to focus in the dazzling sunshine.

A sea of souls stretched before him like painted figures on a giant canvas. They covered the hillocks in the near distance, where green grass was starting to show through the snow. Many had taken station in the nearby trees, standing or sitting on limbs. It was impossible to tell how many were there. Hundreds at least. Between them they cast a flickering luminescence, different colors snapping like Zippo flames at a rock concert, then turning to mist of faded hues. They were as visible in the afternoon glare as stars in the night sky.

Ancestors of every age, race, and era appeared in the shimmering husks of their former bodies. Tall men wore traditional African headdress and beaded necklaces of red, yellow, and white. They carried spears adorned with animal talismans. These Ancestors joined the souls of Jean-Paul's villagers, who'd died of AIDS after taking Duschene's drugs in vain. The warriors stood shoulder-to-shoulder with their descendants whose thin, faces were pocked with sores.

Taking in the richness of the Ancestors presenting themselves to him, Noah realized his mind connected to these spirits with no exchange of words. He understood their stories and their bond to the living. Flashes from their past washed through him at the speed of rapid eye movements. He relived highlights of their history, feeling their sadness and fear, experiencing their joy.

The souls of Yompola villagers, who'd perished in the pogrom, rocked and chanted together in small groups at the edge of the parking lot. The women were wearing *babushkas* and the men, beaver hats.

Nineteen souls who'd been poisoned by Duschene drugs shipped from China hovered on the horizon, murky vapors of yellowish-gray. Men, women and children, from babies to grandparents.

A fifties-era housewife with big hair and wearing a blue shift, apron, and pearls, was an Ancestor of a woman who'd been violated by Charles Dalton III. She was huddled with another victim, a young, weeping woman, who'd committed suicide after Dalton defiled and then fired her.

Noah struggled to withstand this tsunami of awareness. The sensory overload took his breath away. He felt dizzy. His head throbbed. He closed his eyes, blocking visual images. He covered his ears, shutting out the sounds of nature—birdcalls, the rustle of leaves, the flap of wings. He breathed in their spirit, allowing their stories to anoint him.

Some souls yearned to be honored. No one had grieved their deaths or spoken their name in remembrance. "We have lessons to teach. Learn from us. We can guide those in power." All had been drawn here out of love for their descendants.

Chaim appeared, his eyes crinkled to slits, his dark beard and hair neatly trimmed beneath his tall, round hat. Hadassah stood beside him. She looked decades younger, a woman in her thirties. Her babushka hung loose around her shoulders, revealing a thick braid of shiny black hair. Her empty eyes were gone, and she beamed loving energy that caused Noah to tingle.

She held hands with a copper-haired, girl with eyes of cobalt blue, no more than eight years old. Noah recognized her, laughing with happiness at the sight of this child, his Great-Grandma Sara.

Holy Einstein, how blessed he felt to be aware of these Ancestors. But what did they want? Did they all have individual missions for him to perform? This thought humbled and terrified him. It had taken enormous energy to find Chaim, and the whole purpose of his journey still loomed ahead. Three priorities: expose Dalton's crimes, get help for Jean-Paul's people, and stop the sale of Selexikote.

He faced Jean-Paul. "Why are they here?"

"You are a shaman now. Ask."

Noah sighed. He shut his eyes, listening to the beating of his heart. It thumped wildly. It wanted to escape. Flee from all responsibility. He pressed his hands to his chest, sending calming energy. His heart slowed. Lub-dub. Lub-dub.

Then, he knew. The Ancestors yearned to heal the world one corrupt place at a time. They would start here.

A message thundered from the sky. It echoed from the hills and ricocheted off the trees. The ground vibrated. The Ancestors shouted, "We're here to help."

"What do I do?" Noah asked.

"When the call to arms comes, you will know where your sword is," said Jean-Paul.

Noah opened his eyes. The pines danced in the warm breeze. A flock of robins circled overhead. Most of the Ancestors were gone.

Jean-Paul placed a hand on his shoulder. "Are you ready, my brother?"

Noah raised his fist in solidarity.

Jean-Paul raised his and the two men stood together, ready for a fight.

The August heat had returned. The group of six shed their jackets, ski pants and boots, stripping down to their jeans and t-shirts. They piled the clothes into a mountain of fleece and Gore-Tex.

Noah studied his corporeal troop of foot soldiers during this silent ritual, grateful for the synchronicities that bound them. Each had a special gift to deliver for this mission. Noah vowed not to let them down.

Sally caught his eye. They both smiled. In jeans, a tee, and with no make-up, she looked like a teenager. Bernard had placed a protective arm around her, and she leaned into him. Apparently reeling from her paranormal ability to see spirits, she stood speechless. A reaction Noah had never witnessed.

"Let's get into Duschene's building before the board leaves," he said.

Fleck pointed to the pile of gear. "What should we do with this stuff?"

Noah surveyed the area they'd used for his initiation. Smoke tendrils rose from the fire pit they'd lined with logs. Jean-Paul's sacred zebra hide and the _kuor_ lay on the grass. Noah looked to Jean-Paul for direction, but he stared back in silence, his arms folded over his chest.

"Spirits will protect the space," Noah said. "Later, we'll fill in the fire pit and gather everything. Follow me." Noah cut through the trees and marched down the hill, a natural leader steering the group out of the woodlands to the office park. Some souls still present floated close behind—a swat team rising from the dust to say no to injustice.

The snow had melted. Their shoes sank into patches of mud where the summer sun had scorched the grass. Streams of water ran downhill and pooled in the asphalt parking lot packed with cars. Chunks of snow evaporated off their steaming hoods.

They arrived in front of the glass entrance to Duschene Headquarters. Noah stood on the serpentine path, his arms outstretched, his palms turned toward the sky. He closed his eyes, focusing his energy to receive messages from the Ancestors.

The call to arms had come.

Prepared for battle, Noah and his patchwork band of followers—and mother—marched through the glass entry doors of Duschene's headquarters. Fleck's camcorder swung from his neck; Bernard wielded a briefcase.

Noah heard a flap of wings, felt something soft brush by him. A flock of chirping robins, a dozen or so, soared to the top of the lobby atrium.

The security guard who'd blown the whistle on Noah that morning sat behind the front desk, his stuffed cheeks working on a bagel. He stared up at the birds. "What the fuck," he mumbled through the dough. A large white plop splooshed onto his forehead. He groused, still chewing, and mopped himself with a napkin. He made eye contact with Noah and his brow creased. "Naked man." He shook his cream-cheesed finger. "Nunh hunh. Can't come in here."

Crap. Noah had hoped to gain access to the boardroom before creating a scene. He felt a firm grip on his shoulder.

"I'll handle this," Woods whispered in his ear. "Get going."

Noah feigned nonchalance, ignoring his pounding heart. Walk, don't run. Go slow to go fast. He forced his body to obey.

Woods ran over to the desk, flashing his F.A.A. badge to the guard. "We're here on a matter of Homeland Security. It's your patriotic duty to admit us."

"What? Who're you?"

A purplish, hazy spirit stood sentry at an open elevator, motioning the group toward it.

Woods talked up the guard, while the others strolled into the elevator. Noah pushed the button for the sixteenth floor. He blew out his breath. At the last minute, the robins flew between the doors and hovered at the ceiling.

The misty soul floated off as the bronzed doors clamped shut. The cab rose. A string intro and Louis Armstrong's gravelly voice filled the padded space. *And I think to myself, what a wonderful world.*

Sally laughed nervously.

Fleck and Bernard joined in.

"I do not understand this humor," Jean-Paul said, straight-faced.

"Cultural differences." Fleck clapped the shaman on the back. "Most jokes don't translate."

The elevator jolted to a stop. Noah's stomach lurched. Ding. Sixteenth floor.

Show time.

Noah crouched toward the rear of the group, shielding his face. The birds fluttered around him, hiding him from view. He couldn't chance the blonde receptionis recognizing him. As he prepared to leave the elevator he saw two Watusi spirits, impossibly tall, wearing feathered headdresses, beads and carrying spears standing sentinel at each side of the elevator door.

"Welcome back, Ms. Friedman," Blondie bubbled. "Mr. Dalton and the executive committee are behind closed doors."

"Thank you, Gretchen."

"Oh, Mr. Goldberg." Gretchen wrinkled her nose. "Sorry, but you're not allowed to go—

"He's expecting us," Bernard cut in.

Suddenly, the 1950s lady spirit and her weepy counterpart appeared on either side of Gretchen. Both souls placed their hands on her shoulders.

"Totally." Gretchen smiled. Dazzling teeth.

They were in.

Sweat trickled down Noah's forehead. His t-shirt clung to his chest and armpits. Holy Einstein, would he never run out of juice? Three days of constant stress, but his sweat glands kept soldiering on, commanded by the audacity of his stalwart hypothalamus.

He was flanked by the Watusi, Fleck, and Jean-Paul

as Bernard and Sally led the group through the board-room doors. She limped slightly, leaning on Bernard for support.

Dalton sat at the end of the conference table. Baller with a baditude. He looked as though he'd freshly showered. Not a bead of sweat, the lucky bastard. Perfect hair. Starched blue pin stripes matched his tie. The smell of his over-zealous cologne—the fragrance of av-arice—wafted across the room. His jaw sliced the air as he tilted his head to inspect the interlopers.

Ten board members remained. An embossed leather tent-sign stood on the conference table, announcing, "Executive Session," as if they needed to be reminded. In the center of the maroon granite slab rested open wine bottles, a decanter, stemmed crystal, and a silver tray piled high with cheese and shrimp.

"Sally, you've returned," Dalton said in a snide voice. "You must have sniffed cocktails."

Her cheeks grew pink.

His lips curled into a thin line. "Looks like you've had a tough day. What happened to you?"

She ran a hand through her hair, then stopped mid-action. "Don't bother to fake concern when we both know what you're really like." She straightened her shoulders. "We have unfinished business."

"Au contraire. In your absence, the purchase of Selex-ikote was approved. Congrats. You're ten million richer."

Noah's stomach tightened. "It's not for sale."

Dalton glanced at Noah with a puzzled look, then shifted his gaze to a piece of lint on his trousers. "I see the prodigal son has returned." He flicked the speck off with thumb and forefinger. "You're dressed. Right out of 'GQ.' Where's DeMarko?"

Probably hooked up to a respirator, Noah imagined. "He's a little choked up at the moment." Noah swallowed hard. "Sends his regrets."

Dalton stared blankly. His eyes narrowed, almost imperceptibly for a brief flicker before he caught himself. "Bernard, what are you doing here?"

"Something I should have done a long time ago," Bernard said. "Getting you fired."

Dalton glanced at his cronies around the table and laughed. They joined in one by one, their laughter building to a crescendo. "Come, Bernard, that's no way to treat an old friend."

"A corrupt heart has no room for friends," Jean-Paul said.

Dalton shifted his gaze up. "You are?"

"Jean-Paul Amon. You supply Telaxiphentol to many people I love. Many who have died because of you."

"Now, just a minute." One of the board members, bald as a hairless terrier, stood. "Telaxiphentol is the most effective HIV drug on—"

Bernard interrupted. "Dalton's diluting the formula for certain markets," He placed his briefcase on the table, opened it, and pulled out a thick file. "Padding his personal pocket with the difference. It's all documented."

Dalton said, "Do you honestly think the board will listen to a murderer? I've got a file on you, too."

"Do you deny this allegation?" Fleck blurted, feverishly scribbling on a note pad.

"Who's the little shit with the camcorder? Is that

on? Get out of here. All of you." Dalton glided over to the wall phone and lifted the receiver. "Frank, we've got a problem in the board room. Homeland Secur...? The White House?" His jaw clamped. "Listen to me, you idiot. I'll have your ass on the street before you can say Krispy Kreme. Get up here. Now."

Noah slowly looked around the room and took a stand. First he relaxed, slightly shaking out his arms and stretching his legs. Then his back stiffened and he clenched his hands, readying for an all-out brawl. His bruises from the morning melee smarted. His flesh pulsed where fingernails had dug in. Remembering how he'd been tossed into the ambulance, a fresh wave of anger rushed through him, hardening his resolve, and he chomped at his bit to expose the true essence of this snake Dalton. There were six of them hell-bent to see justice. Six of them, plus an army of Ancestors.

The Watusi warriors stamped their spears. Noah looked up. They shook their heads. "Do not battle with monsters, lest you become one," they seemed to caution. The phrase the Ancestors had chanted earlier, repeated in Noah's mind. "Let us guide those in places of power." He hadn't understood its meaning. Now... what if...?

He pictured what might happen with a board controlled by people passionate to do the right thing. Help would arrive with the stroke of a pen. Instantly, money would flow to Jean-Paul's village. The Selexikote agreement would dissolve in a New York minute. Would it be possible to win without a fight?

Dalton deserved prison and worse, but that would

entail a drawn-out court case, years in the making. Duschene employed legions of lawyers. For every document Bernard produced, they would fabricate ten, evidencing Dalton's squeaky-clean record and pointing the finger at Bernard. Meanwhile, Jean-Paul's people would wait.

Switch gears. Don't seek revenge.

Taking deep breaths, Noah stilled himself. He closed his eyes, and stretched his arms out and up, palms exposed. His pulse slowed. His sweat glands stopped pumping.

He pictured the fifties-era housewife-spirit and her weepy counterpart floating through Duschene's beehive of cubicles, whispering to the employees, "You have a voice. The board will listen." The employees rise up. They resolve to no longer endure harassment or humiliation.

He pictured the spirits lost in the Yompola pogrom delivering messages one by one to the board members. Their confusion is erased. The truth surfaces. Bernard is a good man, wrongly accused, the board would conclude, and Dalton must be dismissed.

"Sally, what the hell is wrong with your son?" Dalton bellowed.

Noah blocked the volley, dismissing the negativity. He turned a deaf ear to the ensuing buzz of room chatter. The small flock of robins somehow found their way into the room and silently settled themselves on his shoulders and arms.

His energy ballooned, expanding up and out, gliding through the building and across town. At the same time he bridged oceans and traversed continents, gathering souls, drifting with the Ancestors.

He pictured the spirits of victims around the world, and in past times.

Finally, Noah was ready to step into the minds of the board members and drill deep into their psyches. Thoughts would reemerge as the board's fervent conviction. *Ah. We must use our power to help the world.*

"Sally, what is wrong with your son?" Dalton demanded again. "Does he think this is a carnival?'

Sally quelled her desire to leap across the table and knee Dalton in the groin. Stay calm. Professional. He'll get his later.

"There's nothing wrong with my son," she said in a steady voice. "We're here to tell the board what's wrong with you."

Outside the room, noise grew, until the clamor of many boomed and the chestnut doors shot open as twenty or so angry people marched into the room. Employees.

A mini-skirted woman in her thirties flashed a heated look toward Dalton. "Enough is enough."

A paunchy, middle-aged man pushed his way forward through the group. "Where's the chairman?"

Grumbling swelled up from those seated around the conference table. "This is highly unusual." An astonished-looking man with salt and pepper-hair rose slowly. Removing his glasses, he studied the crowd. "Here I am. Peter Everett."

A slight man with a spiked-do stammered. "We're filing a formal complaint of toxic work environment," he said.

"I get queasy when I think of coming here," another man—pocket protector, wire rims—spoke up.

Dalton smiled at Everett. "Disgruntled employees are the bane of all corporations. Especially slackers."

A sloe-eyed brunette pointed at Dalton. "Sexual harassment."

He shook his head. "I don't know this woman."

"Charles, what's going on?" Everett frowned.

"It's about money." Dalton strolled over to Everett. "It always is."

"Rapist." A redhead, shoulder-length bob, pushed forward through the crowd. "Said he'd fire me if I spoke up."

"He promised me a promotion." Chunky blonde, dark highlights.

Fleck rotated the camcorder. "Can you give me dates? Specifics?"

The board members yammered, leaning toward one another in groups of two or three.

"Lies." Dalton held his ground, a stony faced, consummate con artist. No trace of tension or embarrassment marred his chiseled, botoxed features.

Sally needed to ensure Dalton never harmed anyone else. Ever. She braced herself. He'd humiliate her in front of everyone, call her a whore and make it clear she was the one who threw herself on him. Bernard would defend her now, but he would have second thoughts a few weeks or months down the road. She hated for Noah to hear the sordid story. The thought of disappointing them both knotted her stomach, but she pushed through it. "They're telling the truth." Sally limped closer to Everett. "He raped me, too." Sally removed the scarf from her neck and raised her chin, so the board could get a better look at her bruises. "And he choked me."

Hushed whispers rose from the table. Someone laughed.

"Do you think that is funny?" Jean-Paul asked the man, who shrank back in his chair.

Bernard pressed her arm. "Sally, you don't have to do this."

"Bernard, yes I do."

Dalton shot her a demeaning look. "She's framing me. She's slept with everyone she's ever done business with."

"You son of a bitch." Bernard raised a fist and lunged at Dalton.

Jean-Paul caught him, pulling him back. "Patience, my friend," he whispered. "Let Noah handle this. It is happening." He pointed. "Look."

Noah stood on the opposite side of the room. His arms were outstretched, birds still perched on them. His chest lifted as his back arched. He looked transcendent, as though he'd stepped through a portal from another, more peaceful world. His only movements were the twitching of his closed eyelids and the rise and fall of his chest. Almost imperceptible, but Sally saw. He appeared to glow from below, from above, from within, as though encircled by an aura of radiant light.

Sally's throat tightened. Her heart swelled at her realization that, somehow, her son had summoned this group into the boardroom. He'd avenge her. Her son, the shaman.

Noah's torso arched forward, his outstretched arms like wings. An unseen force jerked him fully upright for a moment, then thrust him forward again. The birds scattered and rose to the ceiling.

Everett nodded. "Perhaps we shouldn't listen to Dalton," he addressed the board. "I don't trust him."

"What are you talking about, Peter?" Dalton's face flushed.

Fog seeped in through the conference room windows, crawling up the walls, growing to a thick cloud of silver haze that clung to the ceiling. Then, it separated into smaller billows, spirits drifting over the board members' heads. The fog slipped down, misty tendrils encircling, then meshing into the men. One of the spirits whispered in Everett's ear. Noah spoke simultaneously, making it appear as though the spirit lip-synched to his words.

"To see and listen to the wicked is already the beginning of wickedness," Noah said, the pitch of his voice raised an octave.

"Peter, I've made you a wealthy man. I've got your support, right? Dalton's sense of ease was beginning to crack.

"Mama, is that you?" Everett sat down. His expression softened.

"Yes, my son," Noah's voice lilted high and sweet. "You hung my painting over the fireplace. I noticed. Please, I'm trusting you to do the right thing."

Everett nodded. "We should fire Dalton."

"What did you just say?" Dalton's face tightened

with unconcealed rage.

A gentleman wearing a bow tie laughed. "Dad? Dad?"

"I'm here," Noah's tone deepened to a rich timbre. "I watch you read to Connor every night. You have an opportunity to make me proud."

"Perhaps you're right, Peter," Bow Tie said.

"Have you all gone crazy?" Dalton banged his fist on the table.

"Helen, I've missed you so much," a man cried out, wiping his eyes and nose with his jacket sleeve.

"Darling, marry Doris. She's nice. Be happy." Noah's face glowed. "Help others."

Every board member sat transfixed in their respective sense of blessing from communicating with their own Ancestors. Some grinned. Others wept, cradling their moist cheeks with both hands.

The fog spirits floated off.

A band of thin and swollen-bellied souls materialized along the windows and took up stations behind the board members, placing their hands on the men's shoulders.

"Help my brothers," Noah said in an otherworldly voice. "No one should suffer when you hold the solution."

"What is keeping security?" Dalton raced to the wall phone and lifted it. "Frank? Frank? God damn it." He slammed the receiver against the wall. It cracked, launching splinters of plastic into the air.

Peter Everett banged his gavel on the granite. "I make a motion to fire Charles Dalton, III."

"You can't be serious." Dalton raced back to the

conference table.

"I second it." Stout Man shouted.

"All those in favor?" Everett asked.

"I made a lot of money for you bastards." Dalton shook his fist.

"Aye," chorused from the table.

A Yompola spirit appeared behind Everett, whispering in his ear, his lips matching the cadence of Noah's words. "Bernard is a good man." Torso and back arch. "I propose we hire Bernard Goldberg to be president," Everett said.

"You've gone nuts, all of you." Dalton's face contorted as he looked from man to man.

Loud discussions sounded at the table.

"I'll second it."

A choir of aye's.

"I have friends in high places." Dalton pounded the granite. "Senator Rupert. Congressman Sinclair."

"Bernard, will you accept the position?" Everett asked.

"On certain conditions," Bernard said. "I want three hospitals built in Africa. I want clinics and free drugs supplied for the next decade."

"You're making a huge mistake." Dalton jabbed a finger at Everett. "I'll have you tied up in court for years."

"Doctors and nurses to train my people," Jean-Paul said.

Bernard nodded. "A teaching hospital."

"I'll take every dollar of business with me." Dalton jumped up and down like a toddler.

"You have my word," Everett banged his gavel.

"Bernard," Sally said. "Don't forget Selexikote."
"I want the Selexikote purchase canceled with no penalties. That drug should never see the light of day."

"Aye. Aye. Aye."

Dalton screamed and catapulted himself on top of Bernard. The two fell to the ground. Jean-Paul stood over Dalton, easily pinning his arms and pulling him onto his back.

Frank, the security guard, burst into the room. "I'm here, Mr. Dalton."

Woods barreled through the door behind him, tackling Frank by the legs. Both men went sprawling.

An impeccably dressed spirit, wearing a thirties-style suit and suspenders, materialized out of thin air in front of Dalton.

"Stop it, Charles." Noah's voice boomed in a deep timbre, reverberating off the walls.

Dalton stopped twitching. "Grandpa?"

"You've embarrassed the family. You've sullied my name."

"I did what the others didn't have the nerve to do. I earned huge profits."

Jean-Paul released Dalton and helped Bernard to his feet.

Suddenly, the spirit flew over the table and jumped inside of Dalton, who flopped onto his back, looking dazed.

"Want to make a full confession, Mr. Dalton?" Fleck moved in with his microphone.

"What?" Dalton stammered, climbing to his feet.

"Do you have a statement?" Fleck thrust the mic in Dalton's face.

Dalton shoved him aside. "I deserve a huge bonus," he muttered, his voice sounding weak.

"No, Charles. Enough." Noah shouted.

Dalton staggered. "I....I don't feel well. I've got to lie down." He ran through the doors and out into the hall.

Fleck pursued him, aiming his microphone like a sword of justice.

The chestnut doors swung shut.

The sun dipped toward the horizon, softening the sky to a powder blue haze and filling the woodlands behind Duschene International Headquarters with a tranquil glow. Pine tree branches swayed in the light breeze, casting dancing shadows of violet against the grassy floor.

Noah edged his shovel into a mound of damp earth. He lifted a blade full, arced it over to the smoldering fire pit, and tilted the loam to refill the hole he'd excavated earlier in the day. Secret scents of the primeval forest released into the air—the mossy odor of plant roots, fungus, and bacteria. He breathed in, catching the molecules and tethering himself once more to solid ground.

Fleck and Jean-Paul carried rocks and logs to their pre-ritual locations. Sally removed twigs and collected items—a mitten, a pair of goggles, a wool hat—to add to the pile of jackets, pants and boots. She hitched along, using a ski pole for support like a gondolier. She'd insisted on helping to restore this sacred space.

Noah dumped another shovelful onto the smoky heap and tamped it. He stopped, eyeing a worm struggling to escape the blade. Bending down, he offered his finger. When the annelid climbed on board, he lowered it a few yards away onto terra firma. He watched it wriggle toward the shade in pursuit of its destiny. Go forward and die, little dude. Anything is possible.

He felt a deep peacefulness settle into him. Bone tired. Burned out. Barely any sleep in over three days, but he didn't care.

Hadassah had been reunited with Chaim. Bernard's good name had been restored. The Selexikote deal was dead. Jean-Paul's people would receive help. Fleck had gotten his story.

Life held such delicious promise. Some purpose greater than completing his research loomed ahead. He didn't know what, but he'd be open to whatever synchronicities came his way.

Sally snuck up behind him, carrying a pile of folded skiwear. "I'm headed back to the hotel."

He turned toward her. "I won't be much longer. Dinner about eight?"

She nodded. "Bernard should be done with the board by then. Woods is bringing his wife. I'll make a reservation for seven of us."

Noah noticed how much younger her face appeared. "It was a good day," he said.

"The best. We've got a lot to celebrate." She smiled, and yes, she definitely looked years younger. Stress was missing, that was it. Not a line on her face.

"When are you going home?" Noah asked.

She shrugged, shifting her eyes toward the trees.

"Might hang around Minneapolis for a few days."

"Mom?"

"Yeah?"

"I like him."

Her cheeks glowed pink. She met his gaze. "I'm going to take things slow this time."

"Sure."

"I mean it. I've been thinking a lot about what you said to me."

"What do you mean?"

"When you came to the office to ask me for a job. You said you weren't the only one who needed to be grounded."

"I shouldn't have said that. Sorry."

"No, I'm sorry. You were right to say I haven't been grounded. I've made poor and impulsive personal choices. Over and over again. I have a bad history, and it nearly cost me my son. But I can change. Awareness, right? Your theory that 'awareness is the fifth dimension?' Maybe it starts with self-awareness. For me, maybe it starts with taking stock of who I am and being more responsible."

Noah smiled. "I love that, Mom."

Her eyes glistened. "And I love you. You amazed me today."

"We make a pretty good team."

"Agreed." Sally ruffled Noah's hair and sighed. "So, I'm glad you like Bernard, but it's complicated. We'd have to do a lot of schlepping back and forth."

"No, it's simple."

"You think? He wants me to meet someone who might be interested in buying Friedman Pharmaceutical."

"You'd be free to leave St. Louis."

"A plan worth considering." She reached up again to brush his cheek. "How 'bout I buy you a plane ticket home. Fleck can drive his car."

"Actually, I want to drive back."

"You hate driving. And you don't have a driver's license. Getting here without a ticket was damn lucky."

He shrugged. "I left some unfinished business along the way."

"What?" She looked at him questioningly, searching his eyes.

His face burned. Crap.

"I see." Sally smiled wide. "I hope she knows how lucky she is."

"I'll drive slowly——"

She raised her hand to stop him. "You'll be fine. The Ancestors will watch over you."

Jean-Paul and Fleck walked over, cradling the rest of the clothes.

"We will carry everything to the car," Jean-Paul said. "Are you ready, Sally?"

"I'll take those," Fleck said, accepting the pile from her.

"You want help?" Noah asked the shaman. "I'll carry the *kour* and the zebra hide."

"Leave them for now. Finish covering the pit," Jean-Paul said. "We will return with salt for the ending ritual. I must find some."

"Salt?" Fleck asked.

"To close the space. We opened portals, and we must close them so spirits do not arrive uninvited. I will teach you."

"Cool," Fleck said. "I'll nab salt from the employee cafeteria."

"You are always thinking." Jean-Paul placed his hand on Fleck's shoulder. "I have noticed this about you."

"Really?" Fleck grinned. "Thanks, JP."

Sally kissed Noah on the cheek. "See you later, Sweetie."

"Later."

He rested against his shovel and watched the three cross the greenbelt until they made a turn through a small gap in the trees. The sun sank below the top of the pines, painting the needles with an orange tinge.

Something moved in the distance, unsettling him. Perhaps a wayward spirit lurked in the forest. He turned three-sixty. Nothing. Just the breeze. The trees swayed with renewed rhythm.

He edged the blade into the dirt. Suddenly, a wave of exhaustion swept through him, shutting him down. Communing with spirits had drained him. He'd rest just for a moment. He closed his eyes, imagining the steak he'd eat for dinner. Thirty-two-ounce T-bone dripping with juice. He'd break his moral-environmental resolve to eat vegan. Just this once. Next week, he'd start fresh. Tonight, baked potato, sour cream, all the extras. Hot fudge sundae. Screw his resolution to avoid Diglycerides as well. His body lusted for comfort food.

Then, he'd sleep like a tree sloth. Twelve dreamless hours of uninterrupted REM cycles. He'd hang the "Do Not Disturb" sign on the room door and curl up unconscious until he woke on his own.

Then, he'd ease the car onto the Avenue of the Saints and find his way back to Crystal. He'd apologize, explain what happened as best he could, and hope she'd forgive him. He dreamed of lifting a wayward strand of flaxen hair off her face, and kissing her pouty lips. Softly. Gently.

Something hard poked Noah in the back. He dropped the shovel, startling awake. A rod poked his ribs again.

"Put your hands in the air."

Fear spiked Noah's senses to full alert. The funky smell of Selexikote punched up his nostrils. He raised his arms.

"Turn around slowly," Roger DeMarko wheezed.

Stay calm, Noah told himself, but his heart jumped like a pogo stick. He turned to face his doctor.

DeMarko's handgun shook, but pointed straight at him. "Well, if it isn't the Master of the Universe." His face glistened with sweat. Streaks of ash smudged his cheeks. Fire had singed his eyebrows and moustache. Burn holes frayed his shirt collar.

Noah's heart thwacked against its tight prison. "Hey, Roger, glad to see you're feeling better."

"You couldn't leave well enough alone." DeMarko coughed, but managed to train the gun. "You had to stick your nose into my business."

Despite Noah's fear, sadness welled in him. He remembered, back in the day, when DeMarko still had good intentions. Maybe it wasn't too late to talk some sense into him. "This isn't like you, Roger. The drug's altered your brain chemistry."

"Shut up." His breath escaped in puffs.

Noah's hands tremored. Go slow to go fast. He took a breath. "I've been thinking. You're suffering from Selexikote side effects. It works like Ritalin. Ritalin users who aren't ADD, develop the traits of ADD."

"I've been thinking, too." He pressed the gun to Noah's temple. "I wonder. When I blow your brains out, will I be able to count the extra cells?" He withdrew the gun and stepped back, pretending to shoot, making a guttural, exploding sound in the back of his throat. He laughed wheezily. "You think you're so smart. I've got the gun. Who's smarter now, dumb ass?"

"Listen to me." Noah forced himself to sound calm. "The drug's had a reverse effect on you. It kept me balanced, but it made you delusional. It doesn't have to be this way." He inched toward DeMarko.

"Yes, it does. You've ruined everything. Do you know what I could have done with ten million dollars?"

"Roger, put the gun down." Another step closer. "We'll get help. You'll get well."

"Stay back. I'm going to enjoy killing you. Then I'll go after your mother."

Jesus. Too late. Too far gone. Roger had fallen victim to the drug. Noah stretched out his hand. "Please, Roger, give me the gun."

"Give me ten million dollars, and the gun is yours. You got that kind of cash?"

"Noah," Jean-Paul called from the opposite end of the greenbelt. "Everything all right?"

"Pity. I'll have to start with your friends." DeMarko cocked the weapon. He pivoted and moved toward them, aiming at Jean-Paul and Fleck like they were arcade ducks.

Noah launched into the air. "Jean-Paul, Fleck, get down." He grabbed for the steel. He met the barrel mid-air, yanking it downward. The gun blast reverberated in his ears.

He fell, pulling DeMarko with him.

Noah's anger geysered, blocking all other feeling. A tangle of arms and legs. He scrambled blindly in the grass to find the gun. An anguished scream escaped his lips. "Jean-Paul? Fleck?" His ears rang. "Answer me." He couldn't feel his legs. DeMarko gagged and coughed. Noah punched toward the sound, one hand searching for the gun, the other targeting DeMarko's throat.

Noah prayed he'd blocked the bullet from reaching his friends. If it was his destiny to accomplish anything, ever, please, please let it be this.

DeMarko choked, hacked, but he kept kicking. Noah jabbed, smashed, aiming for the throat until he'd hear a gurgle.

Someone banged the *kuor*.

"Fleck?" Noah looked up.

A smoke spirit sat at the ritual drum, thudding a steady beat. Another one appeared, torso and limbs of thick charcoal fumes, and hefted a dazed DeMarko to his feet. It opened its mouth as wide as DeMarko's head and roared. The sound rumbled the trees. The ground trembled. Birds lifted off their branches, escaping toward an ice-blue moon. Pine needles shook free, raining around them.

DeMarko howled like a feral cat.

The drum beat faster.

The smoke spirit jumped into DeMarko, smoke billowing out of his ears, eyes, and mouth. His legs started to pump. DeMarko pulled at his lower limbs as if to stay them, but the spirit won control and ran DeMarko toward the animal skin.

Two smoke spirits held it aloft. Green ooze dripped out the bottom, boring a portal into the earth. The spirit jumped DeMarko's body high over it and down. The earth swallowed him.

DeMarko's muffled wail of terror escaped up out of the hole, reverberating through the hills.

The drumming stopped. The green luminescence snuffed out. Spirits melted into thin trails of vapor.

The zebra hide lifted off the ground, spiraling black and white, spinning a path toward the fire pit. It dropped onto the tamped mound. Violet flames shot up like a purple volcano. Sparks of ash wafted through the forest, drifting up, up toward a vault of faint stars.

Noah tried to get up. Holy Einstein, he was so exhausted his legs wouldn't move. If he could just get some sleep. Jean-Paul and Fleck reached him, and he saw they were unharmed. The pounding in his chest started to subside. "Thank God. Why didn't you call out?"

"Oh, no." Jean-Paul sucked in a sharp breath and fell to his knees.

Fleck cried out.

"What?" Noah followed their eyes. Blood gushed

from a hole in his left side, seeping a maroon puddle onto the grass. The sight of it confused him more than it scared him. "Funny, I don't feel anything."

The shaman lifted Noah's head and cradled it in his lap. "Do not speak." He stripped off his shirt, balled it, and pressed it to Noah's side.

Fleck fumbled his cell phone from his pocket and punched at it. "My friend's been shot. I need an ambulance at the north end of the parking lot at Duschene International Headquarters. Please, hurry." His voice broke. His forehead beaded with perspiration. "I'm gonna meet the ambulance so they'll know where to go, okay?" He leaned his head close. "Don't you fuckin' leave me, buddy, or I'll never speak to you again."

"Yeah? No duh. Regular genius, McNulty."

Fleck didn't laugh. "Don't you be the story. You're not the story, you hear?" He disappeared from view.

Jean-Paul's brow furrowed and his eyes were moist. "*Por a saminay. Por a saminayo.* Help me Ancestors. Watch over Noah Friedman."

"I'm okay."

"Do not take him to the other world." Sweat streamed down the shaman's torso. "*Ne le prenez pas. Pas maintenant.*"

"You're speaking French. That can't be good." Noah tried to laugh, but it hurt. He wondered at the purpose of this synchronicity. The fate of bullet meeting flesh at the exact, ordained moment. Or had he been wrong all along? Perhaps there was no rhyme or reason for the things that happened, after all. Perhaps, we're just a jumble of quarks and electrons randomly spinning and colliding.

Tears splashed down the shaman's face onto Noah's forehead.

"Cut it out, Jean-Paul."

"I should have given you a talisman to keep you in this world." He yanked free a leather cord on his ankle, and shoved a tiny object into Noah's hand. A carved leopard. "My fault. *Mon défaut. Mon défaut.*"

Noah heard the shrill sound of sirens in the distance. What a coincidence, two ambulances in one day. One, he'd resisted. One, he welcomed.

It took energy to breathe. He just wanted to sleep now. Just sleep. He closed his eyes, let his head sink further into Jean-Paul's lap, and listened to the shaman's frantic prayer. "You worry too much. Stop it." He pictured Crystal sweeping a strand of blond hair from her eyes. He planned what he'd say when he finally found her.

Wailing alarms sounded closer now, the sound speeding toward him as he drifted away. Jean-Paul's voice receded to a far-off place. Noah's world fell silent. Darkness wrapped him like a tight blanket, and he descended into it, relinquishing all desire but to sleep.

HEALING

Autumn leaves lined the Avenue of the Saints in deep piles of umber. Oaks shed their gold finery onto the windshield of Noah's Prius, where toothed edges trembled for a brief moment before rising to flap past. Golden wheat fields and hay bales slipstreamed by, taunting him with longing for a girl with flaxen hair, and urging him to make time.

A season had passed since he'd driven from St. Louis to Minneapolis. Then, he'd traveled this stretch in the early morning hours, but even in that dim light, he'd seen nature's green in full display. Now, the fall landscape had enriched to fourteen karat. Vivid proof that time brought changes.

From the open window, the wind caressed Noah's face and tousled his hair like wayward spirits. A tiny, carved leopard attached to a leather strap swung from the rear-view mirror. A laminated license, courtesy of the state of Minnesota and bearing a photo oddly reminiscent of his features, stared up at him in bemused shock from the console. Above it, taped to the dash, hung an ecru note card hand engraved in navy ink:

From the Desk of Bernard Goldberg, C.E.O, Duschene International. "For my son, Noah. Drive this in the best of health. With love, Bernard."

Noah rocked and sang along to country music blasting from the speakers. *What hurts the most was being so close, and having so much to say, and watching you walk away...*

Sitting in the car for hours had stiffened his left hip, and he shifted his weight to the other side. He was reminded of his injury with small annoyances. It throbbed when a storm approached; it ached when he slept in the wrong position. In an odd way, he liked these mnemonics of his ordeal in the same way he enjoyed the crescent-shaped scar on his left bicep.

Noah had suffered nerve and muscle damage, but the bullet had missed organs and bones. Thank you, Ancestors.

"You're a wonder," his neurosurgeon had said just last week, declaring him completely healed.

Getting shot—an anomalous blessing, but blessing nevertheless—had forced his mom to remain in Minneapolis. After Noah's hospital release, Bernard had moved them into his house, where Sally had boiled endless pots of chicken soup and hovered twenty-four/seven to nag her son back to good health. A month into his recuperation, Sally's relationship concerns with Bernard had melted away. She'd packed up, moved to Minneapolis, and engineered a buy-out of Friedman Pharmaceutical by her employees. She also spearheaded a class-action suit on behalf of a dozen women who told their stories of rape and harassment by Charles Dalton, III. His indictment soon followed.

Noah had served as best man when Sally and Bernard tied the knot in a stellar *Jewitch* ceremony. Jean-Paul had conducted a shamanic, tribal ritual, sharing the pulpit with a rabbi, kuor, zebra hide, and *chuppah*.

Fleck filmed and edited the wedding video in homage to Sally titled, "My Big *Meshugga* Wedding." Then he flew to Atlanta, where he parlayed his fifteen minutes of "The Dalton Scandal" fame to land a job as a business reporter for CNN.

After Sally's wedding, a neurologist had poked, prodded, and scanned Noah one last time, determining that he'd suffered no permanent damage from his years on Selexikote. No signs of early-onset Alzheimer's.

Jean-Paul had already rendered this diagnosis, insisting Noah had been healed by the initiation. "You came into this world with all knowledge. It is in your bones. When the information is needed, you will remember." He'd shared his teachings during countless hours of hospital vigil, refusing to leave Noah's side, acting as his talisman to keep him in this world. The sound of chanting had lulled him to sleep and brought him back. When at last Noah's strength returned, the shaman announced a trip to oversee the construction of a medical facility in Africa. Shaman and disciple said their goodbyes.

"You warned me to get off Selexikote," Noah told him. "You knew."

Jean-Paul flashed a smile, and the room brightened a notch. "Sometimes I get lucky," he said.

"What do you see in my future? Tell me."

"You must experience the dream of life as it unfolds."

"I'm afraid to get on new drugs. Are any of them safe? Won't they change me? But then, I'm afraid I can't control my bipolar disorder without help."

Jean-Paul rested his chin on steepled fingertips. "Ah, yes, this question of drugs versus no drugs is a dilemma. If you lived in my village, we would wrap our arms around you and treasure the powerful messages you deliver from the Ancestors. Our acceptance would be the only pill required to keep your feet planted in the soil. But," he sighed deeply, "you do not live in my village." He lifted Noah's hand and clasped it in his. "Come with me, my brother. Come."

For a moment, Noah longed for that possibility and his heart ached to say yes. But then, he thought of Sally and another woman he'd miss. And his unfinished work burned deep within, waiting to be birthed. "My place is here."

The shaman's eyes watered, and then he smiled, like a shaft of sun breaking through the clouds. "Yes."

"Can I find acceptance here without taking meds?"

"It is difficult in a world of concrete, steel, and wire to surmount the constant buzz of electricity. You might need the drugs to survive a place so separate from nature. Sometimes drugs are necessary. My people need drugs to survive AIDS. I want that for them. And I will not tell my bipolar friend that he will be fine without medication. Because I don't believe that's true. But you must also weigh the consequences. Anything you take enough of to help, is also enough to hurt. Be mindful of your body and your heart."

Noah mulled over Jean-Paul's words. "I want to be my authentic self. But I can't chance another manic episode and dismantling the lives of those I love. I wish you could tell me what to do."

The wise man shook his head. "You have earned the right to advise yourself. So, the only question, my brother, is...What are you going to do about it?"

Noah exited the Avenue of the Saints and pulled onto the winding country road he'd traveled once before. The air felt electric. He looked for signposts indicating he should make another turn, but nothing seemed familiar. It had been night, after all, and she had pointed the way.

A flock of geese flapped overhead, their V formation embossed black against a robin's egg sky. The V banked, aiming for a warmer climate. Then he saw it: a thickly canopied road off to the right.

He turned the wheel. The car bumped along the branch-laced lane until he spotted her graveled crescent drive, pulled in, and stilled the motor.

Thoughts of fleeing breezed through his brain. His mouth dried up like one in a shrunken head. He took a deep breath, opened the car door, and stepped into the brilliant afternoon. He marched through a pile of leaves, lifting a wake of red and orange against the cloudless blue, and made his way to her door.

He knocked. Lub-dub. Lub-dub. He studied the door's peeling yellow paint. He knocked again.

The door cracked open. Blond hair slipped through the breach, then a full view of her sweet face. Aqua eyes widened with a puzzled look. Then, recognition set in. "Oh, it's you."

"Hey." Three months to come up with his opening volley, and *hey* is what gushed out. Contrary to the neurologist's report, he worried anew he'd lost brain cells.

"What are you doing here?" No sarcasm or malice in her tone. Just a question.

"I thought we might talk." He shrugged. "Want to go out for coffee?"

"I don't know." Crystal crossed her arms, studying him.

His breath caught. He wanted to touch her.

"You hurt my feelings." Her tone didn't attempt to inflict guilt. Just a statement. Her eyes glistened, and she flickered wet off her lashes.

"I'm sorry."

"Why did you leave me?"

"It's a long story. But a good one."

"It better be."

He placed his right hand over his pounding heart. "I promise you'll like it. It starts with a ghost. And a shaman."

"This I gotta hear." She unwound her arms, and her face brightened.

"I was hoping you'd say that."

"My parents are out of town. Wanna come in? I'll make you a sandwich."

He smiled. "Sounds great."

She threw open the door.

The scent of lemon shampoo guided him through the living room, past doily-covered armchairs and framed family photos. A band of sunshine streamed through the window to flame her hair, and the golden swath swished back and forth like a pendulum.

She stopped, turning to face him. He nearly bumped into her. Just an inch away, an atom away, but it might as well have been a universe. If he swayed forward, he could close the gap. Later. He'd muster the courage to kiss her after he spilled out his story.

"Almost went out of town with my parents for the weekend. At the last minute, I decided not to." She laughed, flipped her hair and crossed into the kitchen, her beauty beckoning like the North Star.

He was struck anew by the connectedness of all things. Quarks to galaxies to dark matter. Hadassah to Chaim. Bernard to Sally. Noah to Crystal.

She faced him again, and her gaze left him speechless. "It's funny I stayed home. Don't you think?"

Noah thought all things were possible in this astonishing world. He longed to explain himself. Tell her every minute detail of his journey. She'd believe him. Yes, she would. He ached to reveal his secret. Thoughts of her had sustained him through recovery. Words pinballed in his head. He stood tongue-tied, unable to settle on the perfect reply.

He moved closer.

Then, the right response rose on a wave of gratitude, rippling the surface of his consciousness. Before his birth, this phrase had been carved into a pathway of his brain, waiting for him to remember, marking time for the exact moment and the singular person who would understand the importance of its meaning.

"Love creates a synchronicity with what is loved," Noah said.

She chewed on a corner of her bottom lip, seeming to consider this, placed her palms on his shoulders and raised her chin. "I want to learn more. Would you kiss me first?"

He leaned in.

ACKNOWLEDGEMENTS

My gratitude and thanks to:

My husband Chris, who has played the part of both benefactor and cheerleader. This book, indeed all of my stories, would not exist without his unflagging support.

My children and granddaughter, for reminding me there's dinner to get on the table.

Malidoma Somé whose books and teachings have expanded my universe. Thank you for inspiring me to pen this story.

Vicki Bartlett, who heard me and opened the door when I stood outside in the rain.

Daniel Ladinsky, for giving me permission to use his poem, "Then Winks," for my epigraph. And for allowing me to use the first line of the poem "More Inheritance" as the last line spoken by my protagonist. Your brilliant poetry was just too synchronous to pass up.

Nancy Barton, for loving what I wrote and trying to push it out into the world. Even though we couldn't do this together, your imprint is on the pages and in my heart.

Louella Nelson, Laura Taylor, and Barbara de Marco-Barrett for your mentorship over the years. I've been lucky to learn from your diversity of perspective, knowledge, and styles. Special note to Barbara and my readers: I selected the name DeMarko for my villain before I met Barbara. This is no connection to or reflection of my good friend Barbara, just another crazy synchronicity in a world of strewn breadcrumbs.

My writer friends, who have helped me hone my craft with every ding, correction, or occasional gold star. In particular: Rosie Lewis, Joanne Wilshin, Marcia Sargent, and Marrie Stone. And to Brad Oatman, who gifted me with the perfect title.

Kristin Lindstrom of Flying Pig Media, who helped me birth another baby. Let's do it again.

SELECTED BIBLIOGRAPHY

Somé, Malidoma Patrice, *Of Water and the Spirit*. Penguin Books, New York, 1994

Somé, Malidoma Patrice, *Ritual*. Penguin Group, Arkana, New York, 1997

Peat, F. David, Synchronicity, *The Bridge Between Matter and Mind*. A Bantam Book, United States, 1987.

Combs, Allan and Holland, Mark, *Synchronicity: Through the Eyes of Science Myth, and the Trickster*. Marlowe and Company, United States, 1996

Marohn, Stephanie, *The Natural Medicine Guide to Bipolar Disorder*. Hampton Roads Publishing Company, Inc., Charlottesville Va, 2003.

Fieve, Ronald R., *Bipolar Breakthrough*. Rodale, Inc., New York, New York, 2006.

Ladinsky, Daniel, *A Year With Hafiz, Ladinsky Translation*. Penguin Random House, New York, 2010. "More Inheritance."

Ladinsky, Daniel, *The Gift by Hafiz, Ladinsky Translation*. Penguin Random House, New York, 2010. "Then Winks."

About Deborah Gaal

After a career as an entrepreneur, business executive, and business coach, Deborah Gaal turned her attention to the study and pursuit of writing. Her debut novel, *The Dream Stitcher*, was a finalist of the National Jewish Book Awards, and won the IndieReader Discovery Award for literary fiction.

For more information about Deborah's work, visit:

www.deborahgaal.com

CPSIA information can be obtained
at www.ICGtesting.com
Printed in the USA
FSHW021018050920
73599FS